The Renewable Virgin

BARBARA PAUL

The Renewable Virgin

CHARLES SCRIBNER'S SONS

NEW YORK

First published in the United States by Charles Scribner's Sons 1985
Copyright © 1984 Barbara Paul

Library of Congress Cataloging in Publication Data
Paul, Barbara, 1931–
  The renewable virgin.
  I. Title.
PS3566.A82615R4   1984   823'.914   84-20214
ISBN 0-684-18300-5

1 3 5 7 9 11 13 15 17 19 H/C 20 18 16 14 12 10 8 6 4 2

Printed in the United States of America.

CHAPTER 1

KELLY INGRAM

Rudy Benedict and I were just beginning to get something going when I found out he saw himself as David ready to take on the giant. What Rudy didn't know was I'd always been on Goliath's side.

'What is there to fear?' he said, puffing away on his pipe in that writerish way of his. (Anybody else would have said *What's to be afraid of?*) 'The networks are composed of mere human beings motivated by the same fears and ambitions that drive the rest of us. There are no superpowers involved.'

Except that those mere human beings controlled budgets in the millions while good folks like Rudy and me or I had to scrabble for a piece of the pie. 'What are you up to? You're cranking yourself up for something.'

He gave that smug little smile of his that was *just* beginning to irritate me and didn't answer right away. Making me wait for it. 'I'm writing a play. I'm returning to the theater—where I really belong.'

I didn't see how anybody could return to where he'd never been, but I was being polite that night and didn't say so. 'Well, congratulations, Rudy. That's good to hear.'

'I'm not telling everybody, Kelly. But I wanted you to know.'

I nodded. 'Thanks for the confidence. It's important for Leonard and I to keep track.' Leonard Zoff was my agent.

'Me. For Leonard and me.'

Guessed wrong. 'Me, then. What's your play about?'

Rudy took a long draw on his pipe and said, slowly, 'I'm writing about television. So of course there's no chance of getting it produced *on* television. And the

5

movies aren't any better, not any more. You can't beat that system either.'

So it was theater by default. 'Exposé sort of thing, you mean?'

He looked pained. 'Please, Kelly. I don't write sleaze. All I want to do is show that television is merely one fingernail of the multi-armed corporate powers that control our lives.'

I took a moment to work my way through that metaphor and then said, 'Didn't Paddy Chayefsky already do that?'

Rudy waved his pipe dismissively. 'Merely as one episode in an ongoing David-and-Goliath confrontation. Chayefsky always wrote about the little guy fighting the good but futile fight. One small man failing to topple the giant. That's not what I'm interested in. I want to probe more deeply into the nature of the beast.'

'So you're not interested in giant-toppling?'

He smiled in that charming way that reminded me why I'd been attracted to him in the first place. 'I didn't say that, Kelly. But I'm not such a fool as to think my one play will miraculously open everybody's eyes. This country is so addicted to television that people simply *refuse* to believe their attitudes are manipulated every time they turn on the set.'

I thought it more likely they just didn't care. 'So you do want to topple the giant.'

His charming smile eased into his smug one. 'My goals are more modest. Just shake him up a bit.'

So there it was. Rudy Benedict saw himself as a giant-killer, no matter how modest he claimed his goals were. Like David, standing in a place of safety with his long-distance weapon, taking pot shots at the giant with impunity. (Impugnity?) Only Rudy's weapon would be a play instead of a sling. 'Got a part for me?' I asked automatically.

'Maybe,' he answered just as automatically. 'The *dramatis personæ* isn't complete yet. Ever acted on the stage?'

6

'No.' Ever written for the stage? 'Should I do Off-Broadway, Rudy? I keep getting contradictory advice.'

He shrugged. 'Good showcase. Wouldn't hurt. The kind of stage training you get depends on the director you get. Wouldn't hurt, Kelly.'

I nodded, as if thinking it over. I had no intention of committing myself to a not-completely-professional production that would tie me up all summer on the million-to-one shot that some Big Producer would turn up in the audience one night. I had better irons in the fire.

Rudy had already turned the talk back to his play. I'd flattered him by asking his advice and he hadn't noticed. If he'd needled me for trying to stroke him, I'd have respected him for it. If he'd preened himself on being consulted as a figure of superior experience, I'd have accepted it. But when he didn't even *notice* . . . sometimes I think writers are the most unobservant people in the world.

I'd met Rudy three years earlier, in California, when I was still in my second-generation Barbie doll phase. Slit skirts, sprayed-on plastic face, the whole shtick. I hated looking exactly like everybody else but it was the only way to get roles. Rudy Benedict was one of a trio of writers grinding out unfunny scripts for a show in which the actors mostly rolled their eyes suggestively while the laughtrack man punched the button marked 'Dirty Snickers'. The script called for a Playboy-bunny type who for some reason agrees to go out with one of the show's yokel heroes. My agent's West Coast rep happened to be sucking up to the right people that week so I got the part. I appeared in two scenes and had a total of seven lines, one of which was 'Yes.' Rudy swore he didn't write that one. Then I kind of lost track of him for a while, until we ran into each other in New York.

Just then he was lighting his pipe again, the seventeenth time in the past hour. Rudy was a good guy, but his putting on egghead airs was beginning to get on my nerves. I understood he needed those props to help him make the transition from TV hack to Serious Dramatist. Rudy wasn't forty yet; he'd just scheduled his mid-life crisis a little early, that was all. I wished he'd go on and get the damned play written so he could forget about all the posturing he thought was supposed to go with it.

Finally he gave up on the pipe and decided to nuzzle my neck instead.

'Rudy, you ought to stop smoking that pipe,' I told him. 'It's given you another headache, hasn't it? You've got that pinched look again.'

He rubbed his forehead with the tip of his middle finger. 'Now that you mention it . . .'

He left soon after that. Sometimes it works.

After a good night's sleep I allowed myself the luxury of feeling a little guilty about Rudy. I didn't want to dump him; he was good fun when he was thinking about something other than himself. Besides, there was always the chance that he might turn out to be a Big Talent after all. I resolved to be nicer to Rudy Benedict.

But I never got a chance to put my good intentions into practice, because about then somebody came along and murdered him.

When Rudy Benedict decided it would be easier to be a Serious Writer on the East Coast than on the West, he'd moved into an apartment in Chelsea and hated it. He'd told me he'd been looking for a better place to live for almost a year but couldn't find what he wanted; welcome to the club. I'd been to the place once and it was crowded and littered-looking, nothing special. Rudy had taken it only because someone had told him a lot of writers lived in the area.

Rudy hadn't completely broken his ties with the West Coast, however, and that's how I happened to run into him again. I'd moved back east myself because I'd gotten a small continuing part in a series about a private investigator, to be shot entirely in New York City. ('Pea eyes are making a comeback,' my agent, Leonard Zoff, had said.) This one was a sort of Harry O in the Big Apple, and I had the Farah Fawcett role, the Sex Object Next Door. ('Play it sweet,' Leonard told me when I went in for my interview. 'Make it like "Who, me—sexy?" We're in a *conservative* period, darling. Play it real sweet and make sure they know you're not wearing a bra.') So I'd been all bright-eyed innocence, seemingly unaware that my clothing and movements were come-ons. That'd been just what they were looking for and I had my first continuing role in a series.

At first I didn't have any great hopes for it except as a way to get myself seen; I mean, I didn't have much expectation for the *show*. For one thing, it was a Nathan Pinking production ('If it's stinking, it's by Pinking')— and even if it did hit, that was no guarantee I'd be remembered as anything other than the broad in *LeFever* or by some equally unflattering label. That was the name of the show, *LeFever*, just the one word. Hot stuff, you see. One of the writers soberly explained to me the word had been chosen because of its 'rhythmic compatibility'—a three-syllable word with the stress on the middle syllable, like 'McMillan'. Also, 'LeFever' was elegant-sounding, easy to remember, and not too ethnic.

So I'd moved back to New York, right where I'd started out making whee-look-at-me shampoo commercials until I was told at age twenty-three I'd gotten too old for the image. After that had come five frustrating years in Hollywood, taking every shlock TV role and movie bit I could get. Then along came *LeFever* and it was back east again. I was pushing thirty and fully intended to go on pushing it as long as *LeFever* played. ('Stay young,' Leonard had told me. 'Forget Shakespeare, they're still buying youth.')

The initial feedback from the network had been good. They said the mail indicated the viewers wanted to see more of me. Nathan Pinking wasn't sure whether that meant they wanted to see me in more scenes or whether they wanted to see more of me physically, of my own personal bod. So we did it both ways; my role got larger and my costumes smaller. I even did one scene nude. But the network censor wouldn't let it pass, even though I'd played it sweet.

That's where Rudy Benedict came into the picture. Nathan Pinking had signed him some time ago as part of his stable of writers (you're *supposed* to think of horses), and the contract still had a year to run. But this last year Nathan wasn't using Rudy as a regular but instead kept bringing him in to do rewrite work and to fill in on this series or that as needed. Nathan had four series in production, two of them shooting in New York, so Rudy had been able to make the move back east without violating his contract. He told me he liked doing rewrite work — at least it suited him just then. He didn't have the responsibility of a weekly grind, and it was always fun to walk in at the eleventh hour and point out to the other writers what they'd done wrong. Didn't win him a lot of friends, but he said it felt *so good*. Nathan Pinking called him in on *LeFever* when one of our regular writers had to go into the hospital for prostate trouble.

I asked Rudy to give me some comedy lines and godblesshim he came through with some good ones. The ass playing LeFever was so dumb he didn't even know the scene was supposed to be funny until someone showed him a notice in the *Daily News* that said I'd revealed an 'unexpected flair' for comedy. So he'd come in the next morning mad as hell 'cause I'd gotten the good lines and demanding to know why he'd been left out of the fun. But our regular writer was back then and Rudy was long gone, Nathan Pinking had turned invisible, and so I took the heat. Ass.

Thus Rudy Benedict was doing oddjob rewrites for Nathan Pinking while all of what he called his true creative energies went into the Great American Mellydrammer about television, a subject on which everybody in the world considers themselves, ah, himself or herself, or whatever, an expert. But Rudy really was an expert, or as close to being one as anyone who works *for* the medium can be. As opposed to those who make the medium work for them, owners and execs and such. Rudy'd been around almost since the day he'd left college, fifteen, sixteen years maybe. That's a lot of television scripts. Rudy had survived writer burn-out by working only half of each year.

The night after I'd sent him home with a headache, Rudy had failed to show up for a poker game in the same building where he lived. Since Rudy was supposed to bring the chips, an annoyed host had gone up and pounded on the door. There'd been no answer, but the host could hear the radio playing in Rudy's apartment. So he got the super to open up, and the two of them found Rudy crumpled up on the floor.

Rudy Benedict was dead, and he'd been poisoned — the police weren't saying what kind of poison or how it had been administered. It was a hell of a shock. Rudy wasn't what you'd call a threatening man — he was more like, well, like a *supplicant*, a petitioner. Trying to crash the inner circles, you know, that kind of person. He was a moderately successful man within his own field of expertise, but the field was kind of narrow and Rudy was beginning to feel squeezed. That's one reason he wanted to write a real honest-to-God play, I think. Not to get into the theater so much as to get out of television. Although theater has its own inner circle Rudy would have loved to crash. Not the money and muscle you find in TV and the movies, but there were compensations in belonging to that particular club. Poor Rudy never even got close.

Shock's funny, everybody doesn't react the same. For me it was like pulling back to a kind of platform and looking at the world from that slight distance. Things were a different color, too, a kind of yellow around the edges, I don't know why. That faded after a couple of days. Rudy Benedict and I were not close, had never been close. But the potential for *getting* close had come up and that made all the difference.

LeFever was shooting exteriors at the UN Building when the police came around to talk to me. I was waiting for a new camera set-up when the questions started.

'He was writing an exposé of the television industry,' I told the policewoman who was questioning me. 'A play.'

'Gawdalmighty,' she groaned. 'That's the first thing everybody says.' I let my surprise show, so she dropped the other shoe. 'And it wasn't even true.'

'Whoa, wait a minute.' I thought a moment. 'First of all, who's "everybody"? Rudy didn't tell *everybody*.'

'He might have missed a few people in Manhattan,' she said sardonically, 'but not many.' The policewoman was Detective Second Grade M. Larch, her ID had said; she had a gray potato face and was tired and fed-up-looking. Either a long day or a frustrating one, probably both. 'Rudy Benedict told everybody he knew—in strictest confidence, of course—that he was writing a play about television.'

'But he wasn't?'

'Not really—just piddling around. He'd made some notes about the story, but he hadn't gotten very far. He didn't even have names for his characters yet. Just called them A and B and C and like that.'

'Maybe that's all you found . . .'

Detective Larch shook her head. 'That's all there *was*. He did more talking about that play than he did writing. Writer's block, maybe?'

I shrugged. 'Maybe. I thought he really was working on it. How can you be sure there wasn't anything else? Research notes, incriminating letters, all that stuff? Maybe somebody stole them. The same somebody who killed him.'

She smiled, the first time. 'You want it to be an exposé, don't you? All you folks in television, everyone I've talked to wants it to be an exposé. Sorry to disappoint you, but what notes Rudy Benedict left indicate his play was going to be one of those crisis-of-conscience things. Moment-of-truth stuff for the hero. The hero was to be a television writer who was afraid something he'd written might be harmful to young viewers. Autobiographical?'

I answered with a question of my own. 'Something the

hero had written? Like what? Maybe that—'

'Benedict hadn't even figured out *what* yet. He was just doodling. He was writing no exposé, Ms Ingram, believe me.'

'Call me Kelly,' I said absently. 'So he wasn't killed because of his play?'

'Doesn't look like it, although we're keeping that door open. Who were his enemies, Ms Ingram?'

Okay, if she didn't want to call me Kelly, that was her business, what did I care. 'I don't really know, *Detective Larch*, ma'am. I hadn't seen Rudy for a couple of years until I ran into him again a few weeks ago.'

She sniffed at me. 'You've got to have an idea or two. Give me some names.'

'You want me to *guess*?'

Detective Larch looked tireder than ever. 'Yes, Miss Kelly Ingram, guess, if you have to. Give me some names. I've got to have something to report.'

She didn't give a damn what I said, just so I said *something*. Terrific police work. 'His ex-wife, maybe,' I said reluctantly—not out of concern for the former Mrs. Benedict (didn't even know her) but because I hate being bullied. 'But I understood she and Rudy were on good terms. But then, *I* thought Rudy was writing an exposé of television, so what do I know. She's remarried, living in Connecticut. I don't think Rudy ever told me her married name—pretty sure he never mentioned it.'

'Turrell, Mrs. Roger Turrell. She was home in bed with Mr. Roger Turrell the night Benedict was killed. Guess somebody else. Somebody he might have been on *bad* terms with.'

I lifted my shoulders. 'Just about any producer or director he worked with. Writers are always crying about how their scripts are butchered.'

'Name one.'

I looked around; nobody within earshot. 'Start with the one who's running this show. Nathan Pinking.'

'Pinking was a bad enemy of Benedict's? Ruined his scripts, did he?'

'I don't know if Nathan Pinking was any kind of enemy. You said name somebody and I did. Nathan's no worse, no better than other producers. Maybe a little better than most because he's so careless.'

Bloodshot eyes in a potato face, blinking at me. 'How's that?'

'Nathan's always in a hurry, which makes him careless, which keeps him from interfering too much. He's not even here most of the time—just shows up once in a while to make sure we aren't all off playing hookey on his time.'

'Is he here now?'

'No. Just a couple of his lackeys.'

'Who are they?'

I was pointing them out to her when the word came the cameras were ready. All I had to do in the scene was get out of a cab, run up some steps, and hand an envelope to the actor named Nick Quinlan who played LeFever. The first time we did it he dropped the envelope.

Nick Quinlan was a big, hunk-style male with the right haircut and the right mustache. He looked as if he was showing off his bare chest even when he was dressed to the teeth—really gorgeous to look at, if you didn't mind obviousness. But he couldn't talk. 'Hey, make sure I got aholt fore y'leggo, woncha?'

'Ask for some stickum for your fingertips,' I smiled.

I'd only recently got to the point where I'd started complaining out loud about Nick. When we first started shooting *LeFever*, that ox had stepped on just about every line I had. If I had a speech made up of more than one sentence, I had to run them together in a breathy attempt to get everything said before Nick came butting in with his line. But when he did interrupt before I'd finished, I didn't say anything to the director. I just smiled and kept a stiff upper lip and refused to complain. I was being professional, I was being a trouper, blah blah blah. Until I realized that nobody cared. Nobody even *noticed*. So from then on, every time Nick cut off one of my lines, I hollered. I hollered loud.

Right then the director was doing some hollering of his

own, so I went back and got in the cab. Out the door, up the steps, hand over the envelope. Look concerned.

Nick had a line. It was supposed to be, 'You'd think he'd know better than to write something like this, wouldn't you?' It came out, 'Y'd thank he'd write sumpin bettern this, wooden chew?'

Flubbed lines are redone in television only if they are flagrantly wrong, like changing the meaning as Nick's misreading had just done. By then the director had worked with Nick enough to know that once his leading man started out blowing a line in that particular fashion, he'd never get it right. So right then and there the line was changed to read, 'I wish he hadn't written this.' Nick could handle that. In television, everybody was used to disposable writing.

The next time we tried it somebody who wasn't supposed to be there wandered into the scene. The fourth attempt was ruined when Nick stumbled as he stepped forward to take the envelope and grabbed my arm to keep from falling—making me fall instead. But the fifth time we got it. Five tries to get what should have been a one-take sequence. Normal for *LeFever*.

It was the last shot of the day, so we were free to go. Detective Larch was waiting where I'd left her, leaning against one of the camera vans. She was staring at Nick Quinlan as he stood talking to the director. 'What's wrong with him today?'

'Nothing. He's always like that.'

She shook her head disbelievingly but made no comment. She started asking me about the last time I saw Rudy Benedict, the night before he died.

'He went home early, with a headache,' I fudged a little.

'You didn't see him the next day at all?'

'No. Detective Larch, when did he die exactly? The papers didn't say.'

'About an hour before his poker buddy found him. You're sure you didn't see him that day at all?'

'Of course I'm sure. The last I saw of him was about ten

o'clock the night before.'

'What did he talk about?'

'His play. The one you say he wasn't writing.'

She sighed. 'I gave you the wrong impression, didn't I? I meant he hadn't really got started on it, he was still doodling around. But he was planning a play, getting ready to write.'

'And you know for a fact that it wasn't going to be an exposé of any sort. You're *really* sure of that, are you?'

'The Captain is sure. He's told us to look elsewhere for a motive.'

The Captain, as if there was only one in the entire world. 'Captain who?'

'Captain Michaels. He's in charge of the investigation. How did Benedict seem that last time? Upset, nervous . . . ?'

'Just a little headachy. And that wasn't bad. He'd recently started smoking a pipe, and I think that sometimes bothered him.'

Detective Larch's bloodshot eyes stared straight into mine. 'Headache. You said that before. My God, I must be tireder than I thought. Did he take anything for it?'

I thought back. 'No, he — wait a minute. I gave him some, ah, Bromo-Seltzer.'

At that the policewoman's entire appearance changed — her face came to life, her body woke up. 'Bromo-Seltzer. You're sure it was Bromo-Seltzer?'

I stared at her, horrified. 'You mean the stuff I gave him . . . you're saying I gave him the poison?' I could hear my voice rising.

'Take it easy, take it easy,' Detective Larch said hastily, her own voice rising. 'Let's get it straight first. Are you absolutely positive it was Bromo-Seltzer you gave him? Take your time. Think back.'

I took my time and I thought back. I remembered the sample coming in the mail, in a box that was . . . *yellow*, not blue. 'No, it wasn't Bromo-Seltzer! It was some new product, something for headache and upset stomach. I don't remember what it's called, it was just something

16

that came in the mail. A sample.'

'Did you take any of it?'

'No, it just came that day. Was that it? Was—'

'Ms Ingram, try to remember the brand name. Take your time.'

I looked at her closely. She knew the brand but was being very careful not to tell me. Trying not to damage her evidence by putting words in my mouth, I suppose. Evidence for what?

'Think,' the detective said.

It came to me. 'Lysco-Seltzer,' I said. 'Rhymes with disco. Detective Larch. Give me a straight answer—please. Was that what killed Rudy?'

The expression on her face told me the answer before she could say anything. She reached out and touched my arm. 'I'm sorry. You all right?'

'No, I am not all right,' I said numbly. '*I* was the one who gave Rudy . . . somebody wanted *me* to take that . . .' I just stood there and shuddered. 'My God, it's like the Tylenol murders all over again! Some nut out to poison the whole world—'

'No, wait a minute, it can't be the same as that,' she scowled. 'The Tylenol killer substituted capsules full of poison for the headache medicine and then put the bottles back on drugstore shelves. That's entirely different from getting hold of sample bottles going through the mail. Besides, we've got all these new safety packaging regulations now. Your Lysco-Seltzer—there was a seal over the mouth of the bottle, wasn't there?'

'I don't know, I never opened it. It just came in the mail.'

'Well, did it have a—what do they call it—a film-sealed cap? Or one of those plastic envelope-type things around the whole bottle?'

I visualized the bottle. 'No. No, it didn't have anything like that. But if there wasn't any seal inside, Rudy would have noticed, he must have.'

'He could have noticed and not thought anything about it. The bottle came from *you*, not from a drugstore. He probably just thought you'd already opened it yourself.'

'Oh Jeez.' The camera van had packed up and gone, and Detective Larch and I were left standing on a public sidewalk — not the best place in the world to find out someone had mailed you some poison and you'd passed it on to a friend. 'I need a drink. In fact I need two drinks.'

'So do I,' the policewoman muttered. 'Come on.' She grabbed my arm and steered me down the street toward a welcoming watering place.

By the time we'd finished our second drink the detective and I were calling each other by our first names (hers was Marian). She told me a half-empty bottle of Lysco-Seltzer had been found on Rudy's kitchen cabinet. But instead of headache medicine the small plastic bottle had held cyanide crystals.

'That's the part that doesn't make sense,' Marian Larch said. 'Cyanide is fast-acting, damned fast. Matter of minutes. Yet he didn't die until nearly twenty-four hours later. Did you actually see him take it?'

'No, he said he'd wait until he got home. He just dropped the bottle in his pocket and left.'

'Ah.' She nodded her head. 'Then when he got home . . . perhaps he forgot he had the stuff and took a medicine of his own. Or . . .' She must have seen a giveaway expression on my face because she said, 'You know something you're not telling, Kelly.'

On the whole I am more truthful than your average person. Out of necessity. I don't seem to be able to get away with much when it comes to fabricating off-camera. I know people who lie as easily as they breathe and nobody ever calls them on it. But me — the least little fib I tell catches up with me. Like now.

'I don't think he really had a headache the night he was with me,' I admitted, feeling sheepish. 'I just told him he did.'

Marian's eyebrows rose. 'How's that?'

'Rudy was either in a suggestible mood or else he was looking for an excuse to split. I just said don't you have a headache, and he said yes I do, and that was it.'

'You wanted to get rid of him?'

'Well, not really get rid of him, I just wanted him to go home, you know.'

'What's the difference?'

'I didn't want him to stay that night, that's all.'

She smiled wryly. 'Gotta ask you this, Kelly. Were you sleeping with him?'

I shook my head. 'Not yet. But that's where we were heading, kind of. That night, the last time I saw him — well, I had a long, tight shooting schedule the next day and I just wanted to get to bed and *sleep*. I didn't want to have to say no to Rudy if he decided to make his move then. Besides, I like to say when myself, not wait to be asked. It was no big deal, I was only trying to avoid hurt feelings. Just not *that* night.'

Marian nodded, understanding. 'So by the time he got back to his own place he may have decided his headache had cleared up by itself or whatever. But then the *next* night, right before his poker game — yes, that would do it. The next night he did have a headache, a real one. So he opened the Lysco-Seltzer . . .'

'And it killed him.'

The next day was Friday, which meant we had to wrap the week's episode by six o'clock or else go into overtime and Nathan Pinking simply did not *believe* in overtime. He would put a mystery on the air with the mystery unsolved rather than go into overtime. He would tape 'The End' after only four acts of *Hamlet* rather than go into overtime. We'd finished all the indoor shots, so the whole day was spent rushing from one outdoor location to another. I had to make one wardrobe change on the run, in the back seat of a taxi, while the make-up woman frantically tried to restore order to my face and hair — all because that ass Nick Quinlan had taken the only limo the budget provided that week. The cab-driver loved it.

But I was damned grateful for the frantic pace because it kept me from thinking about that weirdo out there who'd sent me cyanide crystals disguised as Lysco-Seltzer, rhymes with disco. But I wasn't going to let it get to me, I wasn't even going to think about it until the day's work was finished, not even then, not until tomorrow when I was rested and more up to tangling with the notion that I was somebody's intended murder victim.

'Go home!' the director screeched joyfully, and we were finished. My feet hurt and my shoulders ached and I was really dragging, and I couldn't even draw any satisfaction from thoughts of a job well done, thenkyew. It had all been mechanical stuff, concentrate on getting it right the first time, the director had said, just don't make mistakes, leave the Emmy performances for next week. That idiot Nick made several flubs of the sort that should have been reshot but we didn't have time. So that week's episode was going to go out even shaggier-looking than usual.

I was turning down the associate producer's invitation to dinner (pleading exhaustion and wondering why he couldn't tell I was dead just by looking at me) when Detective Marian Larch materialized in front of me. The Captain wanted to see me, she said.

'Can't it wait until tomorrow?' I complained. 'I'm bushed, Marian. What does he want to see me about?'

'I don't know,' she said, perhaps truthfully. 'He just told me to bring you in.'

'*Bring me in!*' I shouted, outraged. 'Am I so desperate a character your Captain had to send a police detective to *bring me in?!*'

She stared at me, amused. 'God, you're prickly tonight. It's just a phrase, Kelly. Doesn't mean a thing.'

'I told you I was bushed,' I muttered.

'Yes, you did, and I'm sorry about this. But it has to be done. Look, I checked out this nice, shiny police car to come get you. Tell you what. I'll wait for you, and when Captain Michaels is finished I'll drive you home. Deal?'

'No, it's not a "deal"—it's *coercion*,' I grumbled but started to climb into the front seat. Then I remembered the man whose dinner invitation I'd been declining when Marian Larch showed up and turned to say goodbye.

He'd disappeared.

Marian and I didn't talk during the drive to the Headquarters building at Police Plaza. She took me up to Captain Michael's office in the Detective Bureau and did a fast vanishing act. Michaels was sitting behind what looked like a brand new desk. He was an overweight, fiftyish man who looked first at my breasts and then at my face. 'Siddown, Ms Ingram.'

Why, thank you for your gracious invitation, sir. I sat. 'What is it you want, Captain?'

'That story you told Detective Larch last night,' he said. 'I want you to tell it to me.'

That *story?* 'What's wrong?'

'I'll ask the questions. Start with the last time you saw Rudy Benedict.' He was actually looking down his nose at me.

I couldn't believe this guy. His body posture, his tone of voice — he was behaving as if he thought that was the way tough guys were *supposed* to act. Jimmy Cagney nasty. I did what he said; I told the 'story' again.

'And your sample of Lysco-Seltzer came in the mail when?' Captain Michaels asked.

'The same day I gave it to Rudy. I hadn't even taken it out of the mailing box yet.'

'There was no mailing box in Benedict's apartment — just the sample bottle. How do you account for that?'

'I don't think I have to account for it,' I protested. 'Come on, Captain, what is this? I probably threw the box away myself, when I gave Rudy the sample bottle.'

'*Probably.* Don't you remember?'

'No, I don't remember. Why should I? Do you remember every box and envelope you throw away?'

'I'm asking the questions.' He sounded like a man afraid of losing the initiative. 'How do you dispose of your trash?'

'My trash?'

'Yes, lady, your trash. How do you get rid of it?'

'I throw it down the waste chute in the apartment building.'

'How often?'

'As often as I need to. I don't have a *schedule*.'

'You throw out your own trash, do you?'

'Sometimes. The cleaning service takes care of most of it.'

'What about the Lysco-Seltzer mailing box? When did you put that down the chute?'

'You mean the one I don't remember throwing away at all? Gee, Captain, I really couldn't say.'

He glared at me coldly for a few moments, doing nothing to relieve the tension. Here I was a potential murder victim and he was showing about as much concern for my welfare as he would for Public Enemy Number One. 'Why haven't I been given police protection?' I demanded abruptly. 'That stuff was sent to *me*, not to Rudy. It was sheer accident that he took it instead of me.'

'Was it?'

'What do you mean, was it? Of course it was! Somebody mails you poison, they don't expect you to pass it on to somebody else.'

'If it was sent to you.'

'What "if"? What are you talking about?'

'The stuff that came in the mail could have been exactly what the sample label said it was—Lysco-Seltzer, a patent medicine. We don't know when the cyanide was substituted. It's an old ploy, claiming to be the intended victim. Lots of killers have used it.'

That made me see red. That really made me see red. To come off a rotten day like the one I'd just had and have to sit there and listen to some fat cop hinting that I'd deliberately given Rudy cyanide—then it suddenly hit me what I was being accused of and I was scared. I mean I was *scared*. 'You can't be serious . . . why would I want to . . . and where would I get the . . . you can't be *serious*!'

Captain Michaels came around from behind his new desk and leaned over me, all muscle and authority and don't-mess-with-me, the bully. His breath stank. 'I'm dead serious, lady, and don't you forget it. You could be the intended victim or you could just be putting on an act. I gotta know a hell of a lot more before I can say which. So why don't you start by telling me about *your* enemies? Who would want to kill you? Why are you such a threat?'

Right then I felt more threatened than threatening, but at least Michaels was asking the kind of question I thought he should have started off asking. So I did my best to tell him what he wanted to know. I named all the people who might have a grudge against me, such as a couple of dozen actresses I had beat out for the role I was playing in *LeFever*. It all sounded kind of superficial in that place, full of gun-toting men and women who dealt with professional criminals every day of their lives. But I had to admit Captain Michaels didn't make me feel dumb; he listened carefully, taking notes and asking questions once in a while. Had he deliberately set out to scare me at first just to make sure I'd cooperate later? It went on and on and on.

Finally Michaels decided he'd heard all he needed to hear, and he did something I'd never have expected. He apologized. 'Sorry to put you through this when you're obviously tired. We wanted to talk to you first thing this morning.' He grinned. 'We couldn't find you.'

Couldn't find me? Oh, sure. I'd spent the day rushing from one part of town to another. I made one of those subverbal sounds that can mean anything.

'I'll get someone to drive you home,' the Captain said.

'Detective Larch said she'd wait for me.'

He nodded and thanked me for coming in. So was he a good guy or a bad guy? I was too tired to decide.

Marian Larch tried to talk me into stopping and getting something to eat. 'It's nine o'clock and you haven't eaten since noon. How about it?'

'All I want is to get home and soak in the tub. I'm so tired dinner would just make me sick.'

'A sandwich, then. You need something in your stomach. It'll pick you up, Kelly.'

'I can make a sandwich at home. *I wanna go home,* dammit.'

Her potato face crinkled into a smile. 'Okay. Home it is.'

I wasn't too tired to notice I didn't have to tell her where I lived; she'd looked my address up or read it out of my police file or something. My police file! Christ.

Before long Marian pulled up to the curb in front of my building. 'I'll wait until you're inside.'

The apartment building where I lived didn't have a doorman and depended solely on an electronic security system. We had to unlock two sets of doors just to get into the lobby, and the exterior of the building was always kept brightly lighted.

Well, almost always. Tonight one of the lights was out.

I was fumbling with the first key when a figure stepped out of the shadow. I jumped and started to yell until I saw it was a woman.

'Kelly Ingram?' she asked.

I relaxed. She was an older lady, gray and tired-looking, as tired-looking as I felt. 'Yes?'

'My name is Fiona Benedict. I'm Rudy Benedict's mother. I just wanted to see the woman in whose place my son died.'

CHAPTER 2

FIONA BENEDICT

I hadn't heard from Rudy for almost three months, but that wasn't unusual. Rudy often went for long stretches of time without communicating, and then suddenly would telephone every night for a week. Or write long, single-spaced letters about everything under the sun or sometimes about nothing at all, writing for the sheer pleasure of writing. He did sometimes tend toward excess. In the meantime I kept sending my regular letter every other week, providing what stability I could. Washburn, Ohio, had not been 'home' to Rudy for a long time, neither the town nor the university. Nevertheless I kept him informed about our comings and goings. Whether he acknowledged it or not, Rudy needed a touchstone outside the world of commercial illusion he lived in.

I was in class lecturing on the Crimean War when the call came from the New York police. I remember being annoyed at the interruption and had no foreboding of bad news. When the man on the telephone, a Captain Michaels, told me about Rudy, I made him repeat what he'd said, twice. Then I hung up on him. Later when I'd collected myself, I called him back and asked for details. Poisoned? How?

At that point all the police knew was that Rudy had ingested cyanide crystals under the mistaken notion he was taking medicine. Who had substituted the cyanide for the medicine was not known. 'I'm sorry to have to tell you this, Dr. Benedict,' Captain Michaels had said, 'but it looks like murder.'

I arranged for someone to take my classes, got through the night somehow, and flew to New York the next morning.

When I got to Police Plaza Captain Michaels was out on a case or too busy to talk to me or perhaps just didn't want to be bothered. But finally a nice young man whose name I'm sorry to say I've forgotten helped me find what I needed to know. Rudy's body wouldn't be released until the autopsy report was received from the medical examiner's office; the young man said it was expected late that afternoon. I spent the intervening hours arranging for the cremation of my son's body, in accordance with Rudy's frequently expressed wishes. The process for making such arrangements consisted primarily of proving my ability to pay for the service.

As it turned out the autopsy report didn't come through that afternoon after all—some delay or other. I finally did meet Captain Michaels, though, a florid-faced, overweight man headed for a coronary. By then I'd had enough time to adjust to the idea that someone had hated Rudy enough to want him dead, incredible though that seemed. But I'd no sooner reached that point than I had to make a complete reversal.

'We learned something new just last night,' Captain Michaels told me. 'It looks like the cyanide wasn't meant for your son at all. Seems he took it by accident.'

He couldn't have stunned me more if he'd slapped me.

'His girlfriend gave it to him,' the Captain went on. 'He was complaining of a headache and she gave him a sample bottle of a new remedy that turned out to be cyanide instead. We're checking her out, but it looks like she was the one meant to get it, not your son.'

Looks *as if*, I thought numbly. 'What's her name?'

He hesitated, guessing what I was feeling. 'Look, Dr. Benedict, you can't really blame her. She—'

'I'll find out eventually, Captain,' I said mildly.

He shrugged. 'Kelly Ingram. She's a TV actress.'

I didn't know the name. 'Do you have her address?'

'Dr. Benedict, I know how you must be feeling, but try looking at it this way. It was an accident. Same as if he'd died in a car crash. Crazy and stupid and no reason behind it, but happens just the same. Try thinking of it like he'd died in a traffic accident.'

I'm certain his intentions were good but I loathe being patronized. 'You have the wrong idea, Captain. You say this Kelly Ingram was my son's girlfriend. I want to meet her—she's the one Rudy was spending his time with before he died. I simply want to meet her. Is that an unreasonable request?'

Still he was reluctant. 'I don't like giving out addresses, ma'am, you understand. But I can fix it for you to meet her here . . . maybe tomorrow. Let's see, tomorrow's Saturday, yeah, that'll be all right. Where you staying?'

I gave him the name of my hotel and had to settle for his assurance that he'd contact me as soon as he could arrange a meeting.

It had been a long, horrible day and I should have been

glad to go back to the hotel and collapse. But I was plagued by a sense of something left unresolved, something more I should do. Visitors at Police Plaza all wear badges which are to be turned in at the time of departure. Captain Michaels had assumed I was on my way out, but I didn't want to leave, not just yet. I didn't feel satisfied, somehow. So instead of checking out I found a chair in a waiting area near the Captain's office and sat there.

I wasn't even sure what I was looking for—reassurance, possibly. Rudy had died by accident, the Captain had said. Part of me rejoiced that my son had not turned out to be the sort of man who could provoke murderous hatred in another person. But another part of me said *Are you sure?* What if the Ingram woman hadn't been the intended victim at all? What if she had deliberately poisoned Rudy and simply pretended the rest of it?

A dismaying thought, and probably a calumnious one. It had undoubtedly occurred just as Captain Michaels indicated: someone had aimed at Kelly Ingram and hit Rudy by mistake.

A low snicker brought me out of my musings. Two uniformed police officers nearby were talking *sotto voce* with the kind of snide look on their faces that meant they were making sexual remarks about a woman. I followed their glance to see an absolutely stunning young woman following a policewoman into the Captain's office. Could it be . . . ?

I stood up and walked over to the two officers, watching their faces turn carefully blank. 'Excuse me, could you tell me who that was? The woman who just went into Captain Michaels's office?'

'That was Kelly Ingram,' one of the officers said. 'She's on that show *LeFever*.'

Aha. So she was right here, and Captain Michaels must have known she was coming, and yet he'd put me off with promises of a meeting tomorrow. Why didn't he want me to see her tonight? Probably he had other matters to take care of first; police are supposed to be sticklers for procedure, I understand.

I'd never heard of *LeFever*. The officer had said she was *on* the show, not *in* it. Television instead of Broadway, then. The Captain had said she was a TV actress.

The policewoman who'd taken Kelly Ingram into the Captain's office came back out, a doughfaced woman in her thirties who looked as if she knew her way around. She and the glamour girl she'd escorted into the office were just about as different as any two women could be. The policewoman was homely and tough-looking and undoubtedly could take care of herself. Kelly Ingram was glamorous and soft-looking and probably would never have to take care of herself her entire life. She looked like the kind of woman whose beauty was so extraordinary she'd simply rely on that to carry her through life, never developing any other aspect of herself, not her mind or her personality or any possible talent she might have.

And this was the sort of woman my son had chosen.

If Rudy had been younger, it would have been understandable. But he'd reached the age where seasoned judgment was supposed to have taken over. Rudy would have been forty next month, early middle age. And he was keeping company with this sensual *child*—early twenties at most, barely out of her teens. Not quite Lolita, but too close for comfort. It would appear my son had become conscious enough of his own advancing years to begin hankering after young flesh. It was later than I thought.

Was it Kelly Ingram's beauty that made someone want to murder her? Was it envy? Sexual treachery? Why was I standing there guessing?

The doughfaced policewoman started down the hall, reading from a manila folder as she walked. Without even thinking about it I fell in behind her. At the back of my mind was the idea of waiting until Captain Michaels was through with Kelly Ingram and then catching her as she left. But still I followed the policewoman; I followed her straight into the ladies' room.

28

She'd been carrying several folders other than the one she'd been reading from, plus a stack of official forms of some sort. All in all they made too big an armful to juggle in the small stall, so the policewoman had piled them on the shelf over the washbasins. She'd already gone into the stall before I entered the restroom and so she thought the place was empty; but it was still rather careless of her. The top folder was marked *Ingram, Kelly.*

There were her home address, several business addresses, physical description, age—I was surprised to learn she was twenty-nine. Not the child I'd thought, then, but I'd had only a brief glimpse of her. I had no time to read further as a flush from the stall told me not to linger. I was standing in the hall wondering what to do next when the police officer who'd identified Kelly Ingram for me came up and pointedly asked if I was looking for somebody. It was time to leave.

Once I was outside, waiting for the Ingram woman in the vicinity of Police Plaza suddenly seemed a less than brilliant idea. Besides, I had her address now. I stepped off the curb and held my right arm in the air until a cab squealed up to me.

Kelly Ingram lived in a new-looking highrise in midtown. The building had no doorman; that meant I couldn't wait in the lobby. My plane had left Ohio at 7:10 that morning and I'd been on the go ever since. I was not a young woman, and the day had finally caught up with me. My legs were trembling as I sat down on that part of the steps that was not in direct light.

I think I actually fell asleep. I know she was at the door unlocking it before I realized she had come. I called her name and stepped into the light so she could see me.

And when I told her I wanted to see the woman in whose place my son had died, she attacked me.

I sat in the kitchen of Kelly Ingram's expensive apartment drinking instant Sanka while the doughfaced police-woman made sandwiches, talking nonstop as she worked. Her name was Detective Marian Larch, and it was she who had prevented the Ingram woman from shaking my head right off my shoulders. The glamour girl herself was soaking in the tub.

'She's had a gawdawful day,' Detective Larch was saying. ' 'Course, yours couldn't have been all that great either. But your showing up like that, when you did — well, it was the proverbial straw that broke the camel's back. She was depressed about Rudy to start with, and then she's scared because it sure does look like somebody wants to see her dead — that would throw anybody. She had this long, rotten work day where nothing went right. Then Captain Michaels keeps her in that office for a couple of hours, and he makes it clear she's not off the hook as a suspect herself. She was tired and she hadn't eaten and she was wanting a bath, and then you step out of the shadow and point out your son would still be alive if it wasn't for her. No wonder she went a little crazy.'

'Yes, I should never have said that.' I did regret saying it. It was senseless and self-indulgent and could have accomplished nothing under the best of circumstances. 'I think I was a little crazy myself. I'm glad you were there, Ms Larch. I could never have stopped her.' The shaking had given me a terrible headache, but I wasn't too eager to take something for it. Not in that apartment.

Among Detective Larch's other talents seemed to be an ability to read minds. She opened her bag and took out a sealed packet containing two headache tablets. 'Straight from the dispensary — I took some earlier today. Go on, they're safe.'

I thanked her and swallowed the tablets. Detective Larch placed a platter piled high with aromatic sandwiches on the table. My stomach turned over at the odor; but it had been nine hours since I'd last eaten and I needed something. I found one sandwich containing nothing but a bland cheese and took that one.

Our hostess came in wearing a robe, her hair still damp. With her make-up washed off she looked closer to the thirtyish person she was, but she was still one of the most astonishingly beautiful women I'd ever seen. I found myself staring; she noticed, and had the grace to pretend not to.

She sat down next to Detective Larch and reached for a sandwich. '*Now* I'm hungry. Thanks for making these.'

The policewoman said something unintelligible, her mouth full.

The Ingram woman and I eyed each other warily. We'd both apologized, once we'd come to our senses, but there was still tension between us. I was still blaming her for Rudy's death, and she knew I was. I should have been blaming the murderer — but I didn't know who the murderer was, and I *did* know who should have died instead of Rudy and she was sitting right there across from me. I was offended by the casualness of the scene, by the ordinariness of her sitting there in a mundane domestic setting, eating pastrami on rye. I kept telling myself I should be feeling compassion for this woman who could still be murdered at any time, who might be dead by this time tomorrow. I kept telling myself that, but I couldn't make myself listen.

She'd finished her first sandwich and was half-way through her second with no sign of stopping. Detective Larch said, 'How can you eat like that and stay thin?'

'Chose my grandparents carefully,' the Ingram woman said.

That surprised me. Most of the slender people I knew liked to credit their good figures to their own self-discipline. Yet this woman whose very livelihood depended upon her appearance had casually admitted it was none of her doing; she just happened to get born with the right genes. So the glamour girl could afford to be a big eater, while poor Marian Larch looked like someone who'd put on five pounds if you so much as said the word *chocolate* in her presence.

'When did you get in, Mrs. Benedict?' the police detective asked.

'This morning.'

'Talked to the Captain yet?'

'Captain Michaels? Yes. He said he'd set up a meeting with you, Ms Ingram. He wouldn't give me your address.'

'Call me Kelly,' she said. 'He didn't say anything to me about any meeting.'

'He must have forgotten,' Detective Larch offered. 'Mrs. Benedict — if the Captain wouldn't give you Kelly's address, how'd you find out where she lived?'

Oh-oh. 'Why, I just asked someone else,' I said innocently.

Detective Larch shrugged. 'Okay, if you don't want to tell me. You're here now.' She changed the subject. 'Are you having your son's body shipped back to Ohio?'

'No, Rudy wanted to be cremated. I'm having it done here. But his body hasn't been released yet. The autopsy report hasn't come through.'

'Probably tomorrow,' the detective said.

'I was wondering why the delay.'

'Medical examiner sometimes has a backlog. They get the reports out as fast as they can. It's nothing to worry about, Mrs. Benedict, it happens a lot.' She seemed to hesitate. 'Excuse me if I seem insensitive — but do you plan on taking your son's ashes back with you?'

What a gruesome thought. 'No, I don't.'

'Then be sure to tell the people at the crematorium ahead of time. Otherwise they'll hand you this little box — '

'Oh, good heavens!' I shuddered. 'Thank you for warning me.' Just then Kelly Ingram surprised me for the second time in five minutes; she reached out and touched my arm in sympathy. 'You're a history professor, aren't you?' Getting my mind off Rudy.

I nodded, and wondered what else she knew.

'That's all Rudy told me,' she said. 'That you were a history professor and you lived in Ohio.'

'Is it Dr. Benedict then?' Marian Larch wanted to know.

I said it was, but did not tell them to call me Fiona. Both of these women were part of an alien, violent world that I did not care to be on a first-name basis with. I stared at the table and said nothing. There was one sandwich left on the platter, exuding a spicy odor impossible to ignore. It was an association I have resented ever since, remembering the smell of garlic every time I think of that period of my life when I was arranging for the disposal of my son's body.

Detective Larch said, 'Is there somebody back in Ohio who can help you with all this—the arrangements, I mean?'

'I can manage, thank you.'

'But a little help would make it go easier. Isn't there someone—'

'There is no Mr. Benedict, if that's what you're fishing for,' I said calmly. 'He deserted Rudy and me when the boy was eight.'

The Ingram woman looked surprised at my mentioning so personal a matter but Marian Larch didn't bat an eye. 'No, I meant a neighbor or friend. Or one of your colleagues. Can *I* help?'

I shook my head. 'Thank you for your offer, though. I have to go through Rudy's apartment tomorrow and decide what to do about his belongings, the things I won't want to keep. I won't know what I'll need to do until I see what's there.'

Kelly Ingram said, 'That'll be a big job. I was there once, and the place is crammed with files and papers and stuff. It'll take you a while.'

I'd expected the files and papers, but I hadn't expected that other thing she'd said. 'You were there *once?* Only once?'

She raised one graceful eyebrow. 'That's right.'

'Captain Michaels said you were Rudy's girlfriend. I'd have thought . . .' I trailed off, not really knowing how to finish.

She sighed. 'I was Rudy's *friend*, Dr. Benedict. Not "girlfriend"—did the Captain really use that word? Rudy and I weren't lovers.'

And still another surprise. 'Oh,' I said, trying not to show I was flustered. 'Captain Michaels led me to believe, ah . . .'

'I can't help what Captain Michaels thinks,' she said, an edge to her voice. 'Rudy and I hadn't seen each other for a couple of years, not until just a few weeks ago. We were only getting reacquainted. We weren't lovers.'

She didn't say *yet*, but she might as well have. But she'd made one other thing quite clear: whether they would eventually have become lovers or not, Kelly Ingram quite clearly had not been *in love* with Rudy. She was not crushed by his death. Upset, yes—even horrified, perhaps, but in that distanced way one reacts to the misfortune of someone who is an acquaintance rather than an intimate part of one's personal life. Kelly Ingram was an actress, but I didn't think she was that good an actress. She had not been in love with Rudy.

I accepted Marian Larch's offer of a ride to my hotel.

The next morning the medical examiner's report came through and Rudy's body was released. I notified the crematorium.

Rudy's apartment in Chelsea was what in my younger days would have been called bohemian—arty and cheap. It was the sort of place I could see Rudy living in fifteen or twenty years ago, when he was just starting out. It was a *sophomoric* apartment.

Rudy had five or six pieces of original artwork, but he'd hung none of them. Instead, what wallspace wasn't taken up with bookshelves was covered with posters, most of them advertising theatrical events. Rudy had said he didn't like the apartment and was looking for a better place to live; perhaps that was why he'd never bothered hanging the paintings. I found them in a small pantry off the kitchen that Rudy had used as an all-purpose storage room; they were still in the movers' crates from the time they'd made the trip from California, almost a year ago.

I'd already decided to box up all of Rudy's papers and ship them to Ohio; there I could go through them without rushing, taking as much time as I wanted. The clothes could go to Goodwill Industries or the Salvation Army. Rudy had quite a few pieces of good furniture; I'd ask the

Ingram woman if she wanted any of them. I'd need to get the phone disconnected, notify the utility companies—I decided to make a list.

I was sitting at Rudy's desk trying to think of everything that needed to be done when the door buzzer sounded. As soon as I figured out how the intercom worked, I heard a voice saying, 'It's Kelly. May we come up?'

My heart sank; it was hard enough going through Rudy's things, but having to be polite to that . . . yet I could think of no reason to refuse and buzzed her in. The other part of 'we' turned out to be a successful-looking man whom she introduced as Howard somebody. Each of them was carrying a stack of flattened cardboard cartons.

'The shippers can pack most of what you'll want to send back,' the Ingram woman said, 'but there are always some things you have to take care of yourself. Now, we'll help or we'll get out of your way, whichever you say. Just tell us.'

It was a little thing, showing up with some boxes, but it made me realize that on the whole she'd been behaving better than I had. 'I'd like you to stay,' I said as pleasantly as I could. 'Right now I'm trying to make a list of all the things that need to be done.'

'Did your son have a safe-deposit box, Dr. Benedict?' Howard the mystery man said.

'I have no idea.'

'Have you gone through the desk yet?'

'Not yet.'

'Then that's the place to start. Was there insurance, a will?'

'Howard's a lawyer,' Kelly Ingram explained.

'A will . . . I don't know,' I said. 'I do know there was insurance.'

'He probably had a safe-deposit box, then,' Howard said. 'Look for a key and his bank statements. Then we'll get a court order to open the box.'

'The key might be in the bedroom,' the Ingram woman said and went to look.

I looked at the man named Howard. 'Are you Ms.

Ingram's lawyer?'

'Personal friend.'

One of her men, then.

'Mind if I take a look?' he said.

I yielded the desk to him, and watched as he quickly and methodically went through the papers. Kelly Ingram came back in from the bedroom waving a key just as Howard held up a bank statement. 'Barclays Bank,' he said. 'This is Saturday, Dr. Benedict. I won't be able to get an order to open the box until Monday. If you want my help, that is.'

'I would like your help very much, Mr. . . . ?'

'Call me Howard. Let's see what else we have here.' He took a ledger out of a middle drawer, opened it, and said, surprisingly, 'Glorioski!'

The Ingram woman laughed. 'Glorioski, Howard?'

'The inner child speaks. Do you know what this is?' He meant the ledger. 'It's an inventory of his belongings — location, cost, and so on. Thank the Lord — a careful record-keeper! This will simplify things enormously. And look here. Will, two insurance policies, some stock, title papers to various things like his car and some paintings — the papers are all in the Barclays box. Great. Kelly, do you know where he kept his car?'

'In a garage on Eighth Avenue. I don't remember the name, but I know where it is. What paintings?'

'What's that?'

'Didn't you say paintings were listed there? I don't see any paintings.' She gestured at the postered walls.

'I know where they are,' I said, and led them to the pantry.

'Yup, there they are,' Howard said. 'One, two, three, four, uh, five? That's all? There're supposed to be six. Where's the other one?'

'Perhaps he sold it,' I suggested. 'Although that doesn't seem likely. I don't think they were worth very much.'

'Not a whole lot,' Howard agreed. 'The most expensive was twenty-five hundred. All six together cost less than what he paid for his car. One of them he paid only five hundred bucks for. Who are these people? The artists, I mean.' He held the ledger out to me. 'Do you know any of these names?'

I glanced at Rudy's carefully printed list and shook my head. 'I'm not a good one to ask. I know very little about contemporary art.'

'Don't look at me,' the Ingram woman said.

'Well, let's see which one is missing,' Howard said. Rudy had taken a black felt-tip marker and printed the title of each painting on the crate it was in. The missing painting turned out to be one called *Man and Shadow*, and the artist was someone named Mary Rendell. I'd heard of neither painting nor painter. *Man and Shadow* had cost Rudy only eight hundred dollars.

Howard said, 'If the safety deposit box has ownership papers for just the other five, then I think we can assume he sold the painting. Or maybe gave it away, birthday or Christmas present or the like.'

'And what if the papers are there for all six paintings?' I asked.

He shrugged. 'Cross that bridge when we come to it.'

It went on like that for a while, until we reached a point where only I could make decisions about the disposal of Rudy's personal belongings. I thanked Kelly Ingram as graciously as I could manage for bringing a lawyer to help out. After all, she was doing the best she could to atone for having caused Rudy's death.

The will in Rudy's safe-deposit box listed me as sole heir, and the two insurance policies both named me as beneficiary. One had originally been taken out to benefit Rudy's wife, but even when they divorced he hadn't changed the policy. Only when she remarried did Rudy substitute my name for hers on the second policy. I learned from Detective Larch that Rudy's ex-wife had been notified of his death soon after his body was discovered, almost twenty-four hours before Captain Michaels had contacted me. It was just like her not to call me. Impossible woman.

Howard the lawyer found a buyer for Rudy's car. The offer was low but I accepted just to be done with it. Marian Larch was intrigued by the fact that the deposit box had contained bills of sale for six paintings but only five were in the apartment. I think she had visions of *Man and Shadow*'s turning out to be a priceless American primitive and that there was some sort of crime-within-a-crime just waiting to be discovered. I made it clear I was not sympathetic to her supersleuth ambitions; at a time like that I couldn't be bothered with what happened to an eight-hundred-dollar painting.

Nevertheless Marian Larch had taken Rudy's inventory list and contacted several galleries and museums, trying to 'get a line on the artists,' she said. The experts she consulted hadn't even heard of most of them; none had heard of Mary Rendell, the artist who'd painted *Man and Shadow*. She'd tried to track down the California dealer whose name appeared on the bill of sale, but his gallery had gone out of business several years ago. So Marian Larch asked permission to make one final search of Rudy's apartment before the packers and shippers took over. I told her yes just to get her to stop bothering me.

She found nothing, of course. 'It's odd,' she said, as we waited for the men from the shipping company. 'The first thing you think of in the case of a missing painting that everybody says isn't worth anything is that it *is* worth something. If not for itself, then maybe somebody painted over an old painting that *is* valuable. A Corot or a Manet or something like that.'

'It's the first thing *you* think of,' I pointed out to her. 'The first thing I think of is that the movers lost the painting when Rudy came here from California. Or he did give it away but didn't bother passing on the bill of sale. Or he got tired of looking at it and threw it out. Rudy wasn't a collector. He'd just buy something now and then to hang on a bare wall.'

'Did you ever see the painting?'

'I've been trying to remember. The last time I visited Rudy—let's see, I spent most of last year in London, and . . . it must be close to five years, the last time I was in California. And I just don't know whether I saw *Man and Shadow* then or not. I didn't pay much attention to the paintings, I'm afraid. I know I didn't ask Rudy their titles.'

'Do you remember seeing one of, well, a man and his shadow?'

I didn't. 'To tell you the truth, Ms. Larch, I don't really remember any of them.'

Just then the shippers showed up, to finish the packing and clear the apartment. They were rough and noisy and couldn't seem to work without a transistor radio blaring away, but they were fast. I appreciated their being fast.

At last it was done. Marian Larch drove me back to my hotel. She told me that when I got back home if I thought of something I'd forgotten to do, just give her a call and she'd take care of it. Belatedly it occurred to me the police detective had shown a lot more consideration than her job required her to, so I tried to thank her but she wouldn't let me. Strange woman, Marian Larch. But nice.

In my hotel room I'd just finished locking my suitcase when there was a knock on the door. It was Captain Michaels—whom I'd thought I'd seen the last of.

'Could we sit down, Dr. Benedict?' he said. 'I have something to tell you.'

I didn't like the sound of that and said so.

He plunged right in. 'We've just had the final report from the crime lab. They go over the scene of the crime pretty thoroughly, you know.'

Scene of the crime—Rudy's apartment, which I'd just closed. 'And?'

'And they found some undissolved Lysco-Seltzer crystals caught under the surface rim of the drain. The drain in your son's kitchen sink.'

I failed to see the significance. 'And?' I repeated.

'Don't you see what that means, Dr. Benedict? Somebody dumped out the Lysco-Seltzer right there in Rudy's sink. That bottle hadn't been tampered with before it went through the postal service and ended up in Kelly Ingram's mailbox.'

I began to see—dear God, I began to see.

'What probably happened was, your son came home from visiting Kelly, put the Lysco-Seltzer on the kitchen cabinet, and just left it there. He may have taken part of the bottle that night or he may not have, the medical examiner can't tell us that. But some time the next day somebody emptied out whatever medicine was left in the bottle and substituted cyanide crystals.'

'So the poison wasn't meant for Kelly Ingram at all,' I said woodenly.

Captain Michael's florid face was drawn into a scowl. ' 'Fraid not. It seems your son was the intended victim all along.'

CHAPTER 3

KELLY INGRAM

I was so relieved when Rudy's mother went back to Ohio I felt like celebrating. I know that sounds callous and I can't help it, but I was glad she was g-o-n-e, *gone*. She'd had one bad shock after another, enough to flatten most people, she'd handled it all with considerable aplomb, I think I'm using that word right, and she'd been courteous to me after that first meeting when I went off my head and flew at her. *Stiflingly* courteous. She drove me nuts.

And I'm not going to say how sorry I was to hear poor old Rudy was the 'right' victim after all, because for starters nobody would believe me. I was truly sorry Rudy was dead and I hated the idea that his murderer hadn't been caught, but I still liked that scenario better than the one that cast *me* as the body on the floor. So I'm thick-skinned and unfeeling—okay, that's too bad, I'm sorry. But I'm also alive and likely to stay that way, and I'm happy about that part of it.

Now that I've got that out of my system, I can say I did feel sorry for Dr. Benedict, in fits and spurts. (Starts?) She made it hard for you to feel sorry for her, being so formal and remote like that. She did it on purpose, that *don't-touch-me* bit. I don't like people getting too close either, unless I say so, but I'm no ice lady like Dr. Mrs. Fiona Benedict. No wonder Rudy didn't talk about her much. I tried to help; I even took Howard Chesney along to handle the legal details for her. She thanked me, but it was obviously killing her to make the effort.

She was still blaming me for Rudy's death, right up to the time Captain Michaels told her about the Lysco-Seltzer in the sink. I saw her only once after that; she stayed on for a few more days to answer what questions she could about Rudy, but then she had to get back to her classes. That couldn't have been easy for her, going back home with all those questions about Rudy's death still not answered. And then having to stand up in front of a classroom with all those students knowing—well now, wait a minute, maybe they didn't know. Would the murder have made the Ohio papers? Dr. Benedict sure as hell wasn't going to make a public announcement if she didn't have to.

Marian Larch seemed to think Rudy's death was somehow tied up with a cheap painting that was missing from his apartment, but she admitted nobody else at Police Headquarters thought so. Captain Michaels had told her to stop wasting time on it. *I* still thought the play Rudy'd been going to write had something to do with it, but I couldn't get Marian interested in that at all. I kept trying to tell her the whole thing seemed wrong, somehow. Rudy Benedict just wasn't the *type* of person to get himself murdered, it seemed to me.

That amused Marian, in a morbid sort of way. 'Oh?' she'd said. 'Tell me, Professor Ingram, what do you consider the right *type* to get murdered?'

'Don't get smart, I'm serious,' I told her. We were on a break in shooting *LeFever*; Marian Larch had gotten into the habit of dropping in—continuing her investigation, she said. I think she just liked to watch what was going on. Or maybe she liked watching Nick Quinlan; lots of women did, Lord help us. 'Rudy wasn't a threatening person,' I said. 'Aren't people who get murdered supposed to be a threat of some sort?'

'You'd be surprised,' Marian said. 'Some of the people who get killed were so mousy when they were alive you could forget they were there at all.'

'I didn't say Rudy was *mousy*—'

'I know, I know, that was just an example. Don't be so loose and easy with that word *type*. Kelly, there just aren't any murder victim *types*—not really. A guy overhears something by accident that makes him a danger to the mob so they put out a contract on him . . .'

'Yecch,' I said.

'. . . so what does this guy's "type" have to do with anything? He just happened to be in the wrong place at the wrong time so they kill him for it. It happens like that, you know, more often than you'd imagine. Couple of months ago an old woman was fished out of the East River, a landlady from Lois Aida—'

'From where?'

'Lower East Side, that's the way they say it. One of her tenants was a pusher and she stumbled on his cache and he killed her. She probably would have kept her mouth shut, but it was easier for him to kill her than worry about her talking. We got the pusher, but that didn't help the landlady any.'

'You know, I was beginning to feel safe again until we started this conversation.'

'And what do you really know about Rudy Benedict?' she plowed on. 'You hadn't seen him for two years, Kelly. You don't know what kind of enemies he might have made in that time. He could have changed completely from the last time you knew him.'

'No, he was the same old Rudy.' I was on firm ground there. 'Putting on the dog a little because of that play he was going to write, but he was still Rudy. Wanting more than he had, but not really knowing how to go about

42

getting it. Trying to change, but not really making any big break from what he'd always done.'

'Well, there—what about that? *Trying to change.* Doesn't that indicate things weren't the same for him as they used to be, that he wanted something different?'

'Aw, no. Rudy was always complaining—even when I knew him in California. He grumbled all the time about the tripe he had to write every week. But the money was good and Rudy wasn't about to throw that away. He didn't really like what he was doing, but he didn't know how to get out of it without giving up the comfortable way of living he was used to.'

'But he had decided to go ahead and write a play. He must have been giving something up for that,' she mused.

'Not really,' I said. 'He was still getting a salary from Nathan Pinking—his contract hadn't quite run out yet. He wasn't taking any risks. Rudy just wasn't the daring type, Marian. If you'll pardon the four-letter word.'

'You mean "type"? I'll pardon it. But there had to be something out of the ordinary in Rudy Benedict's life or else—Kelly, is that man trying to get your attention?'

I glanced across the set of LeFever's office to see a familiar figure jumping up and down and waving his arms. 'That's Leonard Zoff, my agent. He doesn't like coming here—something must be up. Come on.'

We picked our way around the set, Leonard helping us by pumping his arms faster. He wouldn't have dreamed of working his way over to us; too many things to trip over.

'Hello, Leonard, why didn't you just yell, the way you usually do?'

'Laryngitis,' he whispered, and peered suspiciously at Marian. 'Whozis?'

'Marian Larch, of the Detective Bureau. Marian, this is Leonard Zoff.'

'Oh—okay,' Leonard rasped before Marian could say anything. 'Kelly, we gotta talk. We—'

Sometimes he really bugs me. 'Not *Oh, okay*, Leonard. *How do you do* or *Pleased to meet you* or just plain *Hello.*

But not *Oh, okay.*'

Leonard had a standard response for that kind of situation. He slipped an arm around Marian Larch's waist, leered into her face, and whispered, 'Don't mind me, darling. No offense intended—I'm just in kind of a rush, y'know?'

She stared at him. 'I think I liked *Oh, okay* better.'

Rolled right off him. 'Kelly, we got a biggie coming. You ready for this? The Miss America people are considering you for one of the judges. Whaddaya say to that?'

Me, I didn't say anything; I was speechless. But Marian snorted, 'That meat parade!'

'Meat, schmeat, it's *exposure*, darling.' Leonard's eyes were dancing and his lived-in face was one huge grin; he was angling a big one, all right. 'Every year they have one professional beauty among the judges to show the little girls how it's done, and I been telling them how next year it's gotta be Kelly Ingram.'

'This is for next year?' I asked.

'Oh yeah, these things gotta be settled way ahead—you got your foot in the door now because the broad, 'scuse me, the *lady* they had lined up went and got herself preggie. You're still on the pill, aren't you, darling? Anyway, they were thinking Bo Derek but I talked them out of it. By the end of the season, I told them, Kelly Ingram's going to be the biggest thing on the tube. I said you want somebody visible, don't you? Shit, I got other clients, I said, but I'm telling you Kelly's the one you want. How do you like that—I'm in there pitching for you, Kel. You got that?'

'I got it, Leonard.'

'Right. So now all I got to do is persuade Nathan Shithead that it's just what the *LeFever* image needs. And it is, it is!'

Marian was looking puzzled. 'If this other woman is pregnant now and this contest isn't until *next* year . . . ?'

'Why can't she go ahead and do it?' Leonard rasped. 'Because this is her first baby and some women lose their

44

looks when they become mommas. Sorry, darling, but that's the way it is. The Miss America people just can't take the risk.' Leonard's grin had disappeared; he swallowed, painfully—his throat must really have been hurting. 'Nathan Shithead has graciously granted me an appointment, ain't that generous of him? The Miss America Apple Pie folks want a guarantee there's no contractual problems before they'll even negotiate.'

'Why didn't you tell me this was in the works, Leonard?' I asked. 'You know I like to be kept posted.'

'I didn't want to get your hopes up.'

'Meaning you didn't think the pageant people would go for it.'

'Now, darling, don't go putting yourself down like that—you've got to have faith!'

'In myself, I got faith. It's you I'm not so sure about.'

'Don't be so hard on a sick old man,' he rasped. 'Call my office later—I'll leave word. Glad to've met you, uh, Marilyn.' His grin flashed back on for a tenth of a second and he was gone.

'Whew,' Marian said, looking after him. 'Is he always like that?'

'Usually he's noisier.'

Just then they called me to do my half of a telephone scene. The assistant director stood off-camera and read LeFever's lines to me with far more expression than Nick Quinlan would ever be able to manage. When I finished the story editor's secretary came up and handed me some green pages. I groaned.

'Only two lines in your part, Kelly,' she smiled. 'Easy changes.'

I managed to smile back, but I didn't mean it. I hate it when we get as far as green pages.

'What's the matter?' Marian Larch wanted to know.

'Script changes,' I told her. 'Every new set of changes comes through on a different color paper. This week's script already looks like a rainbow and now—well, I guess these aren't so bad.' I read through the new dialogue quickly. Two new lines for me, I already knew them.

Trouble was, I still knew the old ones as well. The trick was remembering which set to say when you were in front of the camera.

'Kelly—'

'Come into my dressing room, they're getting ready to shoot.'

With the door to the dressing room closed we could talk, if we kept our voices low; the soundproofing wasn't all it was supposed to be. Marian was worrying about what Leonard Zoff had said. 'Is that true about the pregnant woman? That the Miss America people won't take a chance on her keeping her looks after she gives birth?'

'No,' I laughed. 'There's not a word of truth in it. In fact, I'm pretty sure there wasn't any pregnant woman at all—Leonard just made her up.'

Marian Larch's eyebrows climbed. 'But why?'

'To keep me in my place, grateful and grovelling. Notice how Leonard supposedly slipped and said *broad*—and then made a big production of correcting the word to *lady?* Well, that was deliberate, that was. Good old subtle Leonard, reminding me I'm just a package to be sold but *he's* the salesman. Then he came on with this story about the pregnant woman—to make me think I was the pageant officials' *second* choice. And then they only came around to considering me because of Mr. Leonard Zoff's superior powers of persuasion.'

'You mean you might have been their first choice?'

'I mean I'll never know—which is exactly what Leonard had in mind. He knows I don't swallow most of that guff he dishes out, but he likes to keep me off-balance. Figures he has more control that way.'

She just looked at me. Then: 'Why do you stay with an agent like that?'

'Find me a better one and I'll change.'

'You mean he's so good at getting results you're willing to put up with all that other stuff?'

'I mean he's no worse than the rest of them. And Leonard does know everybody. Right now he's in the office whispering in Nathan Pinking's ear about how this Miss America gig will be just what *LeFever* needs next year. And Nathan will loll there in his big leather chair, letting himself be convinced. He likes to see Leonard sweat.'

'Why Nathan Pinking? What does he have to say about it anyway?'

'It's in my contract—it's a personal contract Nathan had me sign before he'd give me the role in *LeFever*. I can't do anything outside *LeFever* without his say-so. He vetoed a greeting card commercial I'd been offered because he said down-home wholesomeness wasn't exactly the image he had in mind for me. Nathan told me to try to get one of those pantyhose commercials—you know, the ones where the models sit down without *quite* putting their knees together.'

'I know the ones,' Marian said sourly. 'Your Nathan Pinking must be a real prince. Kelly, are you really going to do it? Be one of the Miss America judges, I mean.'

'Sure, if Leonard can arrange it.'

'And it doesn't bother you at all?'

Oh boy. 'Look, Marian. A beauty contest is sort of like an audition, you know? It's a recognized way of getting started on a career.'

She snorted. 'It's a *meat* parade. All those young girls offering their bodies for inspection—like prize cows at the county fair. And you sanction that?'

'Hey, wait a minute—nobody's forcing those girls to take part. Hell, that's what they *want*, a chance at the spotlight.'

'Sure, they *want* it—because they're young and just beginning to feel their power and flushed with new success. And because they're taught every day of their lives that girls are supposed to be ornamental. They want it because they don't know what else to want.'

I snorted at that. 'Well, I'm going to do it, and that's that. *If* Nathan Pinking doesn't decide to say no just to bug Leonard.'

'Why would he do that?'

'Notice how Leonard always calls him Nathan Shithead?'

'Could I miss it?'

'Leonard hates Nathan Pinking's guts. And Nathan returns the compliment. Yet each of them is the other's best customer. When Nathan's putting a new show together, he doesn't call a casting office until after he's talked to Leonard. And whenever Leonard manages to sign up an established star who's just fired his old agent, Leonard makes sure Nathan gets first crack at him. They can't stand each other, but they always find a way to do business.'

'A love-hate relationship?'

'More like a hate-hate relationship. They really do loathe each other. But money's money, so they'll keep doing business as long as it's profitable for both of them. But if one of them ever starts to slip, the other one will drop him like a hot potato.'

'What if Leonard's the one to slip? Where will that leave you?'

'With a new agent. I'm not going down with anybody's ship but my own, may it never come to pass. Here, check me on my new lines—read me my cues.'

'Ah, it's time I was getting—'

'It'll take you twenty seconds, for crying out loud. There are only two lines. Come on, read me my cues.'

She grumbled, but she did it.

I didn't see Marian Larch for a while after that. I couldn't tell whether the investigation of Rudy's death was easing off or just heading in a different direction. Or maybe Marian had run out of excuses for dropping in on the *LeFever* set.

When he had a show taping in New York, Nathan Pinking rented space at a converted movie soundstage on West Fifty-fourth Street. We had a few permanent sets, but mostly we shot exteriors. New York wasn't like California, where everything you needed to make a movie or a television series was all right there together in the same studio—the crews, the commissaries, the costume shop, the print shop, the scenery docks, the prop shop, everything. Like a factory. In New York you had to go hunting for all the things you needed in a hundred different places. So, nobody came to New York to make a series *indoors*. You came because of what the city had to offer in the way of location shots. The place was an inexhaustible backdrop. *And* a good filler—for those weeks when the script was a mite on the skimpy side and you had to fill in those empty spots with pretty pictures. That happened on *LeFever* every week, by the way. We never ran long, never went into overtime. Nathan Pinking didn't believe in overtime.

I had a week off from the show. I yelled bloody murder but they wrote me out of the script just the same. The episode was being shot in London and the writers explained in this overpatient way they had of talking to dumb broads that there was no way to justify LeFever's taking a girlfriend along with him on an overseas business trip. *Oh yeah?* I said. *What about all those Congressional junkets?*

But the answer was still no, and the real reason, as always, was money. The episode was being financed by a British production company that wanted to use *LeFever* to introduce the hero of a new series they were making. The British were going to try for a direct sale to American television instead of playing it in England first and then selling it to Masterpiece Theatre fifteen years later. So the deal Nathan Pinking had worked out was that the British would pick up the tab for an episode showing LeFever in London cooperating with *their* hero—but the funds were not limitless. Certain things had to go, and the character I played was still on the expendable list. I wasn't exactly overloaded with job security just then.

I called Leonard Zoff and demanded he do something about it, but he wouldn't even try. 'These things are decided long in advance,' he said. 'I know what the Brits budgeted for and there just ain't no traveling money for little Kelly. Accept it, darling—there's nothing to be done.'

'I'll pay my own way.'

'Like hell you will!' he exploded, causing me to jerk the receiver away from my ear. 'Once you start that, Nathan Shithead'll have you paying through the nose until the very *second* your contract runs out! Don't you suggest it, don't you even *think* it—do you hear me?'

I told him I heard him but he went on hollering until I said okay *okay* and hung up. So I was to be the Invisible Woman that week.

I had a special reason for wanting to be in that episode. Their hero was a hell of a lot more attractive than our hero. I'd seen their leading man in one movie and almost wrote the guy a fan letter. I wanted to meet him, that's all there was to it. And then when Nathan Pinking pretended to be doing me this big favor by giving me a week's vacation in mid season, I almost poked him one.

Nathan had said okay to my being a judge at the Miss America contest, so Leonard Zoff was trying to arrange it. If Leonard could bring it off, I'd go through with it, no question. I know what side my bread's buttered on. It was easy for Marian Larch to sneer at the 'meat parade' side of it. She didn't have to worry about the right exposure at the right time in order to earn a living. So a lot of women didn't like the contest, so that was too bad.

Not my problem.

My problem was a bad case of the fidgets. I could use the time off, though. I had my hair done by somebody other than the *LeFever* people, checked my wardrobe, watched the cleaning service people do their weekly thing in my apartment, read some of my mail, and went dancing. That took care of Monday.

The man I went dancing with also took care of Tuesday and Wednesday, but Thursday he felt he should go back to work. He was an architect, and his boss was quote the most demanding, most unreasonable man in the universe unquote. (He worked for his father.) So on Thursday morning I was thinking of getting on a plane and going somewhere for the weekend when the mail arrived, containing a little something I wasn't expecting at all.

It was a yellow box and it had black and white letters that said 'Sample—Not for Sale' and its name was Lysco-Seltzer.

Now, there's no need to panic, I told myself in the calmest and most rational way imaginable. Somebody intent on murder wouldn't use a Lysco-Seltzer bottle *again*, surely. Would he? No—it was exactly what it appeared to be, it had to be. Thousands and thousands of other New York mailboxes were holding little yellow boxes that morning, *and they were all exactly alike*. There was absolutely no need to panic.

I called Police Headquarters and screamed for Marian Larch.

One thing about Marian, she never tried to brush your anxieties aside as something you just imagined. She always took *me* seriously, anyway, and while I expected her to say things like *You're making a fuss over nothing* or the like, she never did.

What she did do was take one look at the Lysco-Seltzer box and drop it in her shoulder-bag. 'It's been tampered with,' she said.

After one look she could tell that? 'How do you know?'

'The address label. That address was typed individually—it didn't come out of a machine like an Addressograph or some sort of dry-process addressing machine. In mass mailings they use a master list and print from that. This box goes straight to the lab. Why are you home?'

It took me a second to figure out what she meant. 'I'm not in the episode they're taping now. I have the week off.'

'Oh, that's nice,' she said dubiously.

'No, that's not nice.'

'No, that's not nice,' she agreed. 'Look, just sit tight until the crime lab gets finished. Don't go out, keep your door locked.'

'Count on it,' I said grimly.

Marian didn't get back with an answer until the next morning—that was one very anxious day and night I spent, I can tell you. I'd almost talked myself into thinking there was nothing to worry about when she'd pulled that label stunt on me. Well, *she* didn't pull the stunt, of course, but it was the kind of news I could have lived without knowing. Or maybe I couldn't. *Live* without knowing it, I mean. Jesus.

I was sitting and staring at a big cardboard carton that United Parcel had just delivered when Marian showed up around ten Friday morning.

'What's that?' she asked.

'A bomb, no doubt,' I said fatalistically.

'Nonsense.' All brisk efficiency. 'Too big for a bomb. Besides, you'll be happy to learn nobody mailed you any cyanide in a Lysco-Seltzer bottle.'

I perked up at that. 'You mean the bottle wasn't tampered with after all?'

'Didn't say that—it was tampered with, all right. But whoever did the tampering didn't substitute cyanide this time. The lab boys said it didn't even look like cyanide crystals—*or* Lysco-Seltzer. Yellow instead of white, for one thing. So maybe the guy who sent it didn't really intend for you to take it at all. Maybe it was just a joke.'

'Joke? What do you mean, *joke?*' I looked at her closely, but that potato face wasn't giving much away; I've got to stop thinking *potato face*. 'Marian, what was in that bottle?'

'Phenolphthalein. Ever heard of it?'

'Spell it.'

She spelled it. 'It's not hard to get hold of, the way cyanide is. Anybody can buy it in a drugstore—you don't even need a prescription. Kelly, phenolphthalein is used mostly as a laxative.'

I just stared at her. 'Somebody sent me a laxative?'

She nodded soberly, but I suspected she was trying not to laugh. 'Somebody sent you a laxative.'

I was absolutely dumfounded or even dumbfounded,

I'm not going to look it up. 'A laxative.' I was at such a loss I went over and kicked the United Parcel carton, I didn't know what else to do.

'Hey,' Marian said uneasily.

'You said it wasn't a bomb. Nobody's out to kill me. They're just out to give me diarrhea. Isn't that wonderful? What a glamorous ailment to come down with! *Why would anybody send me a laxative?*'

'Maybe simply to get a rise out of you—to make you react the way you are reacting.'

'And they just happened to pick the same means that was used to kill Rudy? A Lysco-Seltzer bottle? Come *on*. That's no coincidence.'

'No—I don't think it is. It certainly could be Rudy Benedict's murderer who sent you the phenolphthalein. Or somebody else who found out it was your Lysco-Seltzer that had been doctored in Benedict's apartment and decided to give you a little scare just for the fun of it. A sadistic practical joker.'

'Great idea of fun, isn't it?'

'Whoever sent you the laxative would have to get pleasure out of what he was doing—there's nothing else to be gained. Do you know anybody with that kind of personality? The kind that would get a kick out of embarrassing you?'

'A couple of hundred,' I said without hesitation. 'Nathan Pinking, Leonard Zoff, Nick Quinlan—'

It was Marian's turn to say, 'Oh, come *on*.'

'Come on, nothing. Most of the people I know would think it was funny to put somebody out of commission that particular way. Using the same kind of bottle that killed Rudy is ghoulish, sure, but that just puts an edge on it. It's the kind of thing Nathan Pinking especially would get a kick out of. He's not exactly nice people.'

'But why would he want to put you out of action for even a day? Wouldn't that cost him—oh, that's right. You're not in this week's episode.'

I said, 'Nathan's always doing things just to show you what he can get away with. Do you remember

Christopher Clive?'

'An actor, sure.'

'Not just *an* actor. He used to be somebody, a Shakespearean actor primarily. An Englishman, same kind of training as Gielgud and Richardson and the rest of them. But he went on the skids, stopped acting for years. You know, one of those alcoholics who have to stop drinking altogether because one more swallow will kill them? Well, he's trying to make a comeback. He takes any role he can get.'

'That's it,' Marian said. 'He was on *LeFever*, wasn't he? Small part. Thought I'd seen him recently.'

'Remember the scene in Central Park where he lost his trousers? That wasn't in the script. Nathan Pinking wanted him to drop his pants for a cheap laugh. Christopher Clive is a man of enormous dignity, even as a reformed drunk. It was painful for him. But he did it—he needed the job. Nathan just stood there and snickered. He humiliated that man just to prove he could. Now, do you think somebody like that would hesitate to send me a laxative disguised as something else?'

Marian shook her head. 'I got to admit, he sounds like a good candidate. But those others you mentioned—what about your agent, Leonard Zoff? How would hurting you benefit him?'

I shrugged. 'Leonard sometimes calls himself a flesh-peddler. I think he dislikes women. His speech is just full of little put-downs—well, you met him, you know what he's like. I don't really know what goes on in Leonard's head. But I take it back about Nick Quinlan. On second thought, I know he didn't do it. He's too dumb. Nick couldn't even manage typing the address label much less all the rest of it.'

'I'm glad you eliminated one suspect,' Marian said dryly. 'Do you really spend your life surrounded by so much ill will?'

'Absolutely. You mean you don't? You're a cop, you should know what it's like. Look what's happened here. Somebody just told me they think I'm shit. How am I

54

supposed to feel about that? What am I supposed to do — take it in stride?'

'Kelly —'

'I can't even hit back! Oh, how I'd love to hit back!' Something occurred to me. 'I wouldn't mind slipping a little of that phenolwhatsit to Nick Quinlan. Is the crime lab finished with that bottle? Do you suppose —'

'No, you may not have it back,' Marian said disapprovingly. 'You shouldn't mess around with chemicals you don't know anything about. What's a safe dosage? Don't even consider it.'

I muttered something at her. She was right, of course. I just didn't want her to be right, not just then; I wasn't in the mood for it. I went over to the United Parcel carton and thought about kicking it again.

'Why don't you open it?' Marian asked. Then, when I hesitated: 'Would you like me to open it for you?'

'No, I'll do it.' I couldn't spend the rest of my life being afraid of *boxes*. The carton was taped shut and I had to get a knife from the kitchen to cut it open.

'You'd think the crown jewels were in there,' Marian said as I sawed away at the tape. But it wasn't the crown jewels inside.

It was toilet paper. Seventy-two rolls of White Cloud toilet paper, three hundred double-ply sheets to the roll.

CHAPTER 4

FIONA BENEDICT

When I got back to Washburn, Ohio, I 'confided' in a few people that Rudy had died of an allergic reaction to a new medicine he was taking for high blood pressure. Some of my high-minded colleagues immediately assumed *overdose*, I'm sure, but I couldn't help that. It was better than putting up with the kind of stares that were bound to come my way if it were known I was even remotely connected with a murder. Washburn, Ohio, was where I intended to live out my retirement, starting in three years' time. I did not intend to live there as an object of curiosity.

Poor Rudy. How hard he'd tried, how much boasting he'd done. He was too bright for that world of flash and glitter he'd moved in, but not really inventive enough for any enduring work. In the beginning I'd thought television would be good for him, mature him a little. By constant exposure to the perfectly horrible example television offered, he'd learn how *not* to write, I'd hoped. Eventually, I thought, he'd move on to better things.

But no, he never did. At first I'd assumed Rudy had been seduced by the easy success he'd found, but later I came to understand it was fear that kept him from venturing farther afield. He never took any real risks in his life, and for that I blame his father. All of Rudy's confidence in himself evaporated the day that cowardly man left us to cope on our own. Rudy was supposed to have been planning a play when he died, and there's always the possibility that he would actually have gone ahead and written it. But I didn't think so; it was all talk. Rudy was a big talker. That New York police detective, the doughfaced woman named Larch — she'd brought up the subject of Rudy's play every time she could. I suppose she was trying to give me a good final memory of him: the serious writer embarking on a major work. But it was a false picture; I knew my son.

Rudy had started rebelling against me soon after his father left us and never quite grew out of it. He blamed me for his father's going; and by the time he was old enough to understand what had happened, it was too late. The pattern was set — he needed to blame me. In the last letter I had from him, he was still telling me (in a disguised manner, of course) how important he was in the world he had chosen — as distinguished from the one I inhabited. His father had also been a historian, but in college Rudy had taken courses exclusively in the soft disciplines, art and literature and music appreciation, the

56

sort of thing in which the student's opinions of works of art are treated as more important than the works themselves. And then midway through his senior year, he quit. One semester away from graduation, and he walked out. Rudy had taken a perverse pleasure in leaving school before getting a degree; it was his way of thumbing his nose at the academic life that he identified with me.

At least, that's what I was supposed to believe. On the surface Rudy and I were always on good terms; the rebelling was more in the nature of needles in the side. And I did believe his walking out of college was basically a defiant gesture directed at me. But not completely. By rejecting the academic world, Rudy would never have to live up to its standards—which weren't all that high even then. But the way he systematically avoided the hard disciplines was revealing. By avoiding them, Rudy never had to risk failing. Rudy didn't like taking risks.

When he first started selling scripts to the various series, I watched every show he wrote for. But even on television Rudy rarely missed a chance to get in his digs at the academic life. Repeatedly he pictured it as a retreat, a hiding out from 'real' life—which on television was always assumed to be violent and exhibitionistic and loud and vulgar. That was 'real' living? Being 'street wise' was the epitome of human achievement?

It's an attitude that has always amazed me. Rudy frequently had his heroes sneer at teachers as head-in-the-sand milksops, people who never really knew what was going on *out there* in the 'real' world. Rudy wasn't alone in claiming that, of course; it's a favorite excuse of dropouts, failures, those too lazy or too afraid to use their brains. But it seemed to me *they* were the ones with their heads in the sand. I know perfectly well that the polite life led by a small, self-contained academic community in the 'safe' state of Ohio is not typical of all human life. I have never claimed that it was. But it's a way of life that does exist and it isn't going to go away, no matter how loudly the outsiders proclaim it isn't *real*.

And what did Rudy know of street life? He loved to

write about wise-cracking private eyes and fast-talking con men and dedicated social workers and crime-busting lawyers and world-weary police officers. None of that Rudy had any direct experience of; his knowledge of his subject matter was second-hand and even his attitudes were borrowed — from other writers, other shows. He was my son, but I'm afraid there wasn't one spark of originality in Rudy. Even when he was writing comedy his protagonists were usually unlettered but 'savvy' people who consistently triumphed over their better-educated adversaries. And that, I think, was the secret of Rudy's success. He was a populist writer. He repeatedly gave voice to enduring folk ideals, such as the one that celebrates getting something for nothing. Or the one about the simple soul who wins out not through superior intelligence or skill but just by being his own wonderful self.

There must be a frighteningly large number of people in this country who need to believe that kind of thing; otherwise Rudy's particular brand of dramatized exculpation wouldn't have been so much in demand. This is the way he'd spent his life, telling TV audiences the self-flattering things they wanted to believe. Rudy did not pretend he was doing great work; he affected a certain cynical nonchalance that said this was the only way to survive in the 'real' world.

So Rudy deceived himself as well as his audiences. He always wrote safe stories, ones that could be counted on not to disturb, not to challenge. He took no risks. And yet he looked down his nose at me for hiding in a safe environment. He never saw that he was doing the same thing himself.

And in the end, it hadn't protected him after all.

The semester would be over in another few weeks, and I had plans to make. I notified the dean I wouldn't be available for either summer session after all, and asked him to find someone to take the two courses I'd agreed to teach. It was late notice and rather put him on the spot, but he told me he'd take care of it and not to worry. A considerate man, and a friend.

I had made up my mind that if the police hadn't caught Rudy's murderer by the end of the school term, I'd go back to New York long enough to hire my own detectives. I was concerned that I might be leaving it too late, that whatever trail the murderer had left might have grown cold. But there were too many obligations keeping me in Washburn just then; the end of the term meant final exams and term papers to grade. Also, I had to finish correcting the proofs of my book, and that was something I simply could not rush. After spending eleven years on research and three more on the writing, I wasn't going to allow hasty proofreading to mar the finished product.

So I really had no time to spare when Captain Michaels called me from New York and told me he wanted to send Marian Larch to look through Rudy's papers.

'Why didn't you do that before I had them all shipped here?' I asked in exasperation.

'We didn't want to delay your departure,' he said blandly. (I translated that to mean he hadn't thought it necessary then.) 'She'll take nothing without your permission — she won't even photocopy anything without your permission. We have no authority in Ohio, but I'm hoping you'll cooperate. I'd like to send her, Dr. Benedict.'

'It'll be a waste of time, Captain. Rudy's papers are mostly writing notes, business correspondence, copies of his scripts. The paperwork any writer accumulates over a period of years.'

'Have you read it all?'

'No, I just sorted through it to see what was there, I haven't had time to read it yet.'

'What about personal correspondence? Do you have his personal letters too?'

'There weren't any. Rudy never kept personal letters.' He certainly didn't keep any of mine.

'Still, there might be something. Dr. Benedict, we've got

to consider everything.'

'That means your investigation has reached a dead end, I take it.'

A brief silence from the other end. 'We aren't getting very far here,' he admitted. 'Let me send Detective Larch. It won't hurt for her to take a look.'

In the end I agreed, on condition that she stay at my house and pass herself off as a personal friend of Rudy's here for a visit. I didn't want to have to explain a New York police detective's poking through my son's papers. So now I had a house guest to concern myself with.

I prepared the way by telling a few people she was coming, friends such as the Morrisseys. Drew Morrissey's field was the American Civil War, and Roberta taught in the English Department — Victorian period, mostly.

'I don't remember your ever mentioning a Marian Larch,' Roberta Morrissey said in that annoyingly straightforward way she had.

'I just met her, when I was in New York,' I said truthfully. 'She was a friend of Rudy's,' not truthfully at all.

We were in the faculty lounge of Cuthbert Hall, going through the morning coffee break ritual. Drew cleared his throat. 'Fiona, I don't mean to be nosy — but did you invite her here?'

'She invited herself.'

'Then why, Fiona?' That was Roberta. 'Why are you letting her come? Intruding on you at a time like this!'

I liked her honest indignation, but I went on with the lie just the same. 'Ostensibly she's coming here to console me, but I think she's really looking for consolation herself.' How glibly it came out. The Morrisseys were my closest friends, and I didn't like deceiving them. But the true story was so unpalatable I couldn't tell even them.

Drew was looking especially concerned. He'd turned almost completely gray this past year, something I'd not realized until I got back from New York; I'd watched it happen, little by little, without seeing it. Drew glanced at Roberta. 'Dinner?' She nodded. 'Bring her over to dinner one night,' he said. 'That'll take up some of the time. When is she getting here?'

That seemed a little risky to me; I didn't know how good Marian Larch was at acting a part. But I could think of no reason to refuse, so we agreed on a time. I was sure I could count on the detective's willingness to go through with the charade; she'd shown herself to be a considerate woman in New York.

'You'll have to call me Marian,' was the first thing she said. 'Although I'll go on calling you Dr. Benedict, of course.' She'd rented a car at the airport and found my house on her own; I didn't even have to meet her.

'Yes, that's probably best, Marian,' I agreed. I don't like calling near-strangers by their first names but it would have looked odd not to, this time.

'Just so we'll be telling the same story,' she went on, 'am I right in assuming you haven't told the people here your son was murdered?'

'You assume correctly.'

She kept her face expressionless. 'Now, if you'll show me where the papers are? The sooner I get started, the quicker I'll be out of here.'

I took her up to the attic where I'd had Rudy's things carried. I'd put up a table and chair near one of the dormer windows; I planned to work there myself when I got around to reading the papers.

She was appalled when she saw how many there were. Fourteen good-sized cartons plus three filing cabinets. She opened one of the cartons. 'I had no idea—so many scripts! And all these other folders—what are they?'

'Notes, outlines. Works he never completed, probably meant to get back to eventually. Some research work—background material, mostly. Rudy rarely threw anything away.'

'You've read all this?' Her dough face plainly said she didn't believe it.

'No, I'd planned to give the summer over to it.'

She scowled down at the carton she'd opened. 'Well, I

61

can't read everything here—I'd be here all summer myself. Where's his business correspondence?'

I indicated one of the filing cabinets. 'By the way, we're invited out to dinner tonight. The Morrisseys, friends of mine.'

She nodded absently as she lifted an armful of folders out of the file cabinet. Then as I started to leave, she said, 'Oh—will we be back by ten?'

I lifted my shoulders. 'I doubt it. Why?'

'This is Thursday—*LeFever*'s on at ten. They're into re-runs now—you did know the episode your son worked on is showing tonight, didn't you?'

'No, I didn't know—and I would like to see it. Thank you for mentioning it.'

'Did you miss it the first time?'

'I don't have a television set. We'll watch at the Morrisseys.' I saw her eyes grow large and hurried to cut her off. 'When my set broke down a few years back, I somehow never got around to having it repaired. I'll call you in time to get ready for dinner.'

I left before she could answer. I knew what she was thinking: *Her son was a TV writer and she didn't even bother to watch?*

Roberta Morrissey had cooked her usual roast beef and Yorkshire pudding, although the weather was getting too warm for so heavy a meal. But Marian Larch loved it; she ate with gusto, murmuring compliments between bites that had Roberta beaming. Both the Morrisseys accepted her without question, although I think Drew had been expecting someone more glamorous.

Marian told them she did secretarial work for Nathan Pinking's production company. 'I read audience mail, type up script changes, things like that.' She told how each new script change was typed on a different color paper to help keep them straight. Color-coded script changes! The kindergarten approach to records-keeping. I'm sure Marian was making it all up as she went along, but on the whole she told a convincing story.

After dinner Roberta took my guest off to show her where the bathroom was while Drew and I cleared the table. 'When is your book due out?' he asked.

'Publication date is November fourteenth. But it will probably be available before then. You know how that goes.'

Drew nodded. His last book—about the Battle of Shiloh—had been published almost four years earlier, but he was through with all that now; he'd said at the time it would be his last book. Since then Drew had published a couple of short follow-up articles, unable to leave it alone—but that was all. Roberta liked to say Drew and I were both unabashedly drawn to violence, since we confined our efforts to military history. We were still talking publications when Roberta came back with Marian Larch, who wanted to know what my book was about.

'It's a biography of Lord Lucan,' I told her, 'not the present one but the Lord Lucan who fought in the Crimean War.' Silence. 'Nineteenth Century?' I wasn't particularly surprised at the blank look she gave me. 'He was one of the four men responsible for that bloody mistake known as the Charge of the Light Brigade.'

'Aha,' Marian said, her face lighting up. 'The raglan sleeve!'

'Very good,' Drew laughed. 'And the cardigan sweater.'

She didn't know that one, so I said, 'Lord Raglan gave the order to charge and Lord Cardigan carried it out. Except that the order Raglan gave wasn't the one Cardigan followed—it was so vaguely worded it was misunderstood. Lucan was the man in the middle. He was in a position to stop the slaughter but didn't.'

'Lord Look-on,' Drew said.

'That's what his men called him,' I told Marian, 'even before that infamous charge. A very cautious, unimaginative man who would do nothing without direct orders.'

'That makes three,' Marian said. 'You said four men

were responsible.'

'Primarily. The fourth was a young officer named Lewis Nolan. Undoubtedly the most intelligent of the four, but he behaved stupidly at the moment of crisis. He was an impatient young man—full of contempt for the slow-moving, incompetent type of British officer that infested Victoria's army during the entire Crimean campaign. Men such as Lord Raglan, Lord Lucan, and Lord Cardigan.'

Marian smiled and shook her head. 'How could Lucan have stopped it?'

'Chain of command. Lord Raglan was up on a ridge overlooking a long valley, and he could see along the ridge to his right where some Russian troops were capturing the few British cannon lined up there. Raglan wanted the Light Brigade to charge up the slope and scatter the Russians. That's what light cavalry was for—quick, darting action. So Raglan dictated an order saying the Light Brigade was to prevent the enemy from carrying away "the guns". What he neglected to say was *which* guns. Raglan forgot that people down at the bottom of a hill can't see the same things that people on top of a hill can see.'

'Or read minds,' Roberta smiled.

'Lewis Nolan carried the message,' I went on. 'He delivered it to Lord Lucan, the commander of the Cavalry Division, who was to pass the order on to the commander of the Light Brigade under him. A confused Lucan asked what guns did Raglan mean. And hot-headed young Lewis Nolan flung out his arm and pointed down the valley to the *Russian* guns, the enemy cannon. "*There* are your guns!" he answered quite insolently.'

That was the crux of the whole affair—that moment between Lucan and Nolan. 'It's been well over a century since that young man flung out his arm and pointed to the wrong guns,' I said, 'and we're still trying to figure out why he did it. But whatever the reason, Lord Lucan passed on the order that the Light Brigade, designed only for quick skirmishes, remember, was expected to charge

Russian cannon. Lucan should have demanded a confirming order.'

'*Cardigan* should have demanded a confirming order,' Drew muttered. 'What an ass. Leading his men into so obvious a death trap.'

'Lord Cardigan was the commander of the Light Brigade,' I told Marian Larch, who kept nodding her head through all this. 'He was the one who actually had to carry out the order, and I don't think there was a more stupid man in the whole British army than Lord Cardigan. The man had the brain of a bird.'

'A peacock,' Drew said.

'So that birdbrain actually led men armed only with sabres in a charge against cannon. Nearly seven hundred men rode into that valley. Fewer than two hundred rode back out. Cardigan himself survived the charge, but the entire light cavalry was virtually wiped out in less than twenty minutes. And the whole thing was a mistake.'

'Responsibility ultimately lies with the commanding officer,' Drew said sententiously.

'Of course,' I said. 'Besides, it was Raglan's vague wording that caused the misunderstanding in the first place. But that's the odd thing about this battle. Everyone who writes about it feels compelled to take sides — it's intriguing the way so many reputable historians forget they are supposed to be disinterested analysts and instead become passionate partisans once they start writing about the Charge of the Light Brigade. Excepting Cecil Woodham-Smith, of course. She just states flatly they were *all* a passel of fools.'

'Why do you write about English history?' Marian Larch wanted to know.

I smiled. 'Why not leave English history to the English, you mean? It used to be that way, but the invention of the airplane changed all that.'

'And the foundations,' Drew added. 'Don't forget the foundations.'

'Lord, no,' I said. 'I'd never have been able to write my *Life of Lucan* without grants to pay for all those trips to

London. But national origins aren't important to historians, not really. The English have turned out to be the best French historians. And the Germans are doing good work in Soviet history.'

Roberta leaned toward Marian. 'Did you know Fiona's book is the first full biography of Lord Lucan ever written?'

Marian looked at me in surprise. 'Really?'

'That's right,' I said. 'Millions and millions of words written about the Crimean War, and nobody ever got around to doing a study of Lucan's life.' I laughed. 'Probably because he was such a stodgy, predictable man.' I stopped; I'd been going to mention something Lucan had done in Ireland but an expression had appeared on Marian Larch's face that I recognized. It was the glazed-eye look of those who don't really care what happened before they were born.

We talked desultorily of other things until ten o'clock, the hour of *LeFever*. The Morrisseys had an elaborate, big-screen television console, purchased at Roberta's insistence back when the BBC first announced plans to produce all of Shakespeare's plays. The set tended to dominate the room.

Rudy was one of three writers listed in *LeFever*'s credits. I'd once thought that meant a big budget, but Rudy had told me the script fees were fixed by the Screen Writers' Guild and more than one writer simply meant the money had to be split. I listened carefully, but I couldn't hear any lines that sounded more like Rudy than any others. That was good from the show's viewpoint, I suppose, that kind of homogeneity. But this episode was of the sort that had caused me to drift away from watching television in the first place.

It was the kind of story in which the viewer quickly learned to stop listening and just watch. The lines were dull, the plot slow and disconnected. There was no meaning to be found; the script discouraged active participation, it discouraged thinking. It was as bland as oatmeal. The people and the settings, on the other hand, were *beautiful*. Envy-arousing beautiful. The hero, LeFever, was a vain, muscular young man who posed his attractive body against a variety of luxurious backgrounds. No scenes took place on dirty streets or in slum buildings. The fad for picturing New York as a sewer must have passed; these things probably went in cycles.

And then there was Kelly Ingram. Her role was a lot smaller than LeFever's, but when she was in a scene with the hero, *she* was the one you looked at. I wondered if the actor playing LeFever knew that; he didn't strike me as being particularly bright.

'What a *beautiful* woman,' Roberta murmured. Drew, who'd been in danger of falling asleep, opened one eye.

'That's Kelly Ingram,' Marian Larch said. 'She's even more beautiful in person.'

'Oh, that's right—you know all these people, don't you? Do you know her, Fiona?'

I said I'd met her. There *was* something about Kelly Ingram; if appearance was all it took, she was bound to become a star. Her movements were graceful and unstudied. She walked like a dancer—no, that's wrong; dancers waddle like ducks when they walk. Kelly Ingram walked *as if she were dancing;* that was better.

Her role was that of an adjective describing the noun hero. She was the sexually available but eternally fresh female, experienced innocence personified, the kind of woman whose virginity is renewable upon demand. We were supposed to think that if LeFever could have a woman like that gazing upon him adoringly, then he must be one hell of a man. The same little-boy notion of manhood that has always kept women prone in a male society. I wasn't too surprised to find the Ingram woman helping perpetuate the notion.

The show came to its bland conclusion. Marian Larch and I thanked the Morrisseys and took our leave. On the way home my guest started to say something but stopped. I think she was going to ask me what I thought of the show but then changed her mind.

Marian winnowed a few letters out of Rudy's business correspondence that she wanted to take back with her. They were all concerned with details about scripts Rudy had contracted to write and didn't seem especially significant to me—but historians never give up papers without a fight, so I told Marian I'd take them to school with me and get them photocopied. That was agreeable to her.

She was making plans to leave early Saturday when I asked her to tell me honestly what progress had been made in finding Rudy's killers. I told her I was considering hiring detectives.

'That's your privilege, of course,' she said. 'But it's my opinion you'd just be wasting your money, Dr. Benedict. This isn't one of those cases where a private operative can go in and do things the police can't. In fact, we have resources private agencies don't. It's the lack of motive that has us stumped. We can't find even a hint of a reason why anyone would want your son dead.'

'Then you are stumped.'

A pause. 'Yes. We are. I'm sorry. Rudy had the usual number of people in his life who didn't particularly like him, but nobody hated him—which I'm told is unusual in television. Of all the people he knew, there's not one you could call a real enemy. There was no woman in his life at the moment—he and Kelly Ingram were just beginning to get together. He wasn't engaged in any illegal money-making scheme we could find out about. The medical examiner said he wasn't a user. There's nothing. That's why Captain Michaels sent me here—in the hope there might be something to give us a lead.'

'What about those letters I had photocopied? Anything there?'

She sighed. 'Not really, just a sort of side issue. Look—you can help. There's no way the Captain is going to let me sit in your attic for the next few months. You said you were going to give the summer over to reading Rudy's papers?'

'Yes, that's what I plan to do.'

'Then how about reading for anything specifically out of the ordinary? Help us out.'

'But it's all fiction, Marian—television scripts, plot outlines, something the industry calls story treatments . . .'

'I know. But maybe one of those plot outlines will tell you something. Or maybe a letter got misfiled. You never know. Will you do it? Will you watch for anything the least bit unusual?'

'Well, of course I'll do it. It's just that I don't think anything will come of it.'

We left it at that. Friday had been a hectic day for me; I didn't even have a chance to read my mail until breakfast early Saturday morning before Marian's flight. Once again I had no premonition, no anticipation of disaster. The letter was from my publisher.

We have just learned that Walter Cullingham, Ltd., plans to publish Richard Ormsby's biography of Lord Lucan on October tenth, a month before we will be ready to release your *Life of Lucan*. Cullingham plans simultaneous British and American editions; and our source informs us that while the book is not quite in the coffee-table mode, it is lavishly illustrated and written in Ormsby's usual breezy style.

While Ormsby's book will undoubtedly cut into our immediate sales, we feel there is no long-range need for concern. We expect your *Life of Lucan* to be a steady seller over the years that will outlast the initial impact of Ormsby's version. We were surprised that no word of his work-in-progress had reached us; but we understand Ormsby had once planned a BBC television series about the Crimean War which he had to abandon as unfeasible. Then rather than waste the research he'd had done, he put together a hasty biography of one of the participants. The fact that Ormsby calls his book *Lord Look-on* should give us a fair indication of the profundity of his work.

These things happen, unfortunately. But let me repeat that we feel the long-range reception will be in our favor.

The next thing I knew I was on my knees on the floor fighting for breath. I heard Marian Larch's voice as from a great distance, demanding to know what was wrong. She forced me to lie on the sofa, although I didn't feel faint. It was just that *breathing* had suddenly become so difficult.

Some time evidently passed, because the next time I was fully aware of my surroundings, the Morrisseys were there; Marian must have called them. Drew stood around looking helpless, but Roberta was fussily taking over, apparently under the impression that lowering my body temperature was the thing to do: ice cubes on my wrists, cool wet wash cloths on the back of my neck. Oddly, it did seem to help.

I sat up and apologized for creating such a fuss. When they all wanted to know what had caused it, I just pointed to the letter I'd dropped on the floor.

The Morrisseys understood immediately. Marian Larch had some notion of what it meant; but not being a scholar herself, she couldn't quite appreciate the way fourteen years' work on my part had been neatly undercut by a pop historian whose specialty was providing simplistic explanations of complex matters. Through his use of television, Richard Ormsby had made his face and name familiar to people who hadn't looked at a history book since high school. How could I compete with that?

Drew, the eternal optimist, jumped on the one bright note in my publisher's letter. 'He doesn't seem at all worried about the long-range sales, Fiona,' he said. 'You and Ormsby won't be selling to the same market—he writes for the dabblers, the amateurs. Yours is the study that will become the standard—perhaps even the definitive work. In the long run you won't have anything to worry about.'

'Drew,' I said, 'I'm sixty-two years old. I may not be

around for the long run.'

He didn't have anything to say to that.

Marian Larch missed her flight because of my little fit; that meant she had to stay over until Monday, as there were only two flights a day out of Washburn—one eastward, one west—and none on Sundays. She kept watching me the whole weekend, trying to get me to eat when I didn't want to eat, or talk when I wanted silence.

'You just had an anxiety attack,' she said kindly. 'Like a pressure valve letting off steam. It'll be all right.'

Anxiety attack—a fancy name for getting news so shocking it literally takes your breath away.

Richard Ormsby was a youngish, blond, upper-class Englishman who was carefully articulate and consciously charming. He was one of those 'popularizers' who have sprung up in just about every discipline lately. I'd watched him several times at the Morrisseys', always on BBC mini-series (horrid neologism). At first Ormsby had won cautious praise from historians for creating a new interest in a subject that usually evoked nothing but groans from the non-readers around us. But then it became clear that Ormsby was marketing *himself*, and even that faint praise disappeared.

He'd followed the usual procedure in such matters—first the TV series, then the book based on it. All ballyhooed by means of press interviews and frequent appearances on television and radio talk shows. Ormsby was more a media personality than a historian, but his efforts were well-funded. He did virtually none of his own research, hiring professionals rather than depend upon graduate students whose work would have to be checked. Both television series and book were then written up in a chatty, informal style that reduced momentous decisions and actions to one-dimensional matters that could be understood with a minimum of effort. My publisher had said that Ormsby's proposed series on the Crimean War hadn't worked out and rather than waste the research, he'd tossed off a book about Lord Lucan. I was certain the only reason he'd chosen Lucan was the lack of competition. In well over a hundred years no one had yet published a biography of the man; maybe Ormsby had heard about the woman in Ohio who'd just finished a study of Lucan's life, maybe he hadn't. Somehow I didn't think it would have made any difference.

You spend years learning and working toward a goal and doing your best to create something of quality—and some glib, pretty, young person comes along and with a laugh and a wave of his hand *dismisses your life*. And not only is he allowed to get away with it, he's rewarded for doing so. Richard Ormsby was everything I hated about contemporary life—the cheapening, cashing-in quality that polluted everything it touched.

Some of this I tried to explain to Marian Larch. There were rivalries in all fields, of course; but I could think of a lot of people I'd rather be in competition with instead of Richard Ormsby. I didn't doubt for one minute that mine was the superior book; but hustle and hype had invaded the study of history, and I could be hurt by it.

Marian caught the one eastbound flight Monday morning. Tuesday's mail brought another letter from my publisher, this one gently informing me that the History Book Club had decided to distribute Ormsby's book instead of mine.

CHAPTER 5

MARIAN LARCH

Captain Michaels had a standard way of dealing with lack of progress in a case, and that was to yell at people who couldn't yell back. The day after Fiona Benedict went back to Ohio, he let us have it with both barrels. He called in those of us assigned to the Rudy Benedict murder and gave us a dressing-down that I stopped listening to after the first ten seconds because it was so foolish. Abusive language wouldn't create new leads for us.

He ended with his usual unhelpful instruction: *Get out there and scrounge.* I did what I usually did in such instances—I swapped interviewees with another investigator. Ivan Malecki would go talk to Kelly Ingram while I gave Nathan Pinking a try. Ivan allowed as how he wouldn't mind too much.

Pinking had just got back from London and quickly let me know he was doing me a big favor by fitting me into his busy, busy schedule. We were in his office on West Fifty-fourth, a suite that was smaller than I'd expected. A framed photograph on his desk showed a woman and three teenaged girls. All four looked happy.

Pinking's file said he was fifty-one, but he looked a lot younger. I'd never seen the man before and his face startled me a little. It was the eyebrows you noticed first. The right one was straight and ordinary, just an eyebrow. But the left one was bushy and greatly arched. It made the eye under it look larger—no, the left eye *was* larger than the right. The nose also had that same kind of lopsidedness; the right nostril looked normal, the left one was fleshy and flared. Same difference in the two sides of the mouth. The left side of the upper lip lifted and seemed more curved than the right; the lower lip was full only on the left, and it drooped a little. Nathan Pinking had two halves of two perfectly good faces that just happened not to fit together. I resisted drawing conclusions about the proper Dr. Jekyll right side and the sensuous Mr. Hyde left.

'I don't know what this is for,' Pinking said. 'I've already told everything I know to that other detective, Ivan somebody.'

'Ivan Malecki. Just a couple of questions, Mr. Pinking. How long had you been buying scripts from Rudy Benedict?'

'Oh God, years.'

'Can you be more precise?'

He looked annoyed, but jabbed a finger at the box on his desk. 'Tansy, bring in Rudy Benedict's file.'

A voice said it would and I had to smile. 'Tansy?'

Pinking grinned mechanically. 'They're all called Tansy or Tawny or Silky these days.'

Or Kelly. 'Benedict was on the last year of his contract with you, is that right?'

'Yeah, but I would have renewed. Benedict was a good reliable dialogue man.'

'But would *he* have renewed? He was planning to write a play.'

He snorted. 'Look, Detective, uh—'

'Larch.'

'Yeah, well, Benedict had been threatening to quit television and write for the stage almost as long as I knew him. Ten, twelve years. But it was all talk. He'd never have gone through with it.'

'He'd started. Notes, some plot outlines.'

Pinking shook his head. 'Security blanket. He was always making notes for things he never got around to writing.'

'You sound as if you knew him pretty well.'

'I did.'

Just then pretty blonde Tansy came in looking perplexed. 'Mr. Pinking, the Rudy Benedict folder isn't in the filing cabinet.'

'Bull. Look again.'

Tansy faded out of the room with a whispered *Yes, sir* and I said, 'How long have you known Leonard Zoff, Mr. Pinking?'

His eyes narrowed. 'Too long. Twenty-five years at least. Why do you ask?'

'Did Zoff ever represent Rudy Benedict in his negotiations with you?'

'Zoff doesn't handle writers. He's an actors' agent.'

'Who was Benedict's agent?'

But Pinking had quickly had his fill of answering questions. 'Funny thing—I forget. You'll have to see your friend Ivan for that. He asked the same question.'

Tansy came back in. 'Mr. Pinking, the Rudy Benedict file just isn't there. And Mr. Cameron is here to see you.'

Pinking gave her a look that would have melted a steel

74

girder. 'You're just full of good news, aren't you? Tell Cameron to wait.' He waved her out. 'Now look, Ms, uh, I don't know anything about Benedict's murder. I can't even think of a reason why anyone would want him dead. It was probably a mistake—that stuff must have been meant for Kelly Ingram. She's a much more logical target.'

I explained about the Lysco-Seltzer crystals in Rudy Benedict's sink and emphasized that Benedict was the 'right' victim. 'Why do you say Kelly is a more logical target?'

'Because of who she is. A very sexy, very visible young woman about that far away from being a star.' He held thumb and forefinger a centimeter apart. 'Women like that are natural magnets. It's a special quality they have.'

And men like Pinking were always there to cash in on that quality. 'Still, the cyanide was not meant for her. It—'

I was interrupted by the door bursting open. An angry man I'd never seen before came shooting into the room as if fired from a slingshot. 'Goddamn it, Pinking, I will not sit there cooling my heels awaiting your pleasure! You go too far. You—' He broke off, seeing me for the first time.

He was a lean, black-haired man in his forties with the strangest eyes I'd ever seen. The blue of the irises was so faint as to be virtually colorless, making him appear from a certain angle as if he had no irises at all. It gave him an outer-space look. Not spaced out—just other-worldly.

'I'm sorry, Mr. Pinking, I couldn't keep him out,' came Tansy's faint voice. She was waved out again.

Pinking obviously wasn't going to introduce us so I said, 'I'm Marian Larch, with the New York Detective Bureau.'

Pinking's laugh had a needling edge to it. 'That's right, Cameron. I'm being grilled by the police.'

Good manners struggled with anger, and manners won. 'Ted Cameron,' he said, offering a hand. 'Sorry I burst in on you.'

I shook his hand and said, 'That's all right, Mr. Cameron, I was about finished anyway.' Pinking had already made that clear. 'Are you in television?'

'I advertise on television.' He didn't sound particularly proud of it.

'Cameron is *LeFever's* new sponsor,' Pinking said with a barely concealed smugness I didn't quite understand. 'Or rather his company is. Cameron Enterprises.'

Oho, one of *those* Camerons. Sportswear, sporting goods, radios, other things I couldn't remember. Cosmetics. 'Then this isn't your maiden voyage?'

'God, no,' Pinking laughed before Ted Cameron could answer. 'But this is the first time Cameron Enterprises has deigned to associate itself with a Nathan Pinking production. Ah well, Teddy old boy, we have to take the rough with the smooth.'

'So they say,' the man with the invisible irises said. He'd decided to hold it in until I was gone.

'You're in for an education,' Pinking went on. 'Watch what happens to your profits once Kelly Ingram starts wearing your swimsuits. Through the ceiling! And you'll owe it all to me. Think you can stand it?'

I wasn't too crazy about Leonard Zoff, but I was beginning to understand why he hated Nathan Pinking so. The man was deliberately abrasive, going out of his way to offend just to show you he could get away with it. I stood up. 'You'll get in touch with me when you locate that missing file?'

'Sure, sure,' Pinking said dismissively. He wouldn't.

I said goodbye to Cameron and left through the outer office. Tansy was sitting disconsolately at her desk looking at a magazine. She lifted her head and said, distinctly and puzzlingly, 'Julia Child doesn't like sauerkraut.'

I nodded and went on out. Sometimes it's best not to ask.

At Police Plaza, Ivan Malecki hadn't yet got back from interviewing Kelly Ingram; somehow that failed to surprise me. I called a few contacts in industry and did some checking. Cameron Enterprises had been started three generations ago by Henry W. Cameron, a haberdasher with big ideas. What was originally a small family business had grown rapidly, acquiring smaller companies along the way until now it was a fairly large conglomerate. Various family members were involved in the conglomerate's operation; old Henry's great-grandson, Ted Cameron, currently sat in the president's chair.

What was the president of a company that large doing *personally* overseeing a television series the company was sponsoring? Wouldn't that be a job for the advertising department? Or at least for someone lower down in the hierarchy. And why all that animosity between Cameron and Nathan Pinking? Perhaps the man with the invisible eyes didn't have absolute powers; maybe his board of directors had forced him into sponsoring a show he didn't want. Strange thing for a board of directors to be concerning itself with. Or maybe not; they'd want to use their advertising dollars to reach the highest number of customers possible, and *LeFever*'s ratings had been climbing steadily.

I went in and told Captain Michaels about Rudy Benedict's file that was suddenly missing from Nathan Pinking's office, perhaps conveniently so.

He made a vulgar noise. 'Benedict's papers. We should have gone through them.'

We'd been through this before. 'A writer's papers, Captain. Big job — time-consuming.'

'Got any other suggestions?' he came close to snarling. 'I tell you to go out and scrounge and you come back and tell me a file folder is missing. So what does that mean — our answer is written down on a piece of paper? We got nothing else.' He picked up the phone and started punching out a number he read from a folder on his desk. 'Go home and pack, Larch. I have to get the old doll's permission, but she won't say no.'

I'd never associated Ohio with anything in particular, so the community of Washburn made me revise a few of my ideas about smalltown America. I'd halfway expected a wide place in the road that had no reason for being there except for the university it served. But Washburn smelled of prosperity, and of *taking care*. I don't mean the place was a hotbed of millionaires; but the people who lived there were fussy about their surroundings. Manhattan's Fourteenth Street would have driven them crazy.

Washburn was pretty, in an unremarkable way, and clean. Fiona Benedict lived in a conventional red brick house, white trim, single story plus basement and attic, attached garage, nice yard. She'd taken me up to the attic where Rudy's things were stored—and one look was all I needed to tell me I'd never get through all those papers in the two or three days Captain Michaels had told me to take. So I settled for just the business papers, trusting Dr. Benedict to search through the rest of it for us.

Fiona Benedict was a strange woman. She'd told no one in Washburn that her only child had been murdered. She'd made up some story about accidental death that I agreed to go along with. But I couldn't imagine someone keeping a thing like that to herself. It wasn't that she didn't have any friends; she was liked and respected in Washburn. But the murder of her son was just too painful or too private or too something; she wouldn't or couldn't tell anybody. And the odd thing about it was that I got the impression before I left that she didn't really like Rudy very much.

My first night there was a revealing one; I learned several interesting new things. We went to dinner at the home of two of Dr. Benedict's friends, Roberta and Drew Morrissey. After a marvelous dinner, Roberta Morrissey showed me the way to the bathroom—and displayed a rather disconcerting curiosity about me. She had a very direct way of talking, and we were no sooner out of the dining room than she started pumping me about my supposed friendship with Rudy.

The best way to avoid answering personal questions is to ask questions yourself. 'Rudy never talked to me about his father,' I said. 'I'm sure he remembers him—Rudy was eight when his father left. Did his parents ever divorce, or what?'

Roberta Morrissey shot me a funny look. 'Is that what Rudy told you?'

'That they divorced?'

'No, that his father deserted his family when Rudy was eight.'

Since I'd never spoken to Rudy Benedict in my life, I wasn't sure what I should say. But there was something funny about that question and the way she asked it. 'No, it was his mother who told me that. Rudy never talked about his father.'

Roberta Morrissey looked at me a minute, and then said, 'Rudy's father committed suicide.' I stared at her open-mouthed, and she said, 'Here's the bathroom.'

She was waiting when I came back out. I said, 'You mean Dr. Benedict has rationalized his suicide away? That she calls it desertion to keep from facing up to what really happened?'

Dr. Mrs. Morrissey sighed. 'No, she really does see his suicide as desertion. As an inexcusable abandoning of Rudy and herself. She's never forgiven him.'

'Why did he kill himself?'

I don't think she wanted to talk to me about it, but she felt obligated to finish what she'd started. 'Shame, humiliation. Depression. Evidently Philip Benedict wasn't a very good historian. He'd been taken to task rather severely for some inaccurate translations he'd done—he was a medievalist and he had to deal with archaic language a lot. But then he fabricated some evidence for a book he'd written and was found out. It was pretty much the end of his career. His department head asked for his resignation. Publishers wouldn't take a chance on him after that, and the best teaching position he could ever hope for would be in some small community college somewhere that would consider itself lucky just to get a Ph.D. I never knew Philip Benedict, but from what Drew's told me, I'd say he was just trying to keep up with Fiona. Which was foolish—that need to compete. Fiona is rather special.'

'And you never met Philip Benedict at all?'

'I didn't even know Fiona when all that happened—they were teaching in Indiana at the time. Drew knew them both, from history conventions they all attended. But when Philip killed himself, Fiona wanted to take the boy and start over someplace else. Drew called and told her there was an opening at Washburn, and she's been here ever since.'

So father and son were both murder victims, one by his own hand and the other by a hand still unknown. I began to see why Fiona Benedict hadn't wanted her peers to know how her son had died. Poor woman.

Then that 'poor woman' displayed a side I'd never seen before. The personality she'd always shown me was cool, composed, withdrawn, plainly inaccessible. She had a very good defense system. But then in the Morrisseys' living room she started talking about a new book she'd just finished that had taken her fourteen years to research and write—and the change in that woman was downright spooky. When she spoke of the Crimean War and the Charge of the Light Brigade and idiotic lords and misunderstood orders and fatally foolish actions—well, she was a different person entirely. Her face lit up and her voice became musical and her body was animated—she looked a good fifteen years younger. She was happy and even a little bit excited, but it wasn't a gushing kind of enthusiasm she showed. The lady was simply in her element.

Then we turned on the TV to watch *LeFever* and she changed again, this time into the Bride of Frankenstein—all hiss and sparks and disapproval. The only thing missing was the Elsa-Lanchester-electrocuted hairdo. It was a dumb show, true, but it didn't seem to be Rudy's script that made her so mad; she acted as if she hadn't expected anything better on that score. No, it was Kelly Ingram that got her so riled.

It was easy to see why. I couldn't think of two women more different from each other than Kelly Ingram and

80

Fiona Benedict. Kelly was extroverted glamour and sparkle and good times; Dr. Benedict was privacy and quiet, a thinker. Of course the serious woman would have no respect for the frivolous one.

Yet I thought Dr. Benedict underestimated Kelly Ingram. People see a face as beautiful as Kelly's and they tend to assume there can't be a brain behind it. Kelly wasn't an educated woman by Fiona Benedict's standards, but that didn't mean she was stupid. In fact, she was rather shrewd in her own way. Kelly never kidded herself about what she was doing for a living or tried to pretend it was anything more significant than it was. She never put on airs or played the great actress. I liked Kelly—I liked her energy and her style and her upbeat personality. What Dr. Benedict saw was a useless woman who was getting a free ride through life because she happened to be born beautiful. I thought there was more to Kelly than that.

Kelly struck me as being a halfway woman—no, that's not the right way to put it. Kelly was a woman stuck between time zones, getting messages from the past and from the present at the same time. She was sure-footed in a highly competitive profession where you have to be able to take care of yourself if you intend to survive. But she'd gotten where she was by playing the men's game, by catering to male fantasies. Sure, she did it all tongue-in-cheek—but she still *did* it. I don't think Kelly would ever claim women's only function was to serve as objects of male desire. But her extraordinary beauty had singled her out from birth for just that very role. It's what she knew, it's what she understood—of course it directed her behavior. But she wasn't particularly impressed by any of it.

And, well, to tell the truth, there was another reason I liked her. She'd flattered me. When Kelly got that second Lysco-Seltzer bottle in the mail and was scared half out of her skull, it was me she turned to for help. Not Captain Michaels, *me*. Women don't generally look to other women for help. Men are the protectors, the capable ones, right? We're taught from childhood that women are supposed to be helpless. I mean, women are *supposed* to be helpless; it's expected of us. But when Kelly felt threatened and decided she needed help, I was the one she called. Think that didn't make me feel good?

On the way back to Dr. Benedict's house I'd wanted to talk to her about Kelly, but the look on her face said *No Trespassing* so I didn't.

There was a repetitiousness about Rudy Benedict's business papers that soon had me nodding. I forced myself to pay attention to letter after letter detailing percentages, residuals, kill fees, on and on. Reams of paper spent on correspondence about details of scripts in progress—should the villain be kind to animals, how about discovering the body inside a case of peat moss in the greenhouse, etc. Rudy Benedict had spent so much time writing and reading letters I wondered how he ever got anything else done.

The only thing of interest had to do with satisfying my personal curiosity instead of helping to solve a murder. It was a series of four letters concerning a script Benedict had written twelve years earlier. The contents of the correspondence were about the same as all the others; it was the letterhead I found so interesting. It read: 'Pinking and Zoff Productions, Inc.'

So those two had been partners once—the source of their present mutual hatred? Somehow I couldn't see Leonard Zoff as a producer; he seemed so right in his role of huckster, wheeling and dealing and selling his human products for all he could get. I decided to take copies of the letters back with me; I had to have something to show Captain Michaels for my trip to Ohio.

Then right before I left, Fiona Benedict got some really nasty news: Channel 13 idol Richard Ormsby was publishing a book called *Lord Look-on*. The news hit her so hard I was worried about her; at first I thought she was having a heart attack. I stayed on until Monday, and over that weekend she opened up more than I'd yet seen her do. The *pain* that woman was feeling was overwhelming—I was hurting for her myself. By the time I left Monday morning, she'd withdrawn into herself again; her mouth was bitter.

It was a peculiar thing, and maybe I wasn't being fair in thinking it, but it seemed to me Fiona Benedict was mourning what happened to her book the way you'd have thought she'd mourn what happened to her son. Not that her book was dead, far from it. But what she was feeling was pure and simple grief, no question of that. Yet all the time she'd been in New York seeing about Rudy's cremation and closing his apartment and disposing of his things—she'd been icily calm and collected, never displaying anything of what she was feeling. She was a very private woman.

Perhaps she could handle one horrible thing happening to her, but not two so close together. Or perhaps it was the order in which they happened. If she'd heard about *Lord Look-on* first, then it might have been Rudy's death that caused her to grieve. Or perhaps it was exactly what it appeared to be: the murder was an attack on a son to whom she'd not been close for decades, but the book was an attack on her personally.

Back in New York I made one more visit to the *LeFever* set. They were shooting their last episode and I wanted to find out where Kelly Ingram and Nathan Pinking would be during the rest of the summer. And to see if Nick Quinlan had learned anything about acting yet.

There was a last-day-of-school sort of gaiety on the set, but the laughter was a little too loud and a bit edgy. I guess doing a weekly series does get to be a strain after a while. There were visitors on the set, mostly young women clustered around Nick Quinlan. The director looked harried, but determined to keep his temper.

'Well, there she is, the missing policewoman!' Kelly Ingram's voice bubbled behind me. 'Where've you been lately? I thought you'd deserted us.'

'Blame Captain Michaels,' I told her. 'He decided I

83

wasn't working hard enough.'

'Come along, I've got to do some pickups,' she said, not really listening. 'They might even use one of them, who knows?'

An assistant director fussily positioned Kelly in front of a neutral-colored wall. 'Give us some choice, love,' he said. 'Yes-no-maybe should do it.'

Kelly stood in front of the camera and registered three facial expressions, each one lasting about ten seconds—a smile, a worried frown, and a perfectly blank look that could be anything at all. If the episode ran a few seconds short that week, a shot of Kelly 'reacting' could be inserted.

'Harder than it looks,' Kelly said to me in mock seriousness. 'Have you tried holding a smile without moving for a full ten seconds? Your face starts twitching.'

'What terrible things you're called on to do,' I murmured.

She smiled her big smile, not the one she used for the camera. 'It's those little things that sometimes mean the difference between working and not working. Once I got a role because I was the only woman interviewed who could run down a flight of stairs without looking at her feet, *my* feet. And once when we were . . .' She trailed off without finishing. Then Kelly did an odd thing: she ducked her head in a curiously childlike and vulnerable-looking gesture I'd never seen her make before.

'Kelly?'

She raised her head and peered over my shoulder. 'Who,' she whispered, 'is *that?*'

I turned to see Nathan Pinking introducing the man with the invisible eyes to Nick Quinlan. 'You mean Ted Cameron? That's your new sponsor—haven't you met him yet?'

A barely perceptible shake of the head. '*That's* Ted Cameron?' She seemed surprised. 'My God, what eyes! They do have irises, don't they?' she half-laughed.

'Pale blue ones. *Very* pale. You have to stand at a certain angle to see them.'

'How come you know him, Marian?'

'Met him in Nathan Pinking's office. Last week.'

'Ladies, you're going to have to move,' a tense male voice told us. We moved; a camera was rolled past us, followed by two men arguing quietly.

'Poor Harry,' Kelly smiled.

'Poor Harry' was the director, who looked as if he wanted to lie on the floor and kick his heels and scream a lot. Here he was trying to keep to a tight schedule when the boss showed up with the new money man, wasting valuable shooting time.

'Do something!' Poor Harry hissed to an underling. 'Get them off the set!'

'How can I get them off the set?' the underling hissed back. 'You do it!' I wondered how long *he* would last.

I turned back to Kelly, but she was no longer there. She'd moved off by herself. She stood quietly, watching Ted Cameron.

And then slowly, gradually, he became aware of her attention. Cameron kept on talking to Pinking and Nick Quinlan, but his eyes slid over to where Kelly stood silently watching. Then looking at her became the main thing and the talking with the others slipped to second place. Finally he excused himself and walked over to her.

'Yeah, she can do that all right,' a voice behind me said. It was Poor Harry. 'Make men come to her just by standing still. It's her most marketable commodity.'

I whirled on him angrily. 'What a *vile* thing to say.'

He looked honestly surprised. 'What? I didn't mean anything.'

He probably didn't at that. I muttered something conciliatory and moved over to where Nathan Pinking and Nick Quinlan were standing watching their new sponsor and their leading lady.

'She sure doesn't waste any time,' Pinking snickered. 'Go for the bucks, babe.' Both halves of his mismatched face were busy grinning in their separate ways.

I made my presence known. Strange thing, in all the times I'd come around while *LeFever* was shooting, I'd never yet met Nick Quinlan. But Nathan Pinking assumed I had—and so did Nick Quinlan.

'Hiya,' he said, casually draping an arm over my shoulders. The familiarity was only slightly offensive, because with this man it had about as much meaning as a handshake did with other people. He probably remembered seeing me around the set and thought we were old friends.

I asked Nathan Pinking where he'd be for the next couple of months.

'Here, California, London, goddamned Cairo. You ever been in Egypt this time of year? And someplace cool, if I can squeeze in a vacation.'

'Sorry to push, but I have to have dates and addresses. We need to keep track of where everybody goes once *LeFever* finishes.'

'Hell, I don't remember all that. Ask my secretary—she'll give you a list.'

'Tansy?'

The right side of his face grinned. 'Mimsy. Tansy left.'

Surprise attack. 'When did you dissolve your partnership with Leonard Zoff?'

Surprise defense. 'What partnership? I was never partners with that worm.'

I didn't bother hiding my surprise. 'Well, isn't that interesting. And here I found some correspondence from Pinking and Zoff Productions, Incorporated—right there among Rudy Benedict's papers.'

'Oh, that.' He shrugged. 'Must have been dated twelve, fourteen years ago, right? In a moment of weakness I actually considered going into business with Leonard Zoff. But sanity returned in time. He must have had the stationery printed up—I don't remember it. Whose signature was on the letters?'

'Zoff's.' On all four letters.

'There you are,' Pinking said dismissively. 'Zoff is such a tightwad he'd use the stationery even if the business didn't exist.' Then, with no attempt at subtlety at all, he switched the subject back to what we'd been talking about before. 'See Mimsy. She'll give you my itinerary. I'll be going a lot of places in the next few months.'

'I'm goan' to Wes' Germany,' Nick said helpfully. 'Man, y'looka that? They jus' glommed onna each other.'

I stood there in the quasi-embrace of a TV star watching Kelly Ingram and Ted Cameron discovering each other. I couldn't hear what they were saying, but their talk didn't have the flirtatious look to it you might have expected. Instead it was intense, almost urgent. And private—oh boy was it private, in this very public place. The rest of us just weren't there.

Even Nathan Pinking sensed something unusual going on. 'I never saw two people take to each other quite like that.'

' 'S fast,' Nick nodded.

It was more than just fast. It was *meant*. I realized I wouldn't be talking to Kelly any more that day, so I said goodbye to the two men.

'Y'take care y'self, promise?' Nick called after me.

I promised and left, faintly bemused by what I'd seen. I knew Kelly Ingram was no nun, yet I was still a little surprised by the swiftness with which she'd acted. She'd taken one look at Ted Cameron, decided that was what she wanted, and made her move. I was willing to bet next month's salary it had *not* been like that with Rudy Benedict. Suddenly it became important to know more about Ted Cameron. The one time I'd talked to him, I'd seen only a man restraining his anger in order to be polite—which made me think well of him.

Captain Michaels had been only mildly interested in the Pinking and Zoff letterhead stationery I'd found in Ohio. He'd been disappointed I hadn't uncovered the entire solution to Rudy Benedict's murder in the writer's papers, and he'd even hinted it was my fault the crime was still unsolved. But Nathan Pinking's explanation of the stationery as a leftover from a partnership that had never materialized was peculiar, to say the least. I decided to check with the other 'partner'.

Leonard Zoff's office was on Seventh Avenue, and I

had to get past no fewer than three Tansys (or Mimsys). There were four or five young hopefuls waiting to see the agent, but my gold shield got me in ahead of them.

To my surprise Leonard Zoff remembered me. 'Hello, Marilyn, how's the policing business? Sorry, darling, I can't recall your last name.'

'Larch. And my first name's Marian.'

'Sure, sure, Kelly's friend, I remember. Have a seat and what can I do you for.' The only other time I'd seen Leonard Zoff he'd had laryngitis and had barely been able to whisper. Now he talked in a voice so loud it made me wince. I hate loud voices. I'm surrounded by them constantly—screaming, abrasive voices, and I hate them.

I sat down and said, 'I want to ask you about Pinking and Zoff Productions.'

At that he threw up both hands, palms facing me, fingers spread—as if I'd said *Stick 'em up*. 'Temporary insanity,' he said in an incongruous attempt at wistfulness. 'That's the only possible explanation. I hadda be mad to go into business with Nathan Shithead.'

'Then you *were* in business together?'

'Whaddaya mean "were"? Shit, we're still in business together. I can't get rid of the sonuvabitch. He won't sell me his forty-nine, so I sure as hell ain't gonna sell him mine.'

I couldn't make heads or tails out of that. 'What are you talking about?'

'I'm talking about Nathan Shithead refusing to let go,' he shouted at me. ' "Pinking and Zoff"—what a laugh. It was Pinking and Pinking and Have Some More Pinking and Who the Hell's Zoff? I stuck it out for two years and when I wanted to sell that shithead knew he had me.'

Just thinking about it made him boil, but eventually I got the story out of him. Zoff had wanted out of the partnership about ten years ago; Pinking wouldn't buy him out. Their contract said neither partner could sell to a third party without the consent of the other partner, a consent Pinking had steadfastly withheld. According to Zoff, their production company was more than slightly wobbly at the time, and Pinking had wanted a little insurance. So eventually they worked out a deal. Zoff would start his own theatrical agency, which Pinking would help underwrite in exchange for forty-nine percent ownership. In return, Zoff would retain forty-nine percent of the production company. That way if either enterprise failed, the losing partner would have something to fall back on. It certainly explained why they continued to do business in spite of hating each other; it was to their mutual benefit to do so.

But things had changed in the ten years since Pinking and Zoff had become Nathan Pinking Productions. Both the producer and the agent had succeeded on their own, and that insurance policy didn't look quite as attractive now as it did back in the earlier days. At least not to Zoff. 'I've offered to buy him out a hundred times,' Leonard Zoff told me. 'But he won't give up his piece of my agency. The shithead.'

'Pinking told me less than an hour ago that he and you had never been in business together. Why did he say that?'

Zoff snorted. 'Instinct. Sonuvabitch *never* tells the truth. He lies on principle. How do you think he got to be such a successful producer? He talks shit. Don't you believe anything he tells you.'

'So when he tells me he's going to Egypt next month . . .'

'You can be damned sure he's headed for Australia, darling. Don't believe *any*thing that shithead tells you. How did you know about Pinking and Zoff? It ain't something *I* talk about.'

I told him about finding the letters among Rudy Benedict's papers.

'You went through his papers? I thought his momma took everything back to Michigan.'

'Ohio. I made a special trip there just to read the papers. But I couldn't go through all of them — there are just too many. I had to skip his scripts and story treatments and so forth.'

Zoff was nodding thoughtfully. 'Think there might be anything there? Some clue, I mean. In his scripts?'

I shrugged. 'Long shot at best.'

'Nobody's going to read 'em and see?' He looked mildly shocked. 'Seems to me you oughta check everything. Rudy shouldn't have died—he was a sweet, harmless guy. Who'da needed to kill *him*? You oughta check everything.'

'Dr. Benedict is checking for us. She's giving the entire summer over to reading through all his papers. She gave me her word she'd let me know if she found anything the least bit out of the ordinary.'

That seemed to satisfy him; we both stood up, and he made a production out of shaking my hand. 'Good to see you again, Mary Ann. Any time I can help, you just lemme know.'

This time I didn't correct him, because I'd finally caught on. This important, successful man had so many things on his mind he couldn't be expected to get my name quite right, yet he'd courteously made time for me to ask my little questions. If Nathan Pinking lied as a matter of principle, then Leonard Zoff played one-upmanship games for the same reason.

I should have stopped off in Pinking's office before leaving the *LeFever* set, but I hadn't. So when I got back to my desk at Police Plaza, I dialed Nathan Pinking's number and got this low, velvet voice that assured me I was indeed talking to none other than Mimsy herself. The owner of the voice claimed there was nothing she'd rather do than type up a copy of Mr. Pinking's itinerary for me—and made me believe it. I sure would like to have a secretary like that.

I'd just hung up when Ivan Malecki came over and perched his butt on the corner of my desk. 'Did you hear about your Ohio hostess—our murder victim's mother?'

'Fiona Benedict? What about her?'

'She's here in New York, and—are you ready? She's just been arrested for attempted murder.'

'*What?*'

'She tried to shoot a guy. Some Englishman who's in town to publicize a new book or something.'

'Richard Ormsby? She tried to shoot Richard Ormsby?'

'Yeah, that's the name—hey, how'd you know that?'

But I didn't answer, because I was already out the door.

CHAPTER 6

KELLY INGRAM

I came out of the shower wearing a towel and my dewy-fresh look.

Nick Quinlan looked me up and down with his x-ray eyes and then with a masterful gesture of his head commanded me to come closer. Eagerly I obeyed.

He placed one hand on my hip, leaned down so our faces were almost touching, and whispered softly, 'Doncha got summon more uh uh cum, cumfable more'n 'at?'

'That was fine, Nick,' the director said through clenched teeth. 'But we're running long and we're going to have to cut the line. Just say, "Comfortable?" '

'Cumfable.'

'That's it. Kelly? From the shower, please.'

The next time Nick was concentrating on his change of line and didn't pay enough attention to what his hands were doing and I lost my towel—nevertheless disappointing all the drooling letches on the set who were hoping for a juicy outtake, because I'd had the foresight to wear a bikini underneath. I'd been working with Nick Quinlan long enough to know better than go on to an open set with nothing on under my towel.

I ruined the next take myself. By laughing at the wrong time. Most of the two-shot close-ups you see on television have the two actors impossibly close to each other, their noses sometimes only a couple of inches apart. It's awfully hard not to get tickled when you are supposed to be saying serious lines with your face shoved up into somebody else's face like that. Besides, when Nick is really concentrating, his eyes tend to cross.

The next time we got it. Four takes. We were getting better.

I just realized I've never said one nice thing about Nick Quinlan. I've given the impression that he was beautiful but dumb—a clumsy, slow-witted peacock who liked admiration so long as he didn't have to do anything strenuous to get it. I probably gave that impression because it's true. Oh sure, I know, there are always two sides to everybody, two or more they say, and I'm not going to argue about that, that's okay. But if you want to see something other than Nick's dumb side, you really have to go looking for it. I mean, that's a wild goose chase, why kid ourselves? But still, it doesn't make me look very good when I go around badmouthing the star of the series, the creep.

Therefore I am going to say something nice about Nick Quinlan. Right now.

I'm thinking, I'm thinking.

Ha—got it. He did not smell bad.

I've been rattling on about Nick Quinlan like this because he's the kind of man most people admire and I don't really understand why. A good ole boy with the rest of the boys (accent on *boy*) whose proof of maleness lay (laid?—grammar, not sex)—whose maleness *depended on* the number of women he had at his feet, urf, what a sentence. And he looked and talked and acted just like everybody else, but maybe a little prettier. Yet when somebody really special like Ted Cameron comes along—nobody notices!

The first time I saw Ted I was talking to Marian Larch on the *LeFever* set and honest to God I had to look away. I could not *look* at him, he took my breath away so; excuse the cliché but that's what happened. He was just too good to be true and I was afraid if I looked too closely too soon, he'd melt or turn into the Hulk or something. But when I could look again he was better instead of worse, better even than I'd hoped.

When I'd gotten over my astonishment at those eyes of his, I shot a quick look around the set. There were some visitors, girls mostly, and they were standing and gawking at Nick Quinlan. Ted was only a couple of feet away but they didn't even *see* him, the idiots. I'd had trouble looking at him at first but then I couldn't take my eyes off him. He was slim and together-looking and leaned slightly forward as if ready to take on whatever came next. He wasn't a big man, just medium, and you could tell at one look he wasn't the kind who went around pumping up his chest all the time. His clothes were part of him, not just something hanging on his body. My hands began to itch, I wanted to touch him so much. Then he turned those way-out eyes on me and looked at me. I mean really looked at me. Windows to the soul? Ha. Signals from outer space.

The first thing he said to me was, 'Are you real?'

It didn't take us long to figure out neither one of us was the victim of a one-sided attraction; that's what I was most afraid of. I touched his face, once, for reassurance, then put my hands behind my back. Saving it. He lived in Tuxedo Park and neither one of us wanted to make the drive so we stayed at my place that first night.

In retrospect, I guess it was just glands calling to glands, but never in my life had I wanted a man the way I wanted Ted Cameron. The pressure was unbearable; I ached from wanting him even in the very act of making love. It was not altogether a pleasurable experience. You want contact with the other person so much, you try to get through each other's skin. I wanted Ted with me every minute of the day, I wanted constant physical contact, his body right there next to mine *all* the time. Which of course was impossible. It was very frustrating.

Those first few days were especially troublesome. *LeFever* still had a couple of more days to go, and Ted and I didn't really have time to get to know each other.

What I knew at that point was a lover who seemed to have been made just for me. I spent my time on the set thinking of Ted and bed; I just sleepwalked through my role. And there were complications. Ted had a business to run, and I had some ugly news to deal with.

The very day after Ted and I had met, I went on to the *LeFever* set and learned Rudy's mother had been arrested for attempted murder. I called Howard Chesney and asked him to make sure she had legal representation, send the bill to me.

Ted was with me, concerned and wanting to help. 'Do you want to go see her?'

I shook my head. 'She wouldn't want to see *me*. She doesn't really approve of me, Ted.'

'I thought you said a friend . . .'

'She's the mother of a friend. Rudy Benedict's mother. Rudy was a writer who, oh damn, he was murdered.'

Ted knew about Rudy, but he hadn't known he'd been a friend of mine. Ted slipped an arm around me and said, 'I'm sorry. This can't be easy for you. Who was it she tried to kill? Somebody she thought murdered her son?'

'No, it was Richard Ormsby—you've seen him on Channel 13, haven't you?'

He looked puzzled. 'Why would she want to kill Richard Ormsby?'

'Well, they're both historians—that's the only connection I can see. But historians don't go around shooting guns at each other, do they?'

In the end all I could do was leave it to Howard Chesney. I didn't really want to see her, either. Part of it was I was so absorbed in Ted I didn't have room in my life for anybody else, even people in trouble—yes, I was that selfish about it. But part of it was I just didn't *want* to see her.

Then we finished *LeFever*, and I had some time before I had to start work on a project Nathan Pinking and Leonard Zoff had lined up for me. Time for nothing but Ted Cameron, and he finally began to emerge as a personality instead of this irresistible force looming over my life.

What I saw was a man in thorough, easy-riding control of his life. He was in the driver's seat and he was comfortable there. A man of authority ruling over a kind of kingdom, making decisions, giving orders. And doing it all with such ease and grace that you'd think he was to the manor or manner born. As I guess he was, come to think of it. His personal life was under that same kind of unfussy control; he'd had two not-very-successful marriages that he'd ended, neatly and amicably. Ted's entire life was *neat*.

Little by little I learned more of him. Ted Cameron turned out to be kind, courteous, decisive, intelligent, sexy, generous, knowledgeable, gentle, self-aware, courageous, worldly, reliable, determined, considerate, amusing, resilient, adventurous, playful, straightforward, upright, and steadfast. I liked him a lot.

In spite of what you're thinking, Ted was very human; he did have one serious flaw. He didn't like to dance. (Imagine!) He was so out of it I even had to explain that disco had been passé for some time now. A man whose whole life was a stately dance, a minuet maybe—and he didn't like to dance. Incredible.

But when that first bone-aching obsession with each other began to ease up, we found we had something better, at least I thought I had. I had a partner, a companion. I had somebody to share with.

CHAPTER 7

FIONA BENEDICT

The lump in my stomach did not start small and gradually grow larger. It was just suddenly *there*. Solid stone.

What the romantics call fate and the frightened call

God's will, historians call pattern—mundane, earth-generated pattern, responding to the human need for connections. My pattern: the result of wanting to fill in a gap in our knowledge. The fourteen years of studying the life of George Charles Bingham, third Earl of Lucan. *He* called *his* book *Lord Look-on*. Cute. Dismissive. Cashing in.

The stone grew heavier.

Personal artifacts tell a history. In a box in a drawer in a bureau in my bedroom: one loaded gun. A gift from Rudy; *for protection*, he'd said. Prompted by some feeling of guilt, belatedly being The Good Son. A California gun, he'd said, laughing to make a joke of it. I'd never needed to fire it. Before now.

They must be stopped, the invaders. My life had been violated by a profane Englishman who in all likelihood would go on to rape again. No one would stop him. No one would object. What did it matter, what he'd done to me?

It isn't a matter of loneliness; if the work is good, the cocoon is warm. But when the cocoon is ripped away, the only consolation is the perfunctory sympathy of one's peers. Of *some* of one's peers. Others betray. Garfield of Columbia, in *The New York Times Review of Books*, cashing in on the casher-in. Jumping on the pop history bandwagon, survival of the flightiest. Elsewhere in the out-of-town edition, an announcement of his arrival in New York, spreading the good news about the wonderful thing he's done, how he's saved everyone the trouble of having to read Fiona Benedict's *Life of Lucan*. We are being invaded and we must defend ourselves.

The young woman at the airline counter seemed most concerned over my lack of luggage. Why would I need luggage? But I didn't even get near the aeroplane; I had to turn back. I'd forgotten about those detection devices they use to keep people from carrying guns on to airplanes. The stone in my stomach and I rode the bus all the way into New York City.

No sleep, no food—how long? Doesn't matter; time

seems to have lost its divisions. Uptown is which way? We *are* being invaded, you know.

A talk show at CBS: how to breach the Black Rock? As a member of the audience. Polite words but still pushing and shoving, a man's elbow just missing my eye, *I'll shoot you if you do that again*, I have the means. A woman's high heel on the arch of my foot, not even noticing, too busy showing off for the accompanying man. Pain and dizziness and finally a place to sit down. A seat in the last row.

Then they were all screaming and a light popped out and the pain and dizziness were too much for me and I went down, down. A hand pressing the back of my neck, forcing my head between my knees and consciousness returning. A voice saying *There's the gun*, another voice saying *Don't touch it*. A woman's face peering anxiously into mine, asking if I was all right.

'Is he dead?' I whispered.

'No, that maniac missed him. I *think* he's all right.'

That maniac?

A man's horrified face. 'Hey, lady, you better watch out! She's the one who tried to kill him!'

'Are you crazy?' the woman said. 'It was a man.'

'It was her!'

'It was a man—I'm pretty sure.'

A third voice: 'I thought it was a boy.'

More noise, arguing. My stone and I wanted to lie down, but there was no place. Then a policeman was asking me, all of us, for identification. As a result, one question was answered, at least: he did know who I was, he did know about my *Life of Lucan*.

He stared wide-eyed at me and said in that theatrical English voice, '*You* are Fiona Benedict?' Then he took one of the policemen aside and explained something, earnestly and at great length. I wanted to, I *had* to lie down.

'She's the one, I tell you!' the man with the horrified face kept insisting. 'I saw her!'

A hundred years later I was arrested and charged with

attempted murder.

But still they wouldn't let me lie down. They took me to the nearest precinct station, and asked questions, questions, questions. I couldn't think, I couldn't see straight. I said nothing, nothing at all. Fingerprints, photographs with a number, other indignities. No, I did not want to call anyone.

At last they let me lie down.

CHAPTER 8

MARIAN LARCH

Captain Michaels had said, 'Bullshit. Nobody tries to kill another person over a *book*.' He'd been in the business long enough to know that people do dreadful things to each other for far flimsier reasons than that, but he just couldn't bring himself to believe Fiona Benedict had tried to shoot Richard Ormsby. 'Not her. You, me, anybody else—but not her.'

But then he hadn't been there in Ohio when she first learned about *Lord Look-on*. I knew she could do it, and I understood why. But Ivan Malecki agreed with the Captain; both men were uneasy about the arrest. And with reason.

There was only one positive eyewitness in that small studio audience, a loud-voiced man who kept insisting that he'd seen Fiona Benedict firing a gun at the stage area. Unfortunately, there were half a dozen other people who sort of thought it was a small man or maybe a teenaged boy, they weren't sure. The man who'd fingered Dr. Benedict was the one positive one, but there was only one of him and six of the other kind.

Fiona Benedict was a lousy shot. She'd emptied the gun, executing a lighting instrument and wounding a camera but missing all the people. I wondered if she'd ever fired a pistol before. The gun itself was no help. It was not registered in New York; it was either purchased elsewhere or acquired illegally here. There were no fingerprints, but then there almost never are. Guns don't take fingerprints at all well, despite what the movies and TV say.

The arresting officer had made a really dumb mistake of the sort that occurs more frequently than we like to admit. Whether a suspect has fired a gun or not is determined by performing a test for powder and/or primer residue on the hand *within two hours* of the shooting. After a couple of hours, the residue is absorbed naturally into the skin. And before that, it can be washed off with plain old soap and water. The most reliable method of testing is atomic absorption spectrophotometry or by using scanning electron micrographs linked to an x-ray analyzer. But ordinary precinct stations don't have that kind of fancy equipment; and what with the delay caused by checking everybody in the TV audience, they were getting awfully close to the two-hour limit for testing.

So rather than risk passing that time limit by moving Fiona Benedict to a crime lab, the police decided to perform the nitric acid test for primer residue only, right there in the precinct station. And that's where the dumb mistake came in—not in procedure, which was routine. The nitric acid test reveals the presence of barium nitrate and antimony sulfide and a few other chemicals present in the primer, a residue of which is left on the thumb web and the back of the hand when a gun is fired. But the arresting officer neglected to tell the people performing the test that the weapon in question was a .22 caliber pistol—an evidence-destroying oversight, as it turned out. *Because the nitric acid test doesn't work on .22 caliber residue.* The .22 primer doesn't contain any barium or antimony.

So the nitric acid test was performed and proved negative, Fiona Benedict washed her hands with soap and water, and everyone started wondering if they'd arrested the wrong person. By the time they figured out what had happened, the one piece of hard evidence they might have got had already gone floating down the drain of a washbasin in the precinct station house. If they'd taken her to the lab straight off, there'd have been at least a chance of getting something.

But Fiona Benedict was the only one in the studio audience with a grudge against Richard Ormsby, and the police believed the one insistent witness who claimed Dr. Benedict was the lady with the gun. It was a none-too-sturdy case, but it *was* a case. The DA's office decided to prosecute.

Since the intended victim was a celebrity, the story of the attempted shooting was picked up by the wire services and also broadcast by all three networks. Two of the networks also included the news that Richard Ormsby's attacker was the mother of a victim of an unsolved murder. And one of them aired a hastily scheduled symposium called *What's Happening to America?*—in which the participants all argued about the changes taking place in this country that could lead even civilized people such as college professors to try solving their problems with violence.

All that coverage meant Washburn, Ohio, now knew its quiet and erudite Crimean War specialist was in fact a dangerous woman capable of pointing a loaded gun at someone and pulling the trigger. They also knew that Rudy Benedict had not died by accident, as his mother had led them to believe. Fiona Benedict's carefully constructed safe world had collapsed around her, just as earlier Rudy's had collapsed around him. Even as Rudy's father's had, too, I suppose. You could almost think the Benedicts were cursed—that family certainly seemed marked for tragedy. The father a suicide, the son a murder victim, the mother a murderer—a failed murderer, true, but there was murder in her heart. Fiona Benedict had stood at the back of that studio and fired her pistol over the heads of the seated audience, endangering all those people, in an attempt to destroy another person's life. She was guilty as hell.

100

She was also sick — she hadn't been eating or sleeping and what with the nervous strain and all she was on the verge of collapse. When she was arrested she'd made no statement to the police, had said nothing whatsoever, she hadn't even told anyone her name. She'd offered identification when asked for it, but she just hadn't talked at all — much to the delight of her high-powered lawyer who had suddenly appeared out of nowhere. But the woman was declining visibly. All the fight had gone out of her.

So, once again, I called her friends the Morrisseys.

Drew Morrissey's shock and disbelief were audible all the way from Ohio. 'I couldn't believe it when I heard it on the news,' he said. 'I still don't believe it. There must be some mistake.'

'There's no mistake. She was there and she tried to kill Richard Ormsby. We have evidence.'

' "We"?'

'Dr. Morrissey, I'm afraid I deceived you. I'm a police detective, and I was in Washburn on police business. Dr. Benedict didn't want you to know.' There was a silence. 'Dr. Morrissey?'

'Yes, I'm here. Just one new revelation after another, I'm not too . . . well, I'm stunned.'

'Yes, of course you are. Look, the reason I called is that Dr. Benedict isn't in very good shape, frankly. She's deteriorating physically, and her morale is shot to hell. She's all alone here. The presence of a couple of friends would help, I'm sure of it.'

'Well, ah, that might prove difficult. Ah, I have meetings scheduled all next week, you see, and —'

'I'll be there tomorrow morning,' Roberta Morrissey said on the extension.

I went to the detention cells on Sixty-seventh Street where Fiona Benedict was being held, to let her know Roberta was coming. I had to wait a few minutes as she was talking to her lawyer. When he came bustling out, I heard her call him Howard; Howard looked cheerful. He probably had a good chance of winning this one.

I sat down opposite her at the table in the interview room. 'Hello, Marian,' she said sadly. 'Howard says I'm not to talk to you. He's my lawyer.'

I nodded. 'I saw him leave. What's his last name?'

She dropped her forehead into one hand and laughed shortly. 'I don't know.'

It turned out that Howard the Nameless was a gift from Kelly Ingram — who herself had not been in to see Dr. Benedict. 'She's involved with something right now,' I said, thinking of Ted Cameron.

'Good,' she said with something of her old asperity. 'I hope she stays that way.' Here she was in jail for having tried to kill a man and she still disapproved of Kelly Ingram. But she would have said the two things didn't have anything to do with each other, and perhaps they didn't. I told her Roberta Morrissey was coming to New York and watched her look of astonishment turn into one of gratitude.

'I'm surprised she's still willing to acknowledge me as a friend,' she said. 'But then friends are the ones who come when you need them, aren't they?'

I didn't mention Drew Morrissey's suddenly remembered busy schedule or his continued presence in Ohio. That would occur to her soon enough.

An answer came to a request for information I'd put in with the Securities and Exchange Commission. I'd asked for a disclosure of all listed owners of Nathan Pinking's production company and Leonard Zoff's theatrical agency. Those two men had told me directly conflicting stories and I wanted to know which (if either) was telling the truth.

Leonard Zoff was. Both he and Pinking owned forty-nine percent of the other's business, just as Zoff had said. So Nathan Pinking had lied, and he must have done so knowing full well he'd be found out. The itinerary Mimsy had sent me said Pinking would be out of town until the end of the week, so I'd have to wait to confront him with it.

But at last Captain Michaels was interested. 'A power struggle, a potential take-over?' he mused. 'What's Benedict's connection? Did he learn something he wasn't supposed to know? You may be on to something there, Larch. Keep on it.'

I intended to.

CHAPTER 9

KELLY INGRAM

Ted Cameron was being blackmailed, I was sure of it.

I was staying with him at his estate in Tuxedo Park until it was time for me to go to California to start work on a TV movie I was scheduled to do. Ted played hooky as often as he could, bless him, but he did have to drive into Manhattan now and then to take care of business. I always went along—hah, I guess I did at that. I just wanted him with me all the time but if that couldn't be, then I wanted me with him, if you see the difference. Truth was, I couldn't get enough of him. I was a Ted Cameron junkie.

We eventually passed our hiding-from-the-world phase and started going places—a show and late supper, usually. Ted was just bored by dancing, a shock I was still recovering from. We went to see Abigail James's new play—talk, talk, talk; I'm afraid I drifted off.

But you see, that's all we had—in time, I mean. We'd gotten just that far when this other business took over. Three things made me think Ted was being blackmailed.

Once I'd gone to my apartment to take care of some things while Ted went to a meeting. He came in about the middle of the afternoon, and he was seething with anger. But he didn't want me to know! I felt a sinking feeling when he tried to pretend he wasn't angry, tried to make me think everything was fine. Now I'm not one of those who believe the truth shall *always* make you free, I think

103

everybody ought to have a secret or two. But it's still a blow when a man you're *that* close to deliberately lies to you for the first time — no matter what his motives are. And it didn't make much sense anyway, because what he told me sounded like good news at first.

'You're going to Barbados in October,' he said. 'Nathan Pinking got a commitment from the network for an additional three original episodes of *LeFever*.'

'Additional?' I said. 'You mean plus, also, too? In addition to the regular twenty already in the can?'

'That's right. Plus, also, too.'

'And did you say *Barbados?*'

He smiled naturally for the first time since he'd come in. 'Thought you'd like that. The scheduling is a bit close, but the three episodes will be inserted towards the end of the season.'

'And the network went for it?'

'Sure, why not? A producer goes in with a sponsor already in his pocket, the network isn't going to say no.' He must have heard the bitter tone of his own voice, because he made a conscious attempt to speak more lightly. 'I decided it would be a good opportunity to show our new line of swimwear — as modeled on the show by none other than Kelly Ingram and Nick Quinlan.'

I didn't believe it; he sounded to me like a man backed into a corner. 'Ted? Why are you really doing this?'

His eyes slid away from me and turned invisible. 'I told you, to show our new line of swimwear.'

So he wasn't ready to talk to me about it. He considered himself in Nathan Pinking's pocket, did he — how had that come about? And he didn't want to talk about it. All right, I could live with that, for a while. I put my arms around his waist and hugged hard enough to make him grunt. 'You're coming to Barbados too, aren't you?'

'I have to,' he said with mock resignation. 'Somebody has to make sure Nick Quinlan doesn't put his trunks on backwards.'

That was the first thing. The second thing was a snatch of conversation I overheard in Tuxedo Park.

104

I'd just opened a door to go out on the patio when I heard a man out there saying, 'We can't do it, Ted! Why do you keep insisting? That damned show would take our entire advertising budget. What are we supposed to do, forget about newspapers, magazines—'

'Maybe I can get Lorelei Cosmetics to share the cost in exchange for a few spots,' Ted said worriedly. 'If I can't, then you'll just have to use your whole budget.'

'For a hick sitcom that's never once made the Nielsen top twenty? That's crazy! *Why*, Ted?'

Then they both became aware of me and one of those *horrible* silences developed that go on and on and on and you think are never going to end. For the very first time, I felt like an intruder in Ted's world and I didn't like the feeling at all. The other man turned out to be Roger Cameron, Ted's cousin and the president of Watercraft, Inc., one of Cameron Enterprises' ancillary companies, that's the term Ted used. I was beginning to feel a bit ancillary myself.

The third thing was more roundabout. Ted was thinking out loud, making plans. 'I should be able to take a few weeks off before long—we can go to Scotland. Would you like to go to Scotland?' He laughed, happy at the thought of getting away for a while. 'They say July and August are the best months for spotting the Loch Ness Monster. We can go to Inverness and join the monster-hunt.'

'If we can schedule around my television movie,' I reminded him.

He looked surprised. 'Time for that already? I thought it was later. How long will it take?'

I smiled. 'A Big Production like this one? Nathan has scheduled three whole weeks.' Three weeks to make a movie. And it was important to me because it wasn't *just* a movie—it was also a pilot. 'It can mean my own series, remember.'

He knew; we'd talked about it. 'Make the movie,' he said firmly. 'You should have your own series. I don't like seeing you as a bit of fluff for Nick Quinlan to play with.'

'Yes, sir,' I said, straight-faced.

He grinned, his eyes looking blue instead of invisible for a change. 'Sorry, didn't mean to sound bossy. Kelly—do you like working for Nathan Pinking?'

Strange question. 'Nobody *likes* working for Nathan. Except maybe Nick—they get along.'

He looked dissatisfied. 'You could do better than Nathan Pinking schlock.'

'*You* do business with him,' I pointed out.

'That's different. There are other things involved.'

I decided to take the plunge; this had gone on long enough. 'Ted, it's obvious you can't stand Nathan Pinking and it's equally obvious you don't want to sponsor *LeFever*. So why don't you just cut out? Why are you putting your company's money into a show you don't really want to have anything to do with?'

'Sometimes these decisions are automatic,' he said in a tight voice, and refused to discuss it. He absolutely *refused* to talk about it.

Now, there was only one way I could read all that, and that was that Ted was being blackmailed and it sure as hell looked as if it was Nathan Pinking who was doing the blackmailing. Nathan was clearly forcing Ted to sponsor *LeFever*, and it probably went farther than that. Ted wanted his cousin Roger to put *his* company's money into what Roger called a hick sitcom. One of Nathan Pinking's other shows was titled *Down the Pike* and could be fairly described as a hick sitcom, I think.

There are few things I can think of that would be worse than knowing someone like Nathan Pinking had a stranglehold on your life. I got along with the man by telling myself *constantly* that other producers were worse, whether it was true or not—but Nathan was one of those people you just knew you could never trust. He liked being ugly merely to show you he could do anything he wanted. And if he controlled Ted, that meant he had Cameron Enterprises' assets to draw on, and *that* meant he had somebody to pick up the tab for whatever he wanted to do on television. What a guarantee against failure! An insurance policy to end all insurance policies, the deadbeat creep.

I was sorry about the company, but I couldn't get real worked up about that when I knew what this had to be doing to Ted. My God, it must be eating him up inside! And all this time I'd thought Ted was so in control of his life—the decision-maker, the man who gave orders. I'd just plain misread the signs. It was all a façade, a brave face Ted was showing to the world. How could he stand it? Must be like living in a torture chamber.

I was trying to think of something to do to help. How do you get rid of a blackmailer? Other than, well, *get rid* of him, I mean. The only thing I could think of was to get something on *him*, and then blackmail the blackmailer. But Nathan Pinking had a reputation for being able to protect himself in the clinches, and he wasn't just going to leave weapons laying around you could use against him. (Yes, I got it—*lying* around.) So could I hire a detective to dig up some dirt on Nathan? There *was* dirt; I don't think there could be any doubt of that. But how do you find the right kind of detective? I thought Marian Larch could probably tell me, but how did I go about getting the information out of her without letting it slip that Ted was being blackmailed? Oh, what a mess.

And still . . . and still no matter how I fought it, there was one nasty question that just kept on coming back to me: What did Ted *do* that was so awful he had to give in to Nathan Pinking in order to keep it quiet?

CHAPTER 10

MARIAN LARCH

Roberta Morrissey looked shaken when she came out of the interview room.

'What is it? Did she say something?' I asked.

Roberta shook her head. 'It's just seeing Fiona in a

place like this . . . it takes some getting used to, that's all.'

I understood. Poor lady, she really looked upset. 'Let's go somewhere for, ah, coffee?'

'I'd rather have a drink.'

I took her to a place on Fifth that was fairly quiet. When she started looking steady again, I said, 'There's something I'd like to ask you about. This isn't official, it's only to satisfy my own curiosity. Dr. Benedict was carrying a *Times* review of her book with her. Do you know about that?'

She smiled sadly. 'The infamous *Times* review. Yes, indeed, I know about it. It was probably what tipped her over.'

'But why? I read it. The reviewer said a lot of nice things about her book.'

'He said even nicer things about Ormsby's. That's the trouble with these double reviews—one book always ends up looking inferior. The reviewer acknowledged Fiona's book as the more scholarly piece of work, but it was *Lord Look-on* that got the nod of approval in the final analysis. Ormsby's version was "more fun" to read, he said. He actually said that—"more fun". As if entertainment value were *the* ultimate criterion.'

It still didn't seem that bad to me and I said so.

Roberta looked at me a moment and then asked, 'Marian, when was the last time you bought a history book?'

I grinned sheepishly.

'Did you *ever* buy a history book?' she persisted. 'In fact, have you even read any history since you finished school? Don't look like that, you're in the majority. I write a book about the Brontë sisters and I can count on some slight general interest outside academic circles. Historians don't have even that. Barbara Tuchman's work always sells—but she's an exception. Oh, occasionally a book of contemporary history will be highly touted and have respectable sales, but Drew is convinced most of them are never read beyond the first fifty pages.'

'Not even Richard Ormsby's books?'

'Well, Ormsby has an advantage over people like Fiona and Drew. He has no scruples about oversimplifying things that perhaps ought not to be made simple at all. And that jazzy writing style helps sell his books to the popular market. But the legitimate historians can't write for that kind of market.'

'So they end up writing for . . . each other?'

'For the record, say—for libraries, in a way. You know it's sustained library sales over the years that justifies the publisher's investment. But the way library budgets have been cut to the bone the last few years, librarians aren't going to order two new biographies of Lord Lucan when the world has been happily bumbling along with none at all for over a century and a quarter now. Know how many books are published in this country every year? Almost fifty thousand.'

'Every *year*?' I'd had no idea.

'Every year. So library purchasing departments have to depend on publications like *Library Journal* or *Publishers Weekly* to help them decide what to buy. Both those periodicals gave brief, equally favorable reviews to Fiona's book and to Ormsby's. That means the librarians have to turn to other reviews.' She finished her drink.

I held up two fingers to the waiter. 'So the *Times* review will affect library sales.'

'Undoubtedly.' Roberta Morrissey looked depressed as she thought about her friend's book. 'Do you understand what that means? It means that all over this country *and* in England history students will be consulting Ormsby's book when they're studying the Crimean War. *He* will be the authority, not Fiona. Oh, the large universities with strong history departments will know the difference and they'll order Fiona's book. But the kids won't know. In most schools that assign papers on the war the students will consult Ormsby and maybe never even know about Fiona's work.'

So it was more than just professional jealousy; it was a matter of professional responsibility. Fiona Benedict must have felt her whole life was under siege when *Lord Look-*

on started shooting the foundations out from under her own book. So she'd picked up a gun and started shooting back.

I drove Roberta to her hotel and thought about having another go at Nathan Pinking, but decided against it. I'd talked to him once right after he got back to town. When I confronted him with his lie about never having been in business with Leonard Zoff—he simply claimed he'd never said any such thing. I'd misunderstood him, he said, both sides of his mismatched face equally bland. Leonard Zoff must have been right; Pinking lied automatically. He didn't even care that I knew he was lying.

At Headquarters I found Kelly Ingram waiting for me. She was sitting quietly by my desk, seemingly oblivious of all the attention directed her way. It was the first time I'd seen her since the advent of Ted Cameron.

She seemed nervous about something. 'Marian, I . . . I wanted to ask you, uh, I wanted to, uh . . .'

'Yes?' I put as much encouragement into the one syllable as I could.

'I wanted to ask you . . . could I go see Dr. Benedict?' she finished in a rush.

You're lying, I thought. That wasn't why she'd come in.

But before I could say anything Ivan Malecki came up to the desk and cleared his throat. 'Hello, Kelly, remember me?'

Kelly glanced up. 'Oh hello, Ivan, how are you?' She'd not only remembered him, she'd remembered his name as well. After a minute's worth of inane dialogue, Ivan strutted away, his existence justified.

'You don't really want to see Dr. Benedict,' I said.

'But I do!' she protested. 'I should have been in before this but I, uh . . .'

'Kelly. You once told me you couldn't get away with telling lies off camera. You were right. Now why did you come in?'

'I told you—I want to see Dr. Benedict.'

'Your nose just grew another inch.'

She looked at me disconsolately a moment and then made up her mind. 'All right, here it is. I need a private detective, and don't ask me why because I'm not going to tell you. The yellow pages are full of names, but they don't tell me what I need to know.'

'Which is?'

'The ones that are legit and the ones that are a smidge on the shady side.'

'Uh-huh. And which kind do you want?'

It was hard for her to say it. 'The shady kind.'

Oh my! Now what did this pretty doll-woman want with a shady detective? What had gone so wrong in her glamorous, successful life that she should need expert help from someone who wasn't averse to bending the law a little if the pay was right? There was only one new element in her life that I knew of.

So I said: 'What's Ted Cameron done?'

'Oh, *Marian!*' She looked hurt and exasperated at the same time. 'Are you going to give me a name or not?'

'No, I am not going to give you a name. At least not the kind you want. I'm a policewoman, remember? Sworn to uphold the law? I will give you the names of a few reputable people, if you like.'

'I thought you'd help.'

'I'm trying to. But I can't read minds. Why don't you tell me what's wrong?'

'I can't do that. Damn it, Marian! Just one lousy stinking name.'

'Forget it. Why do you want to have your boyfriend investigated?'

'I don't! Oh, you've got it all wrong.'

'Then set me straight. Tell me what's going on.'

She thought about it a few minutes, but ended up shaking her head. 'I can't tell you. I can't tell anybody.' She sighed. 'As long as I'm here—I might as well go see Dr. Benedict. I'm allowed, aren't I?'

It would be my second trip to the detention cells that day. 'I'll have to take you. This isn't a regular visiting day.'

'Oh—I didn't think of that. Marian, I don't want to put you out—'

'It's okay,' I said. And it was. I was thinking that on the drive over I might get a little more out of her about why she wanted a shady detective.

But what I got was a new lie she'd had time to think up. 'I might as well tell you,' she said. 'I want somebody to find out who sent me the laxative and the toilet paper. You remember that time, don't you?'

I stopped at a red light and just looked at her. The lie was so blatant she had the good grace to laugh at her own clumsiness.

'Won't do, Kelly,' I said.

'Won't do,' she agreed. 'Especially between you and I.' She frowned. 'I?'

'Me, I think. Besides, it's easier to tell the truth.'

But mentioning the laxative had started her thinking. 'I probably never will know who sent it, will I?'

'There's no way of proving it,' I said carefully. 'You can make a reasonable assumption, however.'

'You think you know? Who?'

'Laxative and toilet paper,' I said. 'Who is it among your acquaintance that can't get through a conversation without using the word *shit* over and over again?'

Her eyes grew large. 'Leonard Zoff? Leonard sent me the laxative?'

'He'd be my guess.' The light turned green; I eased the car forward. 'Didn't you once tell me you thought he didn't like women? And here you are, extremely female, one of his brightest prospects for success if not *the* brightest. Maybe sending you that laxative was a way of relieving his own tensions a little—oh dear, bad word choice. But all that's just speculation, Kelly. I may be maligning the man.'

'If he sent *me* a doctored bottle of Lysco-Seltzer . . .' She didn't finish.

'Did he send one to Rudy Benedict too? We don't think so. Whoever substituted the cyanide had to do it the same day Benedict died. Zoff had an alibi for almost the entire

112

day. He was on the go, had a lot of appointments. But we checked all the people he met with, and there just doesn't seem to have been time for him to slip down to Chelsea, make the substitution when Rudy wasn't looking, and keep to his schedule. It's not airtight, so he *could* have found a way of doing it. But it doesn't look likely.'

Kelly accepted that. 'Besides, Leonard would have no reason to kill Rudy. They were friendly. They weren't even working together — they never did, so far as I know.'

'Yes, they did — about a dozen years ago,' I told her. 'When Rudy was writing scripts for that well-known production team, Pinking and Zoff.'

Her head swiveled towards me. 'Pinking and Zoff? You mean Leonard was a *producer?* Wow. And in business with Nathan Pinking?'

'That's right.' The news so surprised her that she was quiet the rest of the way to the detention cells.

Inside the building, we waited in the interview room while Fiona Benedict was being brought up. Kelly began to have second thoughts. 'I'm not sure this was such a good idea.'

'Too late now,' I said as the door opened and a matron escorted Dr. Benedict in.

She stopped cold when she saw Kelly. 'What do you want?' Not a very auspicious beginning.

Kelly stood up, hesitated. 'I, ah, I wanted to see if you were all right. If you needed anything.'

'Nothing.' Fiona Benedict's eyes narrowed and she forced herself to say, 'I suppose I should thank you for sending Howard.'

Well, yes, I suppose you should, I was thinking, but Kelly said quickly, 'That's all right, glad to help. Is there anything else? Anything you want that I can bring?'

The dislike on Dr. Benedict's face was so naked that I wasn't surprised when Kelly flinched. I doubted that she'd ever been looked at like that before in her entire life. 'The role of Lady Bountiful doesn't suit you,' Dr. Benedict said contemptuously. 'Not convincing, not convincing at all.'

'Wh-what do you mean?' Kelly stammered.

'Little Miss Innocence. You forgot to bat your eyes.'

Kelly looked as if she didn't believe what she was hearing. 'Why are you talking to me like this?'

'What are you doing here?' the older woman snapped out. 'Did you come to crow? Go away, Kelly Ingram, go away and don't come back. I don't want to see you or your kind ever again. You and your flashy looks and your cheap obviousness—'

'Now, wait a minute!' Kelly said hotly, stung into defending herself. 'Who the hell are you to call me *cheap*?'

'Oh, I'm sure you put a high price on yourself,' the older woman said heavily. Her shoulders slumped. 'You sell yourself and then you sell out the rest of us.'

Kelly glanced at me; I shook my head—I didn't know what she was talking about either. 'What are you saying, Dr. Benedict?' I asked.

'Look at her, Marian,' she said bitterly in reply. 'So pleased with herself. So willing to adjust to whatever demands a man might make of her. But she's never tarnished and she's always fresh and ready for more. The ideal woman—a renewable virgin. What a role model for young girls!' She took a couple of steps towards Kelly. 'We're *all* teachers—don't you understand that? You go on that asinine show and teach schoolgirls to be exhibitionists. You teach them that their function in life is to display their bodies and never think at all. You're telling them the only worthwhile goal in life is to attract male attention. Yes, I call that *cheap*.'

Kelly was outraged. 'It's only a *role* I'm playing, for crying out loud!'

'And if you don't do it, somebody else will? That's the rest of the argument, isn't it? The same rationalizations women have always used. You made your choice long ago—you're selling yourself, and there's no way you can pretend you're not.'

Kelly looked as if she'd been slapped in the face; you could almost see the fingermarks on her cheek. I decided to interfere. I stepped between the two of them and said, 'Fiona, that's enough. You're being unfair. Don't take it out on her.'

She looked me straight in the eye for a long moment and then without speaking turned on her heel. The matron opened the door and they were gone.

Kelly sank weakly into the nearest chair. 'How can she hate me that much? I never did anything to her.'

'It wasn't really you she was telling off. It was Richard Ormsby.'

'Ormsby? But I don't even know him!'

'You're both attractive, successful television personalities. Dr. Benedict attacked you because you were the handiest representative of a world she feels threatened by. And it's the world her son chose to live in, don't forget—that's mixed up in it too.'

'But all that business about selling myself—'

'Well, she couldn't very well blast you for writing bad history, could she? That's really what's bugging her. She sees it as a form of prostitution.'

'Marian, do you think I'm selling myself?' While I was floundering for an answer, she went on, 'I am going to judge the Miss America contest. It's all set. I'm going to do it.'

I started to say *Oh, Kelly* in exasperation when I realized what she was telling me. Any other woman in her place—myself included—would have been furious, striking out at her accuser, indulging in a long process of self-justification. But Fiona Benedict had said *selling yourself* and Kelly Ingram had thought *Miss America*. A natural link. I always knew Kelly was more self-aware than most glitter girls. She understood the prostitutional aspect of meat parades.

Now if she would only turn her back on it.

But right then she didn't look up to making any decisions at all. 'Come on, let's get out of this place,' I said. 'It's beginning to depress me.'

In the car Kelly asked me to come home with her. 'You're through for the day, aren't you?'

115

I said I was. 'Where's Ted Cameron?'

'Los Angeles. Soothing his Aunt Augusta. Wouldn't you know he'd have an aunt named Augusta?'

I knew of Augusta Cameron; she was the head of Lorelei Cosmetics — one of those *grandes dames* who seem to be the natural rulers in the realm of fashion and cosmetics. 'Why does Aunt Augusta need soothing?' I asked.

'Oh, Ted says every couple of years she gets it into her head she could do a better job of running Cameron Enterprises than Ted and he has to go out and calm her down.'

I was hungry and announced the fact. When we got to her apartment, Kelly called the restaurant at the top of the building and ordered dinner to be sent down. While we were waiting I turned on the news and heard something that made me forget all about food.

And that was that Richard Ormsby had been shot.

It had happened while the Englishman was leaving the NBC studios in Rockefeller Center. His assailant had stood behind a barely open stairwell door and fired at Ormsby from there. No one saw his face. His aim had been perfect: his victim died on the spot. The killer had done his damage and made his escape before witnesses were fully able to realize what was happening.

Richard Ormsby was as dead as they come. And all the time Fiona Benedict had been locked up in a detention cell on Sixty-seventh Street, where we'd left her not more than forty-five minutes earlier.

CHAPTER 11

KELLY INGRAM

Ted gave me the news on Thursday, just after noon. I always knew the end of the world would come on a Thursday.

Look at me, making jokes, ha ha ha. I don't know what else to do so I make a joke about it, how else do you stay away from the funny farm when the sky falls on your head? And it fell, all right, oh *wow* did it fall. Crash, bang, BOOM, noisier than the sound track of a science fiction movie, jokes again. *It has to be this way,* he'd said. Sez who? *Why* does it have to be this way? Where's that written down?

No explanation, no answer, no real reason. Just *we're going to have to stop seeing each other, Kelly.* Stop *seeing* each other? Good God, I'm not a character in a 1940s movie, wasn't even born then. And the worst part was he didn't mean it, I mean he *meant* it, we *would* have to stop 'seeing' each other, but he didn't want to mean it, he didn't want to say it. Ted did not choose to end the affair. He was being forced to end it.

Doesn't that sound stupid? Paranoid, even. Woman gets dumped, thinks up elaborate explanation to save face. *Are you going back to your wife,* I said. *I don't have a wife,* he said. *You've got two,* I said. *Ex-wives,* he said, *and I'm not going back to either one of them,* he said. Then *why,* Ted? Why?

But he had no reason. Just: *It has to be this way.* It was as if he wanted me to know something was wrong, otherwise he'd have made up a believable excuse or tried to make me think he wasn't interested any more or *something.* But there was nothing like that; just *Goodbye, Kelly,* like that. Was he really saying *Help me?* Am I looking for excuses?

He made sure we were in my apartment when he told me—so *he* could leave, I guess, rather than put himself in the spot of having to tell me to go. After he'd gone, I just sat there and stared at the wall until I realized I couldn't see anymore, it had gotten so dark. Wednesday he ordered the tickets for our trip to Scotland, Thursday morning he went to a meeting, Thursday afternoon we were through. So all right, Sherlock, figure out where the change came. I didn't know who or whom his meeting was with; he always told me when I asked but this time I hadn't, damn it. But something had happened that Thursday morning to make me *persona non whatever,* and of course I had to wonder if it had anything to do with the blackmail. Damn Marian Larch, if she'd given me a name when I asked for one maybe all this could have been avoided.

I refused to accept it. It was a temporary separation, that's all, forced on Ted by a villainous blackmailer, Nathan Pinking or somebody else, somebody hateful. *Why* was utterly beyond me, I couldn't even begin to guess. But what was happening now was only an interruption of the normal state of things, an obstacle to be overcome, a thing-in-the-way to be removed, the course of true love never did run on well-oiled wheels or however. It was up to me to do something.

Big talk. Do what? Two little words, floating on top: Marian Larch. That'd do it — sic the police on them. That would do *something* all right, maybe put Ted in jail? (What did he *do?*) Didn't really mean it, I was just thinking nasty things—I was hurt and I wanted to hurt back. Yes, Ted, I wanted to hurt *you.* Why hadn't you managed better? You are a *professional* manager, you should have managed your personal business better.

But I didn't want to call in Marian Larch or Ivan Whatsit or Captain Whoosit for another reason, the best reason in the world, and that was it was too embarrassing. I'd be damned if I'd play a woman-scorned role. Because that's what I'd look like if I went to the police for help, a woman scorned who was getting even—with Ted, with whoever was blackmailing him. With the *world.* And I *wasn't* scorned, dammit! Ted was almost crying when he told me it was all over.

But still he did tell me.

Oh Christ, what a mess. Somebody had Ted's life on a string; all he had to do was pull the string and Ted jumped. *Was* it Nathan Pinking? Whoever it was, he'd come between me and Ted—for what reason? For kicks? Just to prove he could do it? *That* sounded like Nathan Pinking, all right. Nathan didn't particularly dislike me, and that Fiona Benedict was the only person I knew who

118

outright hated me. (I think.) But Nathan had invested money in me, I was one of his more promising 'properties' — why would he want to hurt me? Maybe he didn't; maybe he was just using me to get at Ted; maybe it wasn't Nathan Pinking at all; and maybe I should stop making up fairy tales.

Wish I hadn't thought of that woman. The way she lit into me — my God, so much resentment! Rudy's mother, I mean. As if she'd been storing up grudges against me for *years*, and we'd only known each other a couple of months. The very first time I saw her she accused me of having caused Rudy's death, the old bitch, God, listen to me. I felt like killing her, completely forgot myself. If it hadn't been for Marian Larch —

I don't think I've ever known two women more unalike than Fiona Benedict and Marian Larch. Rudy's mother is awful, just awful — arrogant and disapproving and always looking down her nose at me. At *me!* But Marian Larch doesn't judge everybody by herself, she's friendly and helpful and in her own way a very cool lady, she doesn't get rattled and she always knows what to do. She agrees with Fiona Benedict about one thing, though, the Miss America kind of thing, but she never makes me feel like some kind of worm from under a rock because I don't agree with *her*. But Dr. Benedict makes me feel I could never never never do anything that would please her, not that I want to, please her, that is.

Older people are *always* doing that, it makes them feel superior. If they don't have anything else going for them, they claim *age* automatically gives them answers that are withheld from undeveloped ignoramuses like me. They specialize in being right. No matter what happens, they say in their smug little voices: 'You don't know yet, wait until you're older.' God, is that infuriating! They can tell you *anything*, anything at all, and then stop you from disagreeing with them by saying you're not old enough to know. You mean you believe that ridiculous story about the world being *round*? Oh dear, tee hee. *You don't know yet, wait until you're older.* Fiona Benedict had done something like that to me. She'd taken one look at me and decided *no*. Who the hell is she to set herself up as my judge?

I'll tell you who she is. She's a dried-up old prune who's past it, that's who she is. These women who are always saying *Stop making yourself a sex object,* they're always old or ugly or both. I hate to say it, but if Marian Larch was even a little bit pretty, she might not be so quick to turn up her nose at the Miss America contest. I *like* looking the way I look, damn it, and why should I have to apologize for it? Why is it so wrong to be pretty?

It's not wrong. It's just jealousy, homely women have always been jealous of pretty women, that's all it is, plain jealousy. Well, they didn't actually say it was wrong—she said, Dr. Benedict said, she meant what I was doing with my looks was wrong. Hair-splitting. What does she know about it? What does she *know*? With all her college degrees and her easy life, she never had to put herself on display like some prize cow at a county fair, hoping to God some fat-cat producer would see her and like her. She never had to do that. But Marian had said she wasn't really yelling at me anyway, she was just using me as a substitute for Richard Ormsby. Well, maybe.

Would Ted have tuned in to me like that if I'd been homely? No. He would not have. Would *I* have tuned in to him if *he* was homely? Maybe. I don't really know. Men don't have to be beautiful.

But now one beautiful man by the name of Richard Ormsby was dead, and Fiona Benedict *couldn't* have killed him because she was locked up at the time it happened. In a way that was too bad, I *liked* thinking of that know-it-all woman as a villain. But that must have been why she was so cranky and nasty, because she was in jail for something she didn't do. But Marian said she *did* try to kill Ormsby in the CBS studio, so who did kill him in Rockefeller Center, an accomplice? What was this, a conspiracy of historians? Oh, come *on*.

Dear Mom, nothing much happening here, two murders and a little blackmail, write soon. The more scared I am, the worse the joke. I was scared of what was happening to Ted, and I was scared I wouldn't be able to do anything about it. I was terrified that two murderers were running around out there whose paths had crossed mine and could do so again. Or was it only one murderer? Did the same guy who killed Rudy also shoot down Ormsby? Richard Ormsby—a stranger with whom I had no connection at all, yeah, *whom*. Except that a woman who had tried to kill him also hated me. I was even scared of Fiona Benedict.

Now wait a minute, wait a minute, don't go lumping everything together like that. Three different things had happened. Thing number one was that Rudy Benedict had been murdered. Thing number two was that Richard Ormsby had been murdered. And thing number three was that Ted Cameron was being blackmailed, probably by Nathan Pinking but maybe by someone else. There was no reason to think things number one, two, and three were connected with one another. Trouble was, there was no reason to think they were *not* connected, either.

The only link between the two murders that I could see was Rudy's mother. But Rudy's death didn't have anything to do with the competition between two books about some British officer way back in Queen Victoria's day. (I think it was Victoria.) And what did Ted's blackmailer have to do with either death? Nothing that I could see. Ted didn't even know Rudy Benedict; he knew about his murder, but then he didn't know Richard Ormsby either. Was Marian Larch wrong about Fiona Benedict? Maybe she hadn't tried to kill the Englishman at all. But whether she did or not, that was one set of problems and they had nothing to do with me, thank God. The sooner I saw the last of Fiona Benedict the better.

I couldn't make any sense of it. Best leave it to the police to figure out, don't try to second guess the professionals. Marian and Ivan and Captain—what *is* his name?—Michaels, Captain Michaels, that's it; they were the ones to figure out the mess.

Except that I knew something they didn't know. I knew that Ted Cameron was being blackmailed.

But that wasn't connected to the murders, right? That meant there'd be no real danger to Ted if I told Marian he was being blackmailed, right? I was damned sure of that, right? I was willing to risk Ted's neck on my certainty that he had no connection with either murder. Right?

Well, not *wrong*. But not exactly right either. Could the police investigate a case of blackmail without uncovering what it was the victim had done that made him blackmailable in the first place? What did Ted *do*? — it always came back to that. How much did I trust him?

How much did he trust me? He wanted me to know something was wrong, I was sure of it. It wasn't just business problems either, although things were going bad for him there too. Aunt Augusta and Cousin Roger and Nephew Somebody and a few more sisters and cousins whom he reckoned by the dozens were all ganging up on him, he said, making a bigger fuss than usual in their periodic tries to take the presidency of Cameron Enterprises away from him. But if Ted was kicked out as president, that meant he wouldn't be able to keep on paying off his blackmailer and then what? And Thursday morning something had happened to make him break up with me. Why? To protect me? Was something so horrible going to happen to Ted that he wanted to make sure I was in the clear before it all blew up?

I was still trying to decide what to do when I got a call from someone who identified herself only as Mimsy and who asked me to come to a meeting in Nathan Pinking's office. I hadn't seen Nathan for a while — I was nervous about facing him. I don't know how to talk to *blackmailers*. But when I got to Nathan's office, I stopped worrying about blackmail because something else had come along, something in the person of Leonard Zoff — who'd probably sent me laxative and toilet paper. Besides, Nathan Pinking and Leonard Zoff in the same room at the same time is not my favorite way to spend an afternoon.

Oh yes incidentally and by the way, there was one other little matter that kept me from feeling on top of the world at that particular moment. It was my birthday. Yep, I'd actually done it — I'd turned thirty. I didn't, tell, a, *soul*.

So there I was, feeling elderly, in a room with two men I didn't trust, not sure how I should act toward either of them — because they were in the middle of grandiose plans to make me rich and famous. That's right, rich and famous: *Kid, I'm gonna make you a star.* They were planning a campaign to put me in the public eye, everything from presenting awards at a boat show on the West Coast to narrating a pop documentary about women's hairstyles.

'Your so-called agent has been holding out on you,' Nathan snickered to me. 'Buncha junk lined up for you he didn't tell you about. Afraid you'd kick him out. Guest announcer at a ladies' wrestling match? Haw! Zoff, you've got as much class as a garbage collector.'

'Don't listen to that shithead, darling,' Leonard said loudly around a cigar in his mouth. 'As usual, he don't know what he's talking about. I always have something in the works, but I don't tell you about it til it starts to firm up.'

'Lady wrestlers?' I said dubiously, while Nathan laughed haw-haw-haw.

Leonard gave a long martyred sigh, something he was good at. 'No, not lady wrestlers. I told you not to listen to that shithead. A new series of specials about women's sports, different host every week, different *sports* every week. The network wants you for one of the segment hosts, nothing to do with *announcing* a wrestling match. Might not even be on your segment. See how that shithead twists everything? Couldn't tell it straight if his life depended on it.'

It made no impression on Nathan, who kept right on haw-hawing. 'You watch, you'll end up ringside calling the blows,' he told me between guffaws.

Supposedly I'd been summoned so my agent and my producer and I could talk over plans for my future, but after a while it became clear I could just as well have stayed home. *They* were making the decisions, and I would do what I was told. Somehow those two enemies had agreed that one more year of *LeFever* would be my last, whether the show was renewed or not. By then they hoped to have a new series ready for me, if not the result of the TV movie I was scheduled to make, then something else.

Almost casually Nathan Pinking informed me that rewrite work was being done on the script. It seemed the setting was to be changed, damn it. The original plan was to show me as a bright young thing fresh out of law school who's taken into a big, tradition-bound firm where my unorthodox ways stirred things up a bit. The stirring-things-up-a-bit episodes were to alternate with ones in which I benefited from the experience and advice of older, wiser heads. Something for everybody, you see? Rebellion for the young, triumph over rebellion for the old. With a fair sprinkling of steamy love scenes for everybody.

As shallow as it sounded, I was still looking forward to the role because it would give me a chance to do something other than show off the bod. Being ornamental is okay but not if it's the *only* thing you get to do. There are only so many ways you can pose prettily for the camera. I was always asking the *LeFever* director for things to do, sharpening a pencil, piloting a space ship, anything.

So I was sorry to hear the law office setting had been scrapped. The series format would be kept, but the whole thing would be transferred to a hospital setting. ('Hospitals are back,' Nathan Pinking had announced.) Now Nathan and Leonard were arguing about what my role should be. Nathan suggested brain surgeon.

Leonard's mouth dropped open and he almost lost his cigar. 'I swear to God, Pinking, you must be taking stupid pills,' he said. 'We've been selling her as a piece of tail for two years and all of a sudden everybody's gonna accept her as a *brain surgeon?* I've spent the last twenty-five years listening to your shit, but that's the biggest piece you ever came up with!'

'A *sexy* brain surgeon, you Neanderthal asshole, that's the difference—is that too much for you to grasp? Underneath all that brainy efficiency she's still all woman, she's still a garden of delights for the right man. Got that? No matter how intimidating she is during the day, at night in bed things are like always. You think *that* won't go over, hah? Top of the ratings.'

'We've got a problem,' I said. 'I can't control what you two say to each other when I'm not here, but I cannot sit here and allow you to talk about me like this.' I turned to Leonard. 'Do you realize you just called me a piece of tail?'

He was instantly and unconvincingly contrite. 'Darling, what can I say? You know talking to this shithead always makes me vulgar. You know you're no piece of tail and I know it, don't hold a slip of the tongue against a harried old man. Okay?'

'Right, right,' Nathan said impatiently. He had more important things to concern him than my thin skin.

So they went on with their arguing, quickly forgetting all about my objection to being spoken of as if I were a whore. Four or five years ago I'd have given my eyeteeth to be where I was now, sitting in the office of an important producer while he and my agent worked out the specifics of my career for me. But there was no good feeling to it, there was nothing good about any of it. I felt like a piece of meat.

A piece of tail, Leonard Zoff had said.

You're selling yourself, Fiona Benedict had said.

A prize cow at the county fair, Marian Larch had said.

Nathan gave in on the brain surgeon, and they eventually settled on resident psychiatrist. By then I didn't really much care. How did I get myself involved with these two? I was legally bound to both of them for

125

another few years, and they were giving me the full star build-up. So what the hell was I complaining about? I'd never had to do any of the things a lot of women had had to do in this business. Leonard had never handed me a list of producers with instructions to sleep with as many as I could. And Nathan had never called on me to put in appearances at *that* kind of party. Strictly speaking, they had both left me alone.

So why was I feeling sick to my stomach? I knew Leonard looked on his women clients as so much meat, why was I so surprised? And Nathan had the same kind of respect for his actors that Sherman had had for Georgia. I was a big girl now, what did I expect—soft music and flowers? Girl Scout cookies?

When it was time to go, I was still caught up in my own thoughts and wasn't aware of the fancy footwork going on until it was over — Nathan had maneuvred Leonard out of the office while I was still inside and had quickly locked the door. Leonard pounded on the door and yelled at me not to sign anything, I yelled back that I wouldn't, and I turned to Nathan Pinking to see what it was all about.

He waited until Leonard had given up and gone away, and then said, 'I want you to sign an exclusive management contract with me. Dump Zoff, Kelly. The man has no vision, no class. He thinks small time, he can't help it. That business about calling you a piece of tail—that was no one-time thing. He calls you that all the time. You're just not around to hear it. Why stay with a man who thinks of you like that?'

So there it was; Nathan saw Leonard's slip of the tongue as a chance to undercut his old enemy. Marian Larch had said the two men had once been partners; how could they ever have stood each other? Nathan would have signed a trained seal act away from Leonard if he thought it would cause Leonard trouble.

'Leonard and I have a contract,' I said noncommittally.

'Contracts can be broken. And where has it got you anyway?' he sneered. 'Lady wrestlers! You're too classy for

126

that kind of action, Kelly, but that's something Zoff will never see. You sign with me and you'll never have to do those schlock bits again. You won't have to do anything just for the exposure.'

'Leonard isn't just going to roll over and play dead, you know,' I stalled.

'There are ways of handling these things,' Nathan said with a knowing smirk. 'And I'll tell you something in confidence, Kelly—Leonard Zoff is holding on by his fingernails. He talks a good game and brags about all his successful clients, but he's in hock up to his ears. He's gambling on *you* to hit it big and pull him out of his mess.'

'So if I sign with you, Leonard will go bankrupt?' Nathan grinned, but didn't say anything. Nathan lied a lot, so I didn't completely believe that story about Leonard hanging on by his fingernails. But if it were true, Nathan would be quite willing to lure me away from Leonard *just* to bankrupt him, not because he had any big plans for me. In that case I'd be better off staying with Leonard.

Not to mention the fact that this man hustling me now was probably a blackmailer. I thought of poor Christopher Clive, the Shakespearean actor Nathan had made drop his trousers for a cheap laugh—just to prove who was boss. Had Nathan come between Ted and me for the same reason? Did he want to humiliate me, the way he'd humiliated Christopher Clive? And this was the man I was supposed to trust, the one I was to allow to make *all* the decisions concerning my career! Leonard Zoff sometimes drove me nuts, but he was still a thousand times better than a sadistic creep like Nathan Pinking.

I wanted Nathan's plans for me—the movie, the series—but without Nathan attached to them. How unlucky the two came together, package deals stink. From where I was standing I could see the framed photograph on the desk, the one showing Nathan's wife and daughters. How could they look so happy with an ogre like Nathan Pinking for a husband and father? 'I'll think it over,' I told him.

'I have a whole campaign in mind for you, Kelly. It's keyed to climax during the first season of your new series.'

'You seem pretty certain there'll be a new series,' I said. 'You can't be sure the network will buy it.'

'Oh, they'll buy it,' he said, 'if we go in with a sponsor already sewed up. And don't you worry, we'll have a sponsor.'

Sure. Cameron Enterprises.

'Anyway, the way it works is like this,' Nathan went on. 'All next season, we do this big publicity putsch about your new show, how excited you are to have your own series, the usual gaff. Maybe something about getting Nick Quinlan to do a guest role on your show. But here's where we pull a switch. When the new show starts, you begin dropping hints in interviews and on talk shows that somehow it's not quite as satisfying as you thought it would be.'

'The show is not as satisfying?'

'Not the show—the show's great, the cast is great, the writers are great, you've got a terrific crew, the whole schmeer. But *being a big television star* isn't the rewarding thing you'd thought it would be, and you're feeling a little disappointed. Then along about renewal time, you confide to Johnny Carson that what you really want is a home and family. That if the right man came along you'd give it all up like a shot. You see?'

'I see I'm going to throw up in about two minutes.' I turned to leave.

'No, wait, wait—look, Kelly, it's perfect. Every man in America will feel a little bigger when you say you're willing to give it all up for a man. And every one of them will have a sneaking suspicion that *he's* the man you're waiting for. And housewives all over the country will nod their heads in approval, because the famous, beautiful Kelly Ingram is at last catching on to what they knew all along. They'll be thinking here is this big TV star who wants to be just like *me*. It can't miss! You'll get the men and the women both, and the show'll be good for a long run, Kelly, much longer than *LeFever*. And I can make it all happen. What do you say?'

I said again that I'd think it over and left before I lost control of myself and kicked him in the teeth.

So I was to act out the male fantasy that what a woman really wants is a Strong Man to protect her, was I? Same old con. When I was growing up the style was unwed motherhood à la Vanessa Redgrave. But I remember looking at my mother's old movie magazines, *Modern Screen* and *Silver Screen* and *Photoplay* and a couple of others, and they all had articles about movie actresses who 'really' just wanted to be wives and mothers, all sorts of different people like Lana Turner and Jeanne Crain and Rita Hayworth and even Bette Davis, I think. Even back then it was what people wanted to hear, how celebrities longed to be ordinary and just like everybody else. And here was Nathan Pinking proposing the same slop for me—and acting as if nobody had ever thought of it before. Nathan had never had an original idea in his life and he sure as hell wasn't going to start now.

Stupid part about it, though—before Ted Cameron I probably would have gone along without thinking twice about it. But this man who had thought up my new persona for me was the same thug who had Ted by the balls. And Nathan's little proposal had told me something, that little conference convinced me. Nathan was indeed Ted's blackmailer.

All I want is a home and family, that was to be my line. But it wouldn't be very convincing if I was already married, would it? And Nathan Pinking, watching how much time Ted and I were spending together, had started to see his whole campaign for the new series going straight down the toilet. So one Thursday morning he calls Ted in and tells him to kiss Kelly goodbye.

It had gone too far. Nathan Pinking was controlling lives and money and television shows and indirectly even Cameron Enterprises—and he was getting away with it. The man had no *right* to that kind of power. He was sure to misuse it; Nathan wasn't really a very smart man. He

129

was a *ruthless* man, and self-defensive—that's why he'd gotten as far as he had. Now he had to be stopped. It was clear the only thing for me to do was go to Marian Larch and tell her everything I knew.

And in doing so throw away my chance at my own TV series. My own series. Based on a pilot produced by Nathan Pinking. A chance I might not ever get again.

My own series.

Maybe I should wait until after the movie pilot was made.

CHAPTER 12

MARIAN LARCH

Captain Michaels was openly relieved when he got word from the DA's office to let Fiona Benedict go. The case against her had been shaky to begin with and she never had admitted shooting at Richard Ormsby. Now that it was clearly somebody else who killed Ormsby, the prosecutors knew they'd never make the charge of *attempted* murder stick. Especially since the earlier murder method had been repeated—a public shooting at a television station. 'I always had a feeling she was innocent,' the Captain said.

'Innocent my foot,' I said. 'Innocent of Ormsby's murder, yes, but guilty of trying to kill him earlier. Two different events.'

'Hey, what you got against little old ladies?' the Captain grinned. He was in a good mood since things were working out the way he wanted them to.

'Surely she's not old enough for the little-old-lady label,' I said. 'Early sixties. That's too young.' I refrained from pointing out that Fiona Benedict was only about ten years older than Captain Michaels himself. 'She fired that gun at Ormsby—six times she fired it. The fact that somebody else came along and did the job right later on

130

doesn't change what she did in that CBS studio.'

'Bull,' said Michaels bluntly. 'She should never have been arrested in the first place. That woman's no killer. You're the only one here who thinks she's guilty.'

'Because I was the only one *there* when she first learned about Ormsby's book. It literally put her on her knees, Captain—it hit her that hard.' I didn't particularly want Fiona Benedict behind bars; there were far worse criminals roaming the streets. But any investigation of Ormsby's murder would have to take into account the earlier, unsuccessful attempt by Dr. Benedict. Whoever investigated mustn't make the mistake of assuming the same person shot at Ormsby both times. 'I want to be assigned to the Ormsby investigation,' I told Captain Michaels.

'You and every other gold shield in Manhattan,' he grunted. 'No, you stay put on the Rudy Benedict case—I'm pulling everybody else off, I need the men. Anything new on the Pinking and Zoff power struggle?'

I thought *power struggle* too fancy a term for the sniping going on but didn't say so. 'Only that Nathan Pinking is now indicating his willingness to sell his share of Leonard Zoff's agency. If the price is right.'

'Why the change of mind?'

'Zoff isn't taking the offer seriously. I think it's all part of the same game of cat and mouse those two have been playing for twenty-five years. That's how long they've known each other, a quarter of a century. And they've hated each other every minute of it.'

'So why is Rudy Benedict the one who's dead?' Captain Michaels scowled. 'Pinking bought scripts from him, period. That's the only connection, the whole relationship? And not even that much a one between Benedict and Zoff. There's some other connection we don't know about. Larch, I want you to find it. No more excuses, no more fiddling around. Find that connection.'

'What if there isn't any?'

'Find it anyway.'

Get out there and scrounge. I left the Captain's office

131

and went back to my desk. It was going to take some doing to concentrate; I kept thinking about the Richard Ormsby killing. Whoever had shot the Englishman had certainly done Fiona Benedict a favor. Two favors. Killed her enemy for her and got her out of jail at the same time. Two big favors.

Just exactly how good a friend *was* Roberta Morrissey anyhow?

Feeling an absolute fool, I called one of the investigators assigned to the Ormsby case and asked him about Roberta. He said she'd been talking long distance to her husband at the time Ormsby had been shot; the hotel switchboard records bore her out. I thanked him and hung up, feeling an even bigger fool. Was anyone in the world a more unlikely murder suspect than Roberta Morrissey? Well, maybe on the face of it Fiona Benedict was more unlikely—but look what *she'd* done. Little old ladies just weren't what they used to be.

I forced my attention back to Rudy Benedict. To Pinking and Zoff. Leonard Zoff and Nathan Pinking were involved in a one-upmanship contest that just kept accelerating and accelerating, with no real resolution in sight. Right now it looked as if Pinking was ahead in the success race, but I supposed that could easily change. I wondered if that was what really drove those two—the desire to outdo the other.

I thought about talking to both of them again, but there wasn't any point. Pinking would tell me some new lies and Zoff would call me Miriam and I'd be no further along than I already was. Kelly Ingram was making a TV movie and wouldn't be back in town for another week. Nick Quinlan was making a movie too, in Munich—in German, no less; his part was to be dubbed, fortunately. Fiona Benedict would soon be on her way back to Ohio, and Roberta Morrissey with her.

This might be a good time to go talk to Ted Cameron.

Homework first, though. I called Bill Sewell at Heilveil, Huddleston, and Tippet and invited him to lunch. He accepted; he always did.

Heilveil, Huddleston, and Tippet was a firm of stockbrokers, and Bill Sewell was a very junior partner there. He was a reliable source of useful information, if we didn't tap him too often. I think Bill enjoyed being a police contact, although he said he did it for all the free lunches he got. We met at a restaurant on St. Mark's Place, and I waited until we'd ordered to ask him about Cameron Enterprises.

'Good time to buy in — shares are dropping a little,' he said. 'But that's not what you want to know, is it?'

'It might be. Why are the shares dropping?'

'We're getting rumors of internal dissent. Happens a lot in these third- or fourth-generation family businesses. One small business grown into a conglomerate, squabbling among the descendants of the founder, family unity merely a fond memory from the good old days.'

'Ted Cameron's in danger of losing control?'

'That's about it. Way I hear it, Augusta Cameron and a few of the others haven't been too happy with the way Ted's been running things for some time now. But recently something's brought it all to a head.'

'What?'

'That I can't tell you — the rumors stop there. Haven't really tried to find out, though. But the shares go on dropping, a point or two a week — good indicator of how fast the rumors are spreading. Ted's been challenged before, and he's managed to pull out of it. But this time I think it might be different.'

'Will it hurt the company?'

'Depends on who ends up in charge.'

'Do you know Cameron?'

'Met him. Weird eyes.'

The food came then. I gave Bill a chance to take the edge off his hunger and then asked how the decisions for spending the advertising budget were made at Cameron Enterprises, but he didn't know anything about that.

'Why the interest in Cameron Enterprises?' he asked.

The rules of the game were that you gave something for something — but the something you gave should always be

133

less than the something you got. 'They're sponsoring a television show next season, and we're investigating the death of a TV writer.'

'Sounds pretty thin. Any connection between Ted Cameron and your dead writer?'

'None that I can see. Frankly, we're reaching.'

He grinned. 'I knew that when you invited me to lunch.'

I paid the tab; Bill waved a cheery goodbye and headed back downtown to his office. I went back to Headquarters and did the paperwork for other things I was working on; the Rudy Benedict investigation was no longer a full-time job. At four o'clock I had an appointment with Ted Cameron that had taken me a couple of days to get; Kelly's boyfriend was a busy man.

The corporate headquarters of Cameron Enterprises were on Lexington. The reception area was curiously undistinctive, but the receptionist was expecting me and led me to Ted Cameron's suite—where it took two secretaries working in relay to conduct me into the inner sanctum.

Cameron himself looked *besieged*, that's the only word for it. He made an effort at appearing calm, but his physical mannerisms revealed a lot of inner tension. When he turned from the window to greet me, the movement had a clearly self-protective posture to it.

I reminded him we'd met before, in Nathan Pinking's office. I don't think he remembered me, but he pretended to; whatever his problems, he hadn't lost his manners. 'What can I do for you, Detective Larch? My secretary said you were investigating a murder?'

'Rudy Benedict's murder. Did you know him?'

'I know who he was. We never met.'

'Have you had much contact with television people? I know *LeFever* isn't your first venture into TV advertising.'

'We've done mostly spot advertising up to now. We've sponsored a few specials, but we've never undertaken a series before. So to answer your question—no, I haven't

134

had much contact with television personnel before now. Rudy Benedict's path and mine just never crossed.'

'Who made that decision, Mr. Cameron? To sponsor a series, I mean.' I was looking straight at him and I swear his irises turned invisible as I watched. He didn't move his head or anything, but the blue just vanished.

'A great number of people contribute to a decision like that. Our advertising manager, the budget director, a demographics consultant—'

'But ultimately somebody has to say yes or no. Whose responsibility is that?'

'Mine, of course. Why do you ask?'

Flank attack. 'Why is there so much hostility between you and Nathan Pinking?'

His jaw clenched; one of those giveaway signs. *Too* giveaway, it seemed to me. A successful businessman would have to hide his reactions better than that, wouldn't he? Ted Cameron made me think of a dam about to break. 'I have difficulty in working with a man for whom I have no respect,' he said in answer to my question about Pinking. 'But it's something I often have to do.'

'Then why sponsor *LeFever* if you think so little of Pinking?'

'It's the show we wanted, not its producer. We can reach millions of potential customers through *LeFever*. That's all we're interested in.'

Sounded reasonable. Okay, try the other flank. 'What are your chances for retaining control of Cameron Enterprises? Is Augusta Cameron likely to win this one?'

I had to admire the way he took it. He didn't pretend not to know what I was talking about or stall for time or anything like that. 'So even the police know about it.' He smiled wryly and stood up and began to pace. 'May I ask how you found out?' Still polite.

'One of our sources on Wall Street.'

He nodded, continued pacing. He was harried-looking and obviously under pressure, but he still managed to look, well, *graceful* as he paced the room. I could see why Kelly was so taken with him—the man had style. He was

135

attractive in such a subtle way—nothing obvious or overstated about him. Ted Cameron had a quiet kind of magnetism I'd missed completely when I first met him. But Kelly Ingram had spotted it. She'd spotted it the first time she laid eyes on him.

Finally Cameron decided on an answer he wanted to give me. 'For some time now, Aunt Augusta has been challenging me over the presidency. She does this periodically—about every two years, I'd say. You know she runs Lorelei Cosmetics, don't you?'

'Yes.'

'Well, that's not enough for her. She wants to run the parent company instead of just one of its subsidiaries. At first she was content to try to wheel and deal her way into power—she didn't resort to frontal attack until I moved the corporate headquarters to New York. She—'

'Excuse me—when was that?'

'Ah, thirteen . . . twelve or thirteen years ago. Formerly we were headquartered in Los Angeles, where Lorelei Cosmetics is located. Aunt Augusta felt threatened when I took the business offices to the other side of the country. She changed her tactics.'

'And this time?'

He was silent a moment. 'This time she has new allies. Some other members of the family.'

'Why? Why would they side with her against you this time?'

'Because of certain matters of policy—and that, Detective Larch, is in the nature of being a company secret. Don't ask me to reveal business decisions to someone outside the firm because I won't do it. Besides, what does all this have to do with Rudy Benedict's death? It looks as if you're investigating *me* instead of him. I don't see the connection.'

Neither did I. 'Just a standard procedure of police work, Mr. Cameron. We check everything, even things that don't seem to have any connection at all.' He didn't quite believe me, but that was all right. I made one more try. 'This matter of company policy you don't want to talk about—it wouldn't have anything to do with the way you spend your advertising money, would it?'

'I'm sorry, I'm just not going to talk about it.' His words were calm, but his voice was tight and pinched. He opened the office door and stood waiting for me. Our brief interview was over.

I left wondering if we could get the Los Angeles police to go after Augusta Cameron. Since she was the one who was so bothered by the 'secret' company policy, maybe she'd be more willing to talk about it than her beleaguered nephew.

A few days later I found a note on my desk saying Kelly Ingram was back in town and wanted to see me immediately on a matter that was urgent and important.

Urgent *and* important? Well, certainly mustn't delay, then. On the way over to her place I tried to guess what might be so urgent. (And important.) Another bottle of Lysco-Seltzer? Not likely, not again. Hate mail from Fiona Benedict? Silly.

When Kelly opened the door, the first thing she said was, 'Nathan Pinking is interfering with my sex life and I want you to make him stop.'

Well, *that* was something I certainly hadn't thought of. I invited myself to sit down and waited.

'Nathan's blackmailing Ted,' she said bitterly. 'He's forcing him to sponsor *LeFever*, and he's forcing him to stay away from me.'

I asked her how she knew, and she launched into a long story of improbable events and overheard conversations, all neatly wrapped up with some cause-and-effect deductions on her part that I had to admit sounded pretty plausible.

'So he's afraid I might marry Ted,' Kelly said, still talking about Pinking. 'He busted us up because I'd be no good to his smarmy little promo scheme if I was married. I have to stay fresh and available.'

A renewable virgin? 'What's Pinking got on Ted Cameron?'

'I don't *know*,' she said with real despair. 'Marian, this is just making me sick! Can you nail Nathan for blackmail without . . . without . . .'

'Without exposing what Ted Cameron's done that's made him vulnerable to blackmail?' I sighed. 'If he's committed a felony and that comes out in the investigation, we can't just look the other way, you know that.'

'But if what he's done isn't illegal, if it's just, oh, personal, or something he doesn't want the rest of the family to know about or something like that—you wouldn't have to hassle him then, would you?'

'No, we'd have no reason to.' I couldn't quite figure Kelly. Surely she knew if she blew the whistle on Nathan Pinking the chances were that Ted Cameron would get caught in the blast too. She sounded just a touch angry when she talked about him, I thought. Because he'd allowed himself to be outmaneuvred by someone like Nathan Pinking? 'You must be awfully sure Ted hasn't broken the law.'

'Well, yes.' She didn't sound sure. 'He's a *good* man, Marian. He's not like Nathan Pinking.'

'So what's to keep *him* from blabbing—Pinking, that is? Even if the police do keep quiet.'

'Well, I was thinking maybe plea bargaining. You know, you could promise him a lighter sentence if he'd keep his mouth shut?'

In her own way Kelly was a rather worldly woman, but sometimes she could be so naïve I wanted to scream. 'In the first place,' I said, 'would you trust him to keep his word? I wouldn't. Second, I don't have the authority to agree to plea bargaining, that's up to the prosecutor. Third, we have no evidence of blackmail yet and may not be able to get any. Don't worry, don't worry—we'll give it our best shot.' She'd looked panicky there for a moment. 'But you've got to realize there's a big difference between knowing somebody is a blackmailer and finding evidence that will stand up in court. I believe you're right about Pinking—I already thought his relationship with Ted

138

Cameron had a strong odor of fish about it. That two-sided face of Pinking's should have warned me,' I said facetiously, in a weak attempt at lightening the mood.

All it did was puzzle Kelly. 'Two-sided face? What are you talking about? You mean two-faced?'

'No, I mean his face has two sides to it.'

'Hasn't everybody's?'

Why had I started this? 'Nathan Pinking has halves of two different faces, and they don't fit together. Hadn't you noticed?'

She stared at me. 'No.' Translation: *What are you, a crazy lady?*

'Okay, forget Nathan Pinking's face,' I sighed, pulling out my notebook. 'Now I want you to go over it again, and this time give me all the names you can. Like that cousin who came to Tuxedo Park—which Cameron was that?'

'Roger. He runs Watercraft.'

We kept going over it until I had everything she could give me. Kelly had been suspicious for some time; there'd been a number of incidents stretched out over several weeks that had led her to conclude blackmail was the name of the game. So she'd had plenty of time to think about it. Yet I couldn't help but notice she'd put off calling me until after she'd finished her TV pilot movie. If the Cameron-Pinking-*LeFever* world was about to collapse, Kelly Ingram would not be one of its casualties.

I promised to keep her posted and left.

CHAPTER 13

FIONA BENEDICT

Eventually I learned to ignore the ringing of the telephone, and I stopped answering the door almost entirely. The solicitous expressions of concern proclaimed, no, *de*claimed by acquaintances who spoke too loudly,

too brightly—it got to be more than I could bear. Their
intentions were good, of course, but they were
embarrassed, ill at ease. And why not? Who among them
had prior experience of such a situation? What do you say
to a colleague who has just been released from jail after
having been charged with attempted murder? Most of
them said, *Oh, Fiona, I knew it was a mistake all along!*
That's what their mouths said. But their eyes weren't so
sure.

Drew Morrissey was the worst. Roberta Morrissey had
been the Rock of Gibraltar when I needed her, but Drew
acted as if he wished he'd never met me. He mumbled
and stuttered and shifted his weight from foot to foot and
managed never quite to look me in the eye. He didn't
have the foggiest notion of what to say to me. I knew what
to say to him. *Goodbye.*

Howard—I never will know his last name now—
Howard had given me good advice. *Say nothing at all,*
he'd told me. *Not even 'I didn't do it'—we don't have to
enter a plea yet. Say nothing.* So I'd said nothing; and
when Richard Ormsby was murdered, my immediate
release was not complicated by any statement I might
otherwise have signed. Howard would accept no money;
the Ingram woman's doing again, no doubt.

I'd submitted my resignation the day after Roberta and
I returned to Washburn. The dean said he would just
hold my letter for a while, in case I wanted more time to
think it over. My future was in limbo; it depended upon
decisions I had yet to make. But I didn't see how I could
just pick up and go on at Washburn as if nothing had
happened. The administration and my colleagues were
all being 'understanding'—but I'd still be pointed out to
newcomers as the local criminal. I can't stand being
stared at.

Too much had happened; I couldn't have remained
unchanged by it. I felt a need to take my time, to wait to
find out, to discover what I had left of my old self. I was
plagued by feelings of uncertainty that I either had to
dispel or else accustom myself to living with. There were

too many unanswered questions; I was having difficulty maintaining my sense of balance.

For instance, I had no idea why Richard Ormsby had been killed. Whoever had shot him couldn't have had the same reason for wanting him dead that I'd had. If I'd just waited—oh, that's even more cynical, more reprehensible. Wanting someone else to do my murderous dirty work for me. I *had* tried; I had done my very best to remove that academic trash from the face of the earth, but I'd failed. It needed someone with a steadier hand and a more accurate eye than mine to get the job done.

And I didn't even know who. But whoever it was, he had acted as my surrogate. Some mysterious someone had appeared out of nowhere and had done for me what I'd been too inept to do for myself. I had fired Rudy's gun at that man six times—and I missed six times. Missing doesn't make me innocent; it merely makes me a bad shot. Nothing will ever make me innocent.

I was taking a bath and two showers every day. Roberta Morrissey kept insisting that I was imagining the smell. She was undoubtedly right, but that didn't make it any the less real. I'd heard of the strong disinfectant used in jails but I'd had no idea how astringent and overpowering it was. It stung my mucous membrane and made my eyes water. It permeated everything—my hair, my skin, that rough clothing I was made to wear. Roberta said the odor was long since gone, that I was the only one who still smelled it. I will always smell it.

I wondered if someone had followed Richard Ormsby to New York from London, if his death was the result of some old enmity in his home country. What kind of enmity—personal, professional? Or had my bootless attempt at murder inspired some unstable occupant of the lunatic zone into an act of emulation? An attack upon a public figure breeds further attacks. Even the self-inflicted death of a celebrity stimulates imitations—two hundred suicides in the month following Marilyn Monroe's death, I once read. Had my firing at Ormsby made him suddenly appear a desirable target to some deranged soul in search of an outlet? Where does my responsibility end?

Another remembered smell: garlic. From a sandwich on the Ingram woman's table, the night I first met her. She and Marian Larch sitting there, offering uninvited sympathy for the death of my son. My refusing to tell them to call me by my first name, my resisting an intimacy with them—because they belonged to a harsh and violent world! Something was wrong with me. Something was very much wrong with me. I was not reacting right. The only thing I truly regretted was that someone other than I had had the pleasure of killing Richard Ormsby.

In the meantime I needed something to occupy my mind, or at least distract my attention. I had thought that when my *Life of Lucan* was completed, I'd probably have one more book left in me. I'd been thinking of a problem in connection with the Sepoy Rebellion of 1857 in India, something that had been teasing at me for a long time. But now undertaking work of that nature seemed futile, for reasons I didn't care to stop and examine. What I needed was busy work, not real work.

Rudy's papers.

I'd made only a bare start on his papers when the *Times* review had appeared and started me on my insane mission to New York. So I sat down at the little table in the attic and got to work.

Just about the first thing I learned was that my son had specialized in beginnings. Aside from the opening scenes of over a hundred television scripts that never got written, there were countless folders containing anywhere from two to fifty pages of fiction. Novels, short stories—I couldn't always tell which they were meant to be. Some of the ideas were quite good; but after a powerhouse opening, Rudy would run out of steam. He wouldn't know what to do with his ideas once he had them. It was very frustrating reading; I would have liked to know the endings of at least a few. But if it was frustrating for me, it must have been torture for Rudy—all those promising beginnings that never went anywhere.

But the incomplete stories did the trick. They kept me going, they kept me distracted. *They kept me sane.*

Thank you, Rudy. I wish I could repay you. Thank you.

I'd been reading steadily for almost a week when I came to a folder with the promising title 'The Town That Loved Mozart' written on it. But instead of the usual typewritten pages inside, I found a clipping from *The Los Angeles Times* and two Polaroid snapshots.

The newspaper clipping was nearly fifteen years old; it told of the death by cyanide poisoning of a woman named Mary Rendell. Her body had been found on the grounds of a Bel Air mansion; the owners hadn't known the woman, but said they'd given a large party the night before and the victim could have come in with one of the invited guests. Police were checking the guest list.

Cyanide poisoning. How ironic that Rudy should have kept this clipping about a woman who'd died the same bizarre way he was to die. I read through the news story again. Mary Rendell, Mary Rendell. Why was that name familiar?

Both Polaroid snaps were of a painting, the same painting. It showed a man and his shadow . . . of course! *Man and Shadow*, the painting that was missing from Rudy's apartment — and it had been painted by a woman named Mary Rendell. I looked at the clipping a third time; it said nothing about her being an artist. But I was sure that was the right name, Mary Rendell. Now why would Rudy have been keeping these snapshots and a fifteen-year-old clipping, and why had he hidden them in a deliberately mislabeled folder?

I studied the snapshots. In the painting the man and his shadow had reversed their traditional positions. The shadow was upright and three-dimensional and dynamic; the man was stretched out on the ground and flat and elongated. The shadow was casting the man, not the other way around.

Even in the snapshots I could tell the detail work was extraordinary. This Mary Rendell was not one of those East Village pretenders who spend twenty minutes slapping paint on a canvas and then display the finished 'work' for the tourists to gawk at even before the paint is dry. No, Mary Rendell was painstaking in her work; I wished I could see the original. One of the photographs was a close-up of the man's head—it showed the face had been painted with great care. It was an attractive face, but the eyes didn't seem to have any irises. Intentionally symbolic, or had the photo's color just faded over the years? I couldn't tell.

Well. What was I to make of that? The clipping and the snapshots obviously meant something to Rudy or he wouldn't have kept them. I knew one person who'd be interested—Marian Larch. She'd said right at the start there was some mystery about the painting, this painting of a blank-eyed shadow-man that was still missing as far as I knew. I'd send the snaps and the clipping along to Marian in a few days, the next time I felt up to venturing out of the house. There was a time I wouldn't let anything go without photocopying it first. No more; why bother? I'd just send everything to Marian—let her figure out what it meant.

Not that I expected what I'd found to make any difference. I was fairly well resigned to never knowing who killed Rudy. Even if the police did find out who the murderer was, it would just be a name to me. Someone I didn't know, probably a name I'd never even heard mentioned. But *who* wasn't as important as *why*. Every day it was becoming more important to me to know *why* Rudy was dead.

Why had Rudy been killed? And for that matter, why had Richard Ormsby been killed? Why had I found it so easy to pick up a lethal weapon and use it? Why was I sitting there like a fool in a Washburn, Ohio, attic asking myself impossible questions?

Keep on reading Rudy's papers. Keep busy reading. Keep reading. Read.

CHAPTER 14

MARIAN LARCH

We got a court order to put a tap on Nathan Pinking's telephone, but the judge turned down a similar request for Ted Cameron's phone. He said we couldn't tap in on the alleged victim without his consent. Captain Michaels and I talked it over and decided bringing Cameron in on it at that stage would do more harm than good; so we went with just the one bug.

And what do you know — the tech people who installed it found someone had been there before us. Nathan Pinking's phone contained a multi-directional mike of the sort that picked up everything spoken in the room, not just telephone conversations. It was of standard manufacture, nothing there to tell us who had planted it. We left it, in order not to tip off whoever had put it there that the police were now in on the act.

'Who do you think?' Captain Michaels asked.

'Cameron or Leonard Zoff,' I said. 'The first for self-defense, the second for sheer meanness. But I wouldn't bet on either — it could be someone we don't even know about. Pinking's a man who makes enemies easily.'

So we waited; the calls we monitored were for the most part regular business calls. Pinking did call Cameron twice. The tapes made it clear Pinking was coercing Cameron, but there were no open threats and no talk of payoffs. A man named Rothstein from the DA's office listened to the tapes and said they'd be useful as supporting evidence, but they weren't enough for an arrest warrant.

In the meantime I was busy prying information out of the television networks about their fall schedules. I wanted to find out just how deeply involved Cameron

Enterprises was with Nathan Pinking productions. This is what I learned had been scheduled:

1. *LeFever*—a one-hour crime/action series sponsored by Cameron Enterprises, Ted Cameron, president. *LeFever*'s first-year sponsors had been unwilling to pay the huge increase in advertising rates NBC had decided on (based on the show's steady climb in the ratings). Cameron Enterprises had taken over full sponsorhip.

2. *Crossover Valley*—a trash-passion prime-time soap on CBS, running time one hour. Sponsorship was split between Lorelei Cosmetics, a subsidiary of Cameron Enterprises, Augusta Cameron, president; and Ross Insurance Associates, no connection with Cameron Enterprises. Lorelei Cosmetics was a new sponsor; Ross Insurance was a carry-over from last season.

3. *Down the Pike*—a thirty-minute yokel comedy ABC had planned to cancel until Watercraft, Inc. agreed to pick up the tab. Watercraft was owned by Cameron Enterprises and its president was Roger Cameron.

4. *Gimme an A*—a new half-hour comedy series about high school cheerleaders scheduled to debut on ABC in October. The sponsor was Shakito Electronics, which was owned by Watercraft, which was owned by Cameron Enterprises. The president of Shakito Electronics was Peter B. McKenna, who had married a Cameron and had taken on the presidency of Shakito when his wife died.

5. *On Call*—a made-for-TV movie doubling as a series pilot and starring Kelly Ingram, penciled in for an early December showing on NBC. Three sponsors: Featherlight Footwear, a Cameron Enterprises line of boots and shoes; Mercury Office Machines, a subsidiary of Cameron Enterprises, Robin Cameron, president; and Lorelei Cosmetics.

★

So, with the exception of Ross Insurance's half-sponsorship of *Crossover Valley*, Ted Cameron's conglomerate was footing the bill for everything that came out of Nathan Pinking's production company. Footing the bill and then some; the networks had to make a profit. The nets bought the shows from the production companies, paying less than what it cost the companies to make them and charging the sponsors as much as traffic would bear. A show had to run at least three years before it could go into syndication, and only then would the production company that made it begin to realize a profit—from the residuals. So by locking Cameron Enterprises into full-time sponsorship, Nathan Pinking had found a way to make sure all his shows eventually reached the syndication stage. He might bankrupt Cameron Enterprises in the process, but his own future was secure.

I felt certain that was what Augusta Cameron and the others were up in arms about. Two one-hour series, two half-hour series, and a movie—that must have made a terrific drain on Cameron Enterprises' resources. Pinking also had two more programs in development; rumor at the networks was that he also had sponsors sewed up for them as well (guess who).

Thus when the call came from Los Angeles, it was more in the nature of confirmation than of providing new information. A Sergeant Finley of the LAPD had, at our request, interviewed Ted Cameron's Aunt Augusta—and Aunt Augusta had talked his ear off.

'She's out to stir up as much trouble as she can,' Sergeant Finley said. 'She made no bones about that. Augusta Cameron lives in a constant state of rage—she's furious with her nephew. And all because of the television advertising.'

'I think it goes back farther than that,' I said, 'but it's the TV sponsorship that's got all the Camerons riled up this time. Did she say what her plans were?'

'She got a little coy about that—I think there are still a few Camerons she wants to bring over into her camp. She

147

didn't say so, but I got the impression that if the entire family unites against Ted Cameron, he'll pretty much have to resign. That's what Augusta wants—Ted Cameron's resignation.'

'She has a good chance of getting it.' Ted Cameron was running close to the edge; he might have to resign to avoid a nervous breakdown.

'Why doesn't Cameron just pull back on the TV advertising?' Sergeant Finley wanted to know. 'It can't be worth losing his company over.'

'He can't. It's a long story, but he's committed. Four series and a movie this coming season.'

'Yeah, I know. Augusta says that will come close to bankrupting them because they're just not that big a conglomerate—they can't put that much money into television.'

I thanked him for his help and hung up. Talk about being between a rock and a hard place. Ted Cameron was caught between Nathan Pinking's blackmail on one side and Augusta and her army of Camerons on the other. Pinking's hold over Ted must be herculean to have forced him into a position like that.

What had Ted Cameron done?

The answer came in a brown mailing envelope postmarked Washburn, Ohio.

I looked at the two snapshots of *Man and Shadow* and wondered how Ted Cameron could ever have got himself into such a fix. No question, it was his face in the 'man' part of the painting; those strange eyes with their invisible irises were unmistakable. It wasn't too surprising that the New York gallery owners I'd contacted when Rudy Benedict died hadn't known of the painting or the artist: Mary Rendell had been dead for fifteen years, and she hadn't been old enough to have earned a reputation for herself when she died.

CYANIDE POISONING IN BEL AIR DEATH

The body of the woman found on the Bel Air estate of

148

Ted Cameron, a vice president of Cameron Enterprises, has been identified as Mary Rendell, age twenty, of 1175 Costa Mesa Drive, Santa Monica. Dr. James E. Vernon of the Los Angeles Medical Examiner's office says the cause of death was cyanide poisoning.

Miss Rendell's body was discovered late Monday afternoon by Ernesto Garcia, a gardener at the Cameron estate. Neither Mr. nor Mrs. Cameron knew the victim. Identification was established by means of a medical alert bracelet the victim was wearing; Miss Rendell was diabetic.

Cameron suggested the victim may have come on to his estate with a guest at a party the Camerons had given Sunday night. Lt. Joseph Taylor of the LAPD says police are interviewing the party guests in an attempt to find someone who knew Miss Rendell.

So Ted Cameron had not yet been promoted to president of Cameron Enterprises, and he'd still been married to one of his two wives. Probably the first; fifteen years ago he'd have been about thirty, young for a vice president — but then he had the right surname. I called Sergeant Finley in Los Angeles and asked him to look up the results of the fifteen-year-old investigation into the death of Mary Rendell.

When he called me back he said, 'Unsolved. The investigating officers didn't even have a suspect. Mary Rendell hadn't been in Los Angeles long enough to make much of an impression — only seven months.'

'Where was she from?'

'Little town in Oklahoma called Rushville. She wanted to be an artist, says here.'

'She'd made a good start at it,' I said, looking at the photo of *Man and Shadow*. 'Did the autopsy reveal anything other than cause of death?'

'Like what?'

'Oh, like pregnancy?'

'Nope.'

'Drugs?'

'None. Nothing at all out of the ordinary. "Healthy Caucasian female" — life terminated by ingested cyanide. Now it's your turn. Why are the New York police interested in this old unsolved killing?'

'Because it looks as if Mary Rendell's killer has turned up here. Can't tell you anything officially yet — I have to talk to my boss first.' I promised to let him know when we had something concrete and hung up.

Before going to Captain Michaels, I needed to make one more phone call. I dialed the number of Cameron Enterprises' corporate headquarters and asked to speak to the Public Relations Director. PR people can almost always give you what you need, and they never ask why you want to know.

A woman identified herself as Mrs.Sullivan, and I said, 'Hello, my name is Marian Larch, and I'm trying to get some information about clothing dyes. I know Cameron Enterprises uses a lot of dye — could you tell me who your supplier is? Or suppliers, plural, if you use more than one?'

'We manufacture our own dyes. We have better quality control that way. And we don't have the headaches of late deliveries and the like that we'd have if we contracted out to vendors.'

'I see. And where are your dyes manufactured?'

'We have three laboratories. One here in New York, another in Fort Lauderdale, Florida, and a third in Los Angeles.'

'Thank you, Mrs.Sullivan, you've been most helpful.' If she only knew.

I sat and thought about it. I thought about it a lot. I looked at it this way and that, from every angle I could think of. A few holes, but structurally sound, as they say. I decided to go with it.

I knocked on Captain Michaels's door and opened it before he could yell *Go away*. He was on the phone; he covered the mouthpiece and barked, 'Later, Larch.'

'It can't wait. I've got something.'

He scowled at me but nodded. He finished his phone conversation and then growled, 'This better be good. I got a man up in the twenty-sixth precinct waiting for orders. What's so important it can't—'

'Will you stop snarling and listen? This is important. Ted Cameron killed Rudy Benedict.'

He leaned back in his chair and stared at me, blew air out through his lips. 'Okay, that's the punchline. What's the lead-in?'

'Rudy Benedict was trying to blackmail Cameron. He had a piece of evidence that linked Cameron to an unsolved murder in Los Angeles fifteen years ago. Unfortunately for Rudy, he didn't have the knowhow to deal with a man as dangerous as Cameron. But even though he killed him, Cameron wasn't able to recover the evidence linking him to the old murder. That passed into the hands of Nathan Pinking, who's much more adept at covering himself in a dirty fight than Rudy Benedict ever was. Pinking undoubtedly knows Cameron killed Benedict as well—whether he can prove it or not, it's an added screw he can turn.'

'What was this evidence Benedict had?'

'A painting titled *Man and Shadow*. It was missing from his apartment at the time of his death—the bill of sale was in his safety-deposit box, but the painting was gone. I tried to get a line on it at the time, but nobody had ever heard of the painter. Her name was Mary Rendell and she was only twenty years old when she died. She was the murder victim in Los Angeles fifteen years ago.'

'And Cameron?'

'Probably killed her. Cyanide poisoning again, for one thing. For another, Cameron lied to the police at the time—said he didn't know her. But it's Cameron's face that's in Mary Rendell's painting. He knew her all right—he knew her well enough for her to make him the subject of a painting. Cameron was married at the time, and in line for the presidency of Cameron Enterprises. Mary Rendell must have become an embarrassment to him. I checked with the LAPD—the autopsy report made no mention of pregnancy or drugs. Maybe the threat she posed wasn't sexual. First thing you think of with a man like Cameron. But right now I'd have to say his motive for killing her is in the unknown category.'

'*If* he killed her. You're doing a lot of supposing there.'

'Granted. But Cameron wouldn't be vulnerable to blackmail unless he had some guilty connection with Mary Rendell's death.'

'Okay, that'll play. But how did Benedict get the painting in the first place?'

'Probably just bought it in all innocence. The bill of sale's signed by a small California dealer long since gone out of business—Rudy had a few pieces of inexpensive original art, all of it by unknowns. He picked up *Man and Shadow* when he and Mary Rendell and Ted Cameron were all living in California, fifteen years ago.' I put the newspaper clipping and the two Polaroid snapshots on Captain Michaels's desk. 'Fiona Benedict found these among Rudy's papers.' Poor Fiona Benedict, sitting there alone in her attic going through Rudy's legacy of paperwork. She'd actually held a picture of her son's murderer in her hand and hadn't known who it was.

The Captain looked at the photos first and then read the clipping. 'Rudy Benedict a blackmailer?' He shook his head doubtfully. 'Doesn't fit the profile we got on him. The picture I got was of a cautious man, somebody who didn't believe in taking risks.'

I tapped the newspaper clipping with my forefinger. 'That's not a photocopy. That's the original newspaper item, from fifteen years ago. Rudy Benedict kept it all this time. It took him fifteen years to work up the nerve to do something about his knowledge that Ted Cameron had lied about Mary Rendell. He'd reached some kind of turning point. Rudy was always talking about quitting television and writing for the stage, but he was never quite willing to take all the risks that involved. But his discontent must have reached the point where once in his life he decided he would take a chance.'

The Captain grunted. Not convinced.

'Look,' I said. 'Even attempting blackmail was in Rudy's case a hedge against risk-taking. He wanted to write a play, but he wasn't willing to risk financial failure. So he tried to put the bite on Ted Cameron, to force him to back his play or come up with grocery money or maybe both. He wanted Cameron to provide insurance against failure, one way or another. Rudy Benedict was an ordinary man who attempted one extraordinary thing in his life, and he got killed for his efforts.'

Captain Michaels massaged his chin. 'Maybe. So how'd the painting get into the hands of Nathan Pinking?'

'I'm just guessing here. Maybe Pinking saw the painting hanging in Rudy's California house and made the same connection Rudy did—and either stole or bought or "borrowed" the painting. But I'm more inclined to think a lifetime of playing it safe led Rudy to try covering his back by giving the painting to Pinking for safekeeping. Without telling him why, of course. But when the time for the shakedown came, Benedict didn't handle it right and Cameron killed him—and then, too late, discovered Rudy didn't have the painting. Maybe Rudy had showed him photos of the painting—those two there, or others like them. But the real thing wasn't in Rudy's apartment.'

'So Cameron killed him for nothing.'

'That's about it. He would have been better off in the long run if he'd just agreed to pay Rudy whatever he asked. Rudy would never have bled him dry the way Nathan Pinking is doing—he wouldn't know how, for one thing. By killing Rudy, Ted Cameron just gave Pinking another hold over him. It's ironic, in a way. Cameron killed off the "easy" blackmailer only to end up in the hands of a worse one.'

'Where did Cameron get the cyanide?'

'Cameron Enterprises itself can supply the raw materials a poisoner would need. They manufacture their own dyes—and they have laboratories both here and in Los Angeles. Ted Cameron could just help himself, both

153

places. I'm sure we can prove he had access—that's all we'll need, isn't it?'

Michaels shrugged. 'Should be.' He shifted back to the other man involved. 'I wonder how Pinking protected himself—letter with his lawyer, I suppose. And the painting? He wouldn't leave that in any accessible place—I suppose his lawyer could hold that too. Okay, I think we'll hold off on Pinking until we pick up Cameron. Which one is more likely to talk?'

'Cameron,' I said. 'He's living right on the edge. It shouldn't take much to push him over.'

'That's what I'm afraid of,' the Captain muttered. 'We're gonna have to go careful there. I don't want any psychiatrist up and saying he's not competent to stand trial. Good way to win a little cheap sympathy.'

I found it hard to feel any sympathy at all for Ted Cameron, cheap or otherwise. *He* wasn't the one I was worried about. I was worried about somebody else.

How was I going to tell Kelly?

CHAPTER 15

MARIAN LARCH

I had to hand it to Captain Michaels; he'd played it just right. After first checking with Cameron Enterprises to make sure the boss was in, the Captain and Ivan Malecki and I paid an unannounced visit to corporate head-quarters on Lexington. Three of us to arrest one man—Ivan was along to supply a little extra muscle that nobody really thought would be needed.

What the Captain had done was very simple. He'd put the old *Los Angeles Times* newspaper clipping and the two Polaroid snapshots on Ted Cameron's desk without saying a word. Then, when Cameron had had time to assimilate what they meant, Captain Michaels said, 'We're going to give you a choice. Confess to the murder

154

of Rudy Benedict and stand trial here in New York, where there's no death penalty. Or don't confess, and we'll extradite you to California where you'll be tried for the murder of Mary Rendell. There's no statute of limitations on murder—and California, I need hardly remind you, has the death penalty.'

For a moment I thought Ted Cameron had gone into shock. He stared at Captain Michaels with his mouth open, his blank eyes unblinking for so long that even Ivan began to feel uneasy. 'Is he all right?' he whispered.

Eventually Ted Cameron closed both his mouth and his eyes, but still he did not move or speak.

'Of course,' the Captain went on, 'if you're a gambling man you might want to take the chance that the California DA won't prosecute a fifteen-year-old case too vigorously. And all guilty verdicts in capital cases are automatically reviewed by the California Supreme Court—you might get a break there. But you got to balance that against the fact that you're a big shot, and the newspapers always have a heyday whenever a big shot is on trial, you know, speculating whether there's one law for the poor and another for the rich. They always do that. It might make your prosecutors a little prickly, less inclined to ease up. Personally I think you'd do better here. But it's your decision. It's your life.'

Cameron licked dry lips and said, 'I want my lawyer.'

'Of course you do,' the Captain said in almost paternal tones. 'And you'll get your lawyer, just as soon as we take care of a few little rituals first.' He nodded to Ivan and me. I read Cameron his rights while Ivan put the cuffs on him.

It was the cuffs that finally jarred him awake. 'Are these necessary?' he asked bitterly. 'What am I going to do—shoot it out with you? Run away? Where would I run?'

Michaels walked out of the office without answering. 'Let's go,' Ivan said, nudging his prisoner forward. I brought up the rear. The cuffs were *not* necessary; but then the Captain was trying to get a confession out of Ted

Cameron. Amateur criminals such as those who kill for personal reasons are sometimes intimidated by the accoutrements of the law.

We marched Cameron past his stunned secretaries, one of whom was talking earnestly into the telephone. I wondered whether she'd called Cameron's lawyer or his Aunt Augusta.

I kept waiting for the dam to break, for the bomb to go off. But by the time we got Ted Cameron into an interrogation room at Headquarters, he had an almost beatific expression on his face. His hands were steady, his voice was calm, he had no nervous mannerisms. He was in a state of false euphoria because the impossible battle he'd been waging was at long last over. He'd lost—but the relief of being finished with the struggle was so great that nothing else mattered. The Captain and Ivan and I had seen this before, and we all knew it was a temporary state; if we got anything out of him it was going to have to be quick. So we let him call his lawyer even before we booked him. Confessions signed without the presence of legal counsel had a way of being thrown out of court.

'Tell us about Rudy Benedict,' Captain Michaels said.

Cameron didn't answer—looked at me instead. 'You're Kelly's friend, aren't you? What are you going to tell her?'

'The truth.'

He gave a half-smile. 'Are you certain you know the truth?'

'No, I'm not. Why don't you make sure I've got it straight?'

Cameron's attorney arrived, a pale, white-haired man named Trotter whose field was corporate law and who was clearly out of his league. He demanded we postpone the interrogation until he could get a criminal lawyer for his client, but the law didn't require us to await the appearance of specialists so we said no. Trotter did the next best thing and advised his client not to say anything.

'I don't want to see her,' Ted Cameron said to me. 'I mean, I don't want her to see me like this.'

'I'll take her the message,' I promised.

Then he talked. Somewhere in the midst of his false euphoria Cameron had decided he was better off with us than facing a probable death sentence in California. Or maybe he just needed to talk, to tell somebody about it. His first instinct had been to protect himself, to call for a lawyer. But then when he had a lawyer, he ignored his advice. It happened all the time (fortunately for us). Trotter protested constantly, practically begged Cameron to shut up, *ordered* him not to sign anything. But the president of Cameron Enterprises had given up. He'd had all he could take; he was through. Two murders, the impending loss of his business, the horrors of being blackmailed—it had all finally caught up with him.

His connection with aspiring artist Mary Rendell turned out to be sexual after all. He said she was 'a mistake I once made'—thus casually dismissing a human life in so callous a manner that whatever possible sympathy I had left for him was utterly destroyed. When it was time for their affair to end, twenty-year-old Mary Rendell had been shocked and unbelieving. She wouldn't let go. Cameron himself was only thirty at the time and not as experienced in handling sticky situations as he was later to become. An uncle who was then president of Cameron Enterprises was on the verge of retirement; and Ted, brightest new star in the Cameron firmament, was terrified that an extramarital scandal might queer his chances for the job. Cameron Enterprises was a large conglomerate now, but it was still a *family* business.

So poor, naïve Mary Rendell had to go. Ted Cameron poisoned her, and lived in constant fear of discovery for months afterwards. He became president of Cameron Enterprises over Aunt Augusta's strenuous objections (she'd wanted the job for herself); and as soon as he safely could, he moved the corporate headquarters to New York. A new start in a new place; he even had a new wife by then.

Things went well for him after that; he had years of smooth sailing. Cameron had reconciled himself to the fact that he was a successful murderer. Business was

157

good; he'd turned out to be the right choice for Cameron Enterprises' chief executive—a fact that kept Aunt Augusta at bay. His second marriage failed, but he quickly discovered that the life of a rich, unmarried man in New York City wasn't all that hard to take. No unsurmountable problems in his life.

And then one day a snapshot arrived in the mail, a snapshot of a painting in which Cameron's face was easily recognizable. On the back of the snapshot was written *Man and Shadow, painted by Mary Rendell*. Cameron had not known of the existence of the painting. Mary had probably been saving it as a surprise. 'She was like that,' he said off-handedly.

I wondered—not for the first time—why Mary Rendell had put her lover in the shadow position in her painting. Perhaps she'd instinctively sensed there was something basically insubstantial about Ted Cameron. Or was it just her way of saying she didn't completely understand this man she was so involved with?

It was Rudy Benedict who'd sent Ted Cameron the photo. When the two men met, Rudy was the nervous one. He told Cameron they'd run into each other in California years ago, that, in fact, he'd been a guest at the party Ted and his first wife had thrown the night Mary Rendell was killed. Ted didn't remember him.

The relationship between would-be blackmailer and blackmailee-elect had been a strange one. Rudy Benedict clearly had never tried anything like that before in his life, and he was *very* uncomfortable. His approach, Ted Cameron said, was that of an insecure job applicant while he himself had been cast in the role of prospective employer. Rudy wanted Ted to understand *why* he was putting the screws on him; that was important to him.

So Ted Cameron had nodded sympathetically and listened to poor, second-rate Rudy Benedict's dreams of theatrical and literary glory. This pretended interest Rudy mistook for sympathy; he began to relax a little. All he wanted, he said, was living expenses until he could get one play written and produced. Just one, that was all.

158

When his play opened, he would hand over *Man and Shadow* to Ted Cameron. Whether the play succeeded or flopped made no difference. Rudy just wanted to be taken care of until he had his foot in the stage door. His blackmailing ambitions were so limited it didn't even occur to him to demand that Ted Cameron put up the money for the production of his unwritten play. All he wanted was an *allowance*.

Ted Cameron had deliberately fostered Rudy's need to believe he was a sympathetic listener. That part made perfect sense to me; his naturally courteous demeanor inspired an easy acceptance of Ted Cameron as a thoroughly civilized man. He and Rudy met several times, and Cameron always carried a bottle of cyanide crystals with him, waiting for an opportunity. They'd sit guzzling beer like a couple of stevedores, talking about the best way to arrange Rudy's new income so as not to invite the unwelcome interest of the Internal Revenue people. Rudy wanted the money to appear as legitimate income on which he would pay taxes, so he suggested Cameron buy up a contract for Rudy's services that Nathan Pinking held and which was about to expire. Businessmen could always use writers.

Who was Nathan Pinking, Ted Cameron wanted to know. Rudy told him. By then they'd progressed to Rudy's apartment, and Ted had stared at the postered walls with unconcealed amusement. Rudy had hastened to explain it was only a temporary living arrangement, that he hadn't even bothered to uncrate his paintings but had simply stored them all in the pantry. *In the pantry*, he'd said. That decided Cameron. When Rudy made a beer-necessitated trip to the bathroom, Cameron had picked up a spare set of keys from the top of Rudy's bureau. When Rudy came back in, Ted had agreed to the proposed way of paying off the blackmail. The two men parted on good terms; they'd even shaken hands, Cameron said. But he'd left his cyanide crystals behind in Rudy's Lysco-Seltzer bottle.

As he was telling us this, Cameron seemed more struck

by Rudy's ineptness than by his own perfidy. After Rudy was dead, Cameron had taken his stolen keys and gone back to the apartment. He found the paintings in the pantry, but *Man and Shadow* wasn't among them. It had all been for nothing. At one point he'd seriously considered paying Rudy the blackmail he'd asked; it wasn't all that much. He'd killed him because he decided he couldn't leave anyone alive who knew his guilty secret.

So double murderer Ted Cameron could do nothing but wait. He had no idea where the painting was; the newspaper stories had made no mention of a missing painting. As the days went by and nothing happened, it was beginning to look as if he'd get away with this one too. Then one day a voice on the phone identified its owner as Nathan Pinking and suggested a meeting.

Ted Cameron knew right away his new blackmailer was no apologetic Rudy Benedict. The first thing Pinking had done was explain that he'd left the painting with one lawyer and a letter of explanation with another. He'd come by the painting because Rudy Benedict had put it in a storage locker on West Thirty-fourth Street and had asked Pinking to hold the key. *Just in case something happens*, Rudy had said. Pinking had thought it a bit peculiar at the time but then had forgotten about it—until Rudy Benedict had been murdered.

Pinking had told Ted Cameron he'd recovered the painting from the storage locker but still didn't know what it meant until he saw a picture of him (Cameron) in the newspaper, in connection with Cameron Enterprises' negotiations for a friendly takeover of some small Florida beachwear company. Now that Pinking had a name to attach to the face in the painting, things began to fall into place. Pinking had been living in Los Angeles at the time Mary Rendell was killed, and he vaguely remembered that Cameron Enterprises was somehow associated with an unsolved murder. He sent his secretary to the library with instructions to track it down; and when she did, Nathan Pinking knew he had the ideal sponsor he'd long been looking for.

160

He'd started out easy, Ted Cameron said—if you call demanding full sponsorship of *LeFever* at jacked-up rates starting out easy. Even that took some doing, but Cameron managed it. Then the demands increased, and Cameron understood his company was expected to underwrite anything and everything Pinking wanted to put on the air. Cameron was becoming desperate to find the sponsorship money; he started forcing the ancillary companies to assume part of the burden. Unfortunately for him, Lorelei Cosmetics was in the best financial position of all the individual companies under the Cameron umbrella and the logical one to be tapped for the most funds. So Aunt Augusta was the first to sniff trouble, but soon the whole Cameron clan was up in arms. Ted Cameron was in serious trouble. Not only was his guilty secret in the hands of a totally unscrupulous, totally unreliable man, but Cameron was also in danger of losing Cameron Enterprises. Clearly there was only one thing to do. He was going to have to kill Nathan Pinking.

There was the problem of the two lawyers, though. One had the painting, another had a letter that would incriminate Cameron. He would have to find out who the lawyers were, and then hire someone to burglarize them. The two robberies and the murder of Nathan Pinking would all have to be timed to take place simultaneously, otherwise Pinking would guess what was up if the lawyers were taken care of first. Cameron didn't like the idea of bringing hired criminals in on it, but he could see no way around it. It would take very careful planning. He was working on the plan when something happened that made him change his mind.

He met Kelly Ingram.

The way Cameron explained it, he was obsessed with her. He'd never been fixated on a woman before in his life, and he didn't know how to deal with it. He was completely bowled over. Kelly changed everything; Cameron couldn't chance losing her. He didn't want to do anything, anything at all, that was the least bit risky—like committing a third murder. He began to feel

161

as if his illicit luck had suddenly run out. He was *afraid* to kill Nathan Pinking; because this time, the important time, something might go wrong. He couldn't risk it. Without knowing it, Kelly Ingram had saved Nathan Pinking's life.

So Ted Cameron had to put up with Pinking's control over him; he said he felt he was living in a torture chamber. It was Kelly that kept him going. And then Nathan Pinking, who saw only dollar signs when he looked at Kelly Ingram, had commanded Cameron to stop seeing her. But losing Kelly did not revive Cameron's earlier resolution to kill his blackmailer; by then the fear of failure had become too deeply ingrained. Nathan Pinking gave Ted Cameron an order, and Ted Cameron obeyed. He could no longer make decisions. He could no longer *act*, he could only sit back and be acted upon. He was drained, defused, whipped. He was through.

So when Captain Michaels had put the two Polaroid snapshots on the desk, it had taken Cameron a few minutes to understand it was finally all over. But when he did understand, he was relieved. Nathan Pinking had once speculated that Rudy Benedict might have held back a snapshot or two; but since Rudy's papers had all been shipped to his mother's house in Ohio, there didn't seem to be much danger. Pinking felt sure that the snapshots — if they did indeed exist — posed no threat to the cosy financial arrangement he and Cameron had finally settled on. And that, Cameron said, was all. End of story.

The lawyer Trotter hadn't said anything for a long time. He sat staring at Ted Cameron as if he'd never seen him before.

Cameron had a question. 'Did Rudy's mother find the photos? In his papers?'

'That's right,' Captain Michaels said.

Cameron made a noise that might have been a laugh. 'I have a favor to ask, Captain. When you arrest Pinking, tell him where the photos came from. He was so sure they'd cause no trouble. Will you tell him?'

Ivan Malecki cleared his throat and said, 'Did you have a bug planted in Nathan Pinking's office—a listening device?'

Cameron looked mildly surprised and said no. Somebody else, then. Cameron turned invisible pupils toward me, looking for all the world like a blind man. 'When will you tell her?'

'Now,' I said. 'Before she has a chance to hear it on the news.'

He smiled and thanked me. Politest killer I ever met.

I got up and left.

I'd known it wouldn't be easy, but it was even worse than I'd expected. The words were barely out of my mouth before she started rejecting them.

She didn't take in half of what I said—she didn't want to hear any of it. It was pitiful, the way she kept looking for excuses. She blamed Captain Michaels, she blamed me, she even found a way to blame Fiona Benedict. She was willing to blame the *entire world* before she'd blame Ted Cameron—he meant that much to her. It's hard, admitting you made a mistake that big.

'He's killed two people, Kelly,' I said. 'He's admitted it.'

She refused to believe it, simply *refused*. I decided there was no point in pushing it; she was going to have to have time to accept it. Time by herself, time to ease her way in. Bullying her wouldn't help.

When I left, she looked as if she wanted to kill *me*. I've never felt so bad in my life.

When I got back to Headquarters, the reporters were there. Nathan Pinking had been brought in and charged with blackmail and with being an accessory to murder after the fact (for concealing evidence); Captain Michaels had already made a statement to the press. A blackmailer and a murderer arrested in tandem, and both of them fairly well-known figures. A lurid tale, but even *The Wall Street Journal* was interested in this one.

I sat at my desk waiting for the traffic going in and out

163

of Captain Michaels's office to stop. Ivan Malecki came over, saw the look on my face, and said, 'That bad, huh?' When I nodded, he squeezed my shoulder and went away. For which I was grateful; sometimes a pep talk is the last thing you need to hear. It had been a nerve-racking day and I wanted to go home.

Catching a murderer isn't the cause for celebration you might think. There's no good feeling to it. It's a depressing scene, and the main feeling is one of shame. Shame that we should be like this; you look at a killer and you see a piece of humanity that's failed in its essential nature, that of being *humane*. The last thing in the world you want to do is go out and hoist a few and congratulate yourself for being so clever. Catching killers is just something that has to be done, like carrying out the garbage. They're both disease preventatives.

I felt absolutely rotten about Kelly. I'd have been glad to offer her a shoulder to cry on, but she'd made it clear she didn't want me within ten miles of her. There wasn't anything I could do. I'd just have to rely on her common sense to see her through.

Finally the door to Captain Michaels's office was open and he was in there alone. I went in.

'Good work, Larch,' he said. 'You stuck with it and you came up with a blackmailer as well as the killer.' I must not have had my face rearranged right yet because he said, 'Kelly Ingram didn't take it too well, huh?'

'Not well at all.'

'Give her time. That's a helluva lot to have to swallow all at once. She'll come round.' Back to an easier subject. 'You'll get a commendation for this one, you can count on it.'

'Then am I right in thinking this is a good time to ask for something?'

He stage-sighed. 'Ask.'

'Assign me to the Richard Ormsby murder.'

He looked surprised. 'You still want on that one? It's a dead case, Marian.'

'Maybe. It doesn't need to be.'

164

He squinted one eye at me. 'You think you know who did that one too?'

I shook my head. 'I just have an idea or two I want to follow up. But I can't if you won't assign me to the case.'

He told me he thought I was crazy but okayed the assignment. I thanked him and went back to my desk. One more chore to perform before I could call it a day; my role as bearer of bad news wasn't quite finished.

I called Fiona Benedict in Washburn, Ohio, and told her her son had died because he'd made the mistake of trying to blackmail a murderer.

CHAPTER 16

KELLY INGRAM

It was weird seeing Leonard Zoff sitting at Nathan Pinking's desk in Nathan Pinking's office. Taking care of what used to be Nathan Pinking's business. It was weird thinking of Nathan in jail for blackmail, although I'd done my damnedest to make sure he got there. What it was thinking about Ted, there was no word for.

Leonard looked at me sympathetically. 'Wouldn't hurt you to get back to work, darling. Sooner the better.'

I nodded listlessly; he was right. What I needed was some sort of set daily routine, the kind of thing where you didn't have to think at all. *LeFever* was just the ticket.

'You feel awright?' Nick Quinlan asked me.

'I feel all right, Nick,' I said. 'Just not a whole lot of energy, you know?'

'Yeah, I know.' He nodded somberly. 'Happensa me sometimes. Too bad we doan git to do those three, y'know, the Barbados shows. They'd make ya feel bear. Hey, Leonard, how come we're not goin' to Barbados?'

'Shut up, Nick,' Leonard sighed. The connection among producer Nathan Pinking and sponsor Ted Cameron and the promised extra episodes in Barbados that were nothing more than blackmail booty—it was all too much for Nick to grasp. 'Sorry, Kelly,' Leonard said. 'He means well.'

I shrugged; it didn't matter. Nick looked puzzled. He did that a lot—look puzzled.

It had taken some getting used to, the idea that my ex-lover, the joy of my life and the light of my existence let the drums roll and the trumpets sound ta-taa (idiot idiot *idiot*)—was in fact a cold-blooded killer. And I mean cold-blooded, that's not just a phrase, it means something. Look at what he did: he killed Rudy Benedict. *Rudy Benedict*. Undoubtedly the most miscast would-be criminal on the face of the earth—and Ted couldn't find any way of handling him other than killing him? There were a number of things Ted could have done. He could have paid him off. He could have tried to talk him out of it. He could have stolen the painting. He could have threatened to tell Rudy's mother.

'I know it's early to be starting on the new season,' Leonard Zoff was saying in his loud voice, 'but I'd like to get as much in the can as possible before Kelly's movie airs in December. The network might want us to start taping her new series right away—depends on how fast they can sign up a sponsor. We won't have any trouble there, Kel, I'm sure of it. It's good stuff, a sure-fire series idea. You're lucky you got it finished before Nathan Shithead was arrested.'

'Lucky. Yeah.'

'Whassamadda with *LeFever?*' Nick said sourly. 'Not goodanuff for ya?' Now there he was *pretending* to be dumb. Even he understood about having your own series.

Leonard started stroking Nick and I tuned out. I didn't know Mary Rendell, of course, but Marian Larch said she was only twenty when Ted killed her. A *girl*, for Christ's sake—such a dangerous person that murder was the only answer? Seemed to me Ted Cameron was the big bad successful killer only when he came up against weak opponents like Rudy Benedict and Mary Rendell. But when he faced off against somebody a little slicker, like

Nathan Pinking, *Ted* was the one to knuckle under. A lot of married, upwardly mobile types had Mary Rendells in their lives, but they didn't *kill* them for crying out loud. They either handled the situation and got away with it or they didn't handle it and got found out, but they didn't become murderers rather than face a setback in their professional lives. And if Ted hadn't killed Mary Rendell, he wouldn't have had Rudy to worry about. He killed those two people simply because it was the easiest way to solve his problems—he wasn't willing to make the effort to find another way. And if you don't think that's cold-blooded, I'd like to know what the hell is.

And there I was, Little Miss Stars-in-Her-Eyes-and-Rocks-in-Her-Head. I never knew, I never suspected, I never had an *inkling*. Even when I figured out Ted was being blackmailed, I still didn't believe he'd done anything *bad*. I was so besotted with the man I was even able to rationalize away blackmail. I wanted him to be a certain kind of man and I *made* him that kind of man, in my mind, I mean. It was just that I knew what I wanted and I decided he was it and I never saw what he really was. I never knew Ted Cameron at all.

Do you have any idea what it feels like to find out you've slept with a murderer? And not just once, but repeatedly? Try to imagine it—learning your bed partner is a killer. Kinky thrills, a real turn-on? Maybe for some people. Me—it just made me sick. I threw up every day for a week. Finally Leonard Zoff called and insisted I pull out of my 'mulligrubs'—whatever they are. When I did, I found some changes had taken place in the world.

'I was thinking of a new car for LeFever,' Leonard was saying soothingly to Nick. 'One of the flashier sports models. What do you say to that?'

'I get to pick it out?' Nick asked.

'Who else?'

Sure you do, Nick. Don't hold your breath, Nick.

Nathan Pinking's production company was now Leonard Zoff's production company. The way Leonard explained it, Nathan was still a minor partner and his

167

share of the profits would go toward supporting his family while he was in prison. For some reason that Leonard didn't explain, Nathan had had a choice only of either selling to Leonard or shutting down — which wouldn't pay his family's bills while Daddy was a guest of the state. So the long battle between the two had finally come to an end, and Leonard had won. With Nathan locked up for a goodly number of years, Leonard would have it all his own way.

You'd think he'd be on top of the world, wouldn't you? Well, he wasn't. As a matter of fact Leonard was kind of lackadaisical, going at the early taping of *LeFever*'s third season as if it was every bit as exciting as checking over last week's laundry list. Nick was always half asleep anyway, and what with me just coming out of the blues, it wasn't the most scintillating meeting I ever attended. Leonard was businesslike and all that; we were making plans and getting on with it. But Leonard had lost a lot of what my grandmother would have called his spizzer-inctum — his special up-and-at-'em kind of drive. Maybe it just wasn't the same without Nathan Pinking to scrap with.

'Kelly, darling, pay attention, please. We're gonna do more out-of-city location shooting this time, so you and Nick will have to keep your calendars clear after the twenty-first. Don't even go making a dental appointment without checking with me first. I'm gonna have enough on my mind without schedule conflicts and all that shit.'

All that shit. 'Leonard,' I said abruptly, 'did you once send me a laxative and a carton of toilet paper?'

The color drained right out of his face — and then drained right back in. 'Toilet paper, darling? Why should I send you toilet paper?'

But it was no good; he'd given himself away. 'Why, Leonard?' I asked. 'Do you resent me that much?'

'What are you talking about?'

'You know what I'm talking about. A bottle of Lysco-Seltzer containing a laxative and a carton of toilet paper. You sent them.'

168

Nick said lazily, 'Whire we talkin' toilet paper?'

'You're crazy,' Leonard said. 'I didn't send you that stuff.'

'Okay, Leonard,' I sighed. 'If that's the way you want it.'

Things were a bit edgy after that, even though both of us did this big act about how everything was hunkydory again. Don't know why I let it bother me that much, but it got to me. Hitting on small bad feelings to keep away the big ones, I guess.

The meeting dragged to a close. Nick had come in a limo—it was getting harder and harder for either of us to appear in public without drawing swarms of autograph-hunters. That was good most of the time, *God*, the years I dreamed about it!—but you have to be *on* the whole time and I just wasn't up to performing right then. I asked Nick if he'd drop me at Police Plaza.

On the elevator down, Nick draped one arm across my shoulders in that posture he likes best when he's talking to women. 'Doan look so sad, pretty Kelly,' he said. 'The hurtin' stops soonsya let it. Let it stop, Kel.'

Well. Who'd have thought Nick Quinlan had that kind of compassion in him? He'd said exactly the right thing. I wondered if I could ever get mad at him again after that.

'Asides, it doan help LeFever's image none, you goan round lookin', y'know, unsatisfied.'

Yep. I could.

I wanted to see Marian Larch—strictly personal sort of thing, no police business. It had eventually sunk in on me that I'd been just awful to her when she came with the news about Ted. I was *blaming her* for what happened—actually I should have been thanking her, I guess. It was pretty goddamned clear that *I* didn't have enough sense to see through Ted Cameron. I'd have just gone on drifting along, never knowing. Nathan Pinking aside, what if things had stopped being good between Ted and me? Would he have gotten rid of me the way he did Mary Rendell?

Put him out of your mind. Just stop thinking about him. He slips into your mind, force him out by thinking of other things. It can be done.

Ivan (I have *got* to find out his last name) said Marian was down in the Property Department. I decided to go looking for her rather than wait, because a lot of the good folks at Police Headquarters were giving me the eye. I was a different kind of celebrity here; my ex-lover was a murderer.

Think of other things.

Ivan insisted on escorting me because they didn't like people—'civilians' was Ivan's word—wandering around the Headquarters building and that may even have been true. (If we're civilians, then the police are *military?*) Marian was just coming out of the Property Department when we got there.

'I'm sorry!' I hollered at her.

Marian jumped a foot. 'For what?' she demanded, alarmed.

'For being so nasty the day you, well, you know, when you brought me the bad news.'

Her plain, friendly face crumpled into a smile. 'Oh, that's all right,' she said generously. 'I probably could have found a better way to tell you.'

'No, it was my fault. I acted bad or maybe badly and I'm sorry for both of them and I apologize.'

'Nothing to worry about. We were all tense, it was a tense situation and—'

'Damn it, Marian, I am *trying* to take the blame. Will you shut up and let me feel guilty?'

Ivan looked worried. 'Are you two kidding or are you fighting?'

'I am perfectly content to let you feel as guilty as you like,' Marian said to me majestically, 'so long as your guilt trip does not interfere with my stance of gracious understanding.'

'You're kidding,' Ivan said with relief.

'And you were right about something else,' I went on. 'It was Leonard Zoff who sent me the toilet paper.'

170

'Ah-hah. Did he admit it?'

'No,' I said, 'but he gave himself away when I asked him. Just now, at a meeting.'

'I think it's good that he knows. That *you* know, I mean. It'll make him think twice if he's ever tempted to send out any more toilet paper gifts.'

'He seemed honestly surprised when I brought it up. But then he pretended not to know what I was talking about.'

'*I* don't know what you're talking about,' Ivan complained. 'Why are we talking about toilet paper?'

'You're not by any chance related to Nick Quinlan, are you?' I asked him.

'We're talking about an associate of Kelly's who had trouble getting through the anal stage of his development,' Marian explained to Ivan. Which didn't really explain anything, come to think of it. Neat trick.

'Are you through for the day?' I asked her.

'Lord, no. Tons of work.'

'Then sneak away for a break. You can do that, can't you?'

'I'm almost finished,' Ivan said hopefully.

'Sorry, love, I'm all set for this big dramatic scene with Marian and there's no man's role in it.'

He grinned. 'Is that the actress talking or the woman?'

'Depends on who's asking,' I said. 'The cop or the man.'

He didn't like that much, the implication that cops and men were two different things. (It was okay for him to do the same thing to me, though.) He tried to laugh it off. 'Hey, that's not what you're supposed to say.'

'I know,' I sighed. 'I'm supposed to say something like *I was a woman before I was an actress* and then bat my eyes and smile. Sorry, Ivan, I'm just not up to it today, okay?'

'Okay,' he said dubiously.

Marian was laughing. 'Now, what's got into you? Come on—I think I can sneak a break at that.'

'My family always said "bathroom tissue",' Ivan called after us by way of goodbye.

We went to a private club on East Fiftieth that I didn't much care for except that it sure as hell was *private*. I didn't have to worry about strangers coming up to me there or even being gawked at. Normally I rather like being gawked at, but circumstances were different now. Our private booth had one-way glass in the window; we could watch the passing parade outside without being seen ourselves.

'This place must cost you an arm and a leg,' Marian said in hushed tones. 'All I wanted was a cup of coffee.'

I explained how lack of privacy had suddenly become a real problem. 'I don't even feel comfortable in your office, Marian. People stare there too.'

She nodded. 'So what's this big dramatic scene you told Ivan you wanted to play?'

'What's his last name?'

'Ivan's? Malecki.'

'Malecki, that's right. Couldn't remember it. Did I offend him, do you think?'

'No, but you puzzled him. You sounded out of character.'

'I am. Completely out of character. Not sure what my character is anymore.'

'Oh Gawd, not the existential miseries.'

'No, nothing like that. It's just that everything's shaken up. Leonard sitting behind Nathan's desk and not looking at all happy about it—'

'Really? That's a surprise.'

'Surprised me too. I don't mean he regrets taking over the production company—he's going ahead with everything okay. But he's not getting the kick out of it he should be getting. He should be King of the Hill now, but he's not.'

'Maybe he needs Nathan Pinking as an adversary to spark him. Could be it was the fight itself that kept him going.'

'That's what I was thinking. He and Nathan have been battling for so long, Leonard must feel something is missing from his life now.'

A waiter appeared pushing a trolley laden with about forty fancy finger sandwiches and at least twice that many elaborately iced pastries. That's what you got in that place when you asked for *just coffee*.

When he'd gone, I said, 'Marian, I hope you don't mind my dragging you away from your work. No big scene, that was just to keep Ivan Malecki from coming along. There are just some things I don't understand. Like why did Nathan Pinking sell out to an old enemy like Leonard? Why didn't he sell to somebody else?'

'He couldn't. You had no way of knowing it, but Leonard Zoff already owned forty-nine per cent of Pinking's production company.'

'*What?*'

'And Pinking owned forty-nine per cent of Zoff's theatrical agency. It was a deal they worked out when they dissolved their earlier company— Pinking and Zoff Productions. You remember, I told you about that.'

'Then they were still partners? All this time?'

'They certainly were. And the contract they signed specified that neither partner could sell his share without the permission of the other partner. So once Pinking was arrested, Zoff had him over a barrel. Pinking had to sell to Zoff or see the business fold. If he hadn't been worried about providing for his family, Pinking probably would have just told Zoff to go to hell.'

'That's something that's always amazed me,' I said, nibbling on a pastry. 'How Nathan could be such a monster *and* a good family man at the same time.'

'Never heard of the Mafia, huh?' Marian said wryly. 'Anyway, Zoff bought just a big enough percentage from Pinking to give himself majority control of both the production company and the agency. I think he's going to hire somebody to run the agency for him.'

'Yes, he's already done that. He promoted one of his own people. Leonard's going to keep on managing a few of his clients, though. Including me.' Leonard-the-agent had just negotiated my new *LeFever* contract with himself, Leonard-the-producer. I *think* I came out all right on that one.

'Do you have a new sponsor for *LeFever* yet?'

'Oh God, yes. NBC had to fight 'em off, even though they raised the advertising rate again. It's weird, isn't it? You'd think that once the story became public—well, look. Here's this producer that's been blackmailing somebody into sponsoring his show. The other advertisers *ought* to be thinking that the show has to be a real turkey if that's the only way a sponsor could be found. But no—they're lining up for the privilege of paying for *LeFever*. We're in the news now, and it doesn't matter what that news is. Just so people are talking about us—that's all that counts.'

'What about your movie?'

'Same thing. They've even started negotiating about my new series, the one to be based on the movie. In fact, all of Nathan's shows have been covered except *Down the Pike*—ABC cancelled that one. But if things keep going like this, Leonard Zoff is going to end up a rich man.'

Marian made a vague gesture with her hand. 'Well, that's show biz.'

'No, it isn't,' I said glumly. 'That's the advertising biz.'

A silence grew between us. We drank our coffee and looked out the window. There was something I wanted to ask her, but my mouth had grown suddenly dry. I took a drink of water; it didn't help.

I'd forgotten Marian Larch could sometimes read minds. She said, gently and considerately, 'He's undergoing psychiatric examination. A whole team of doctors, the Cameron clan got them for him. The police psychiatrist has already declared him competent to stand trial, but the date won't be set until the Cameron psychiatrists are finished.'

I nodded; that's what I'd wanted to know. 'I've decided to put him out of my mind.' My voice sounded strained.

Marian smiled sadly. 'Good idea.'

And then I was surprised to hear myself saying, 'I don't want to do any more *LeFever* episodes.'

Marian raised an eyebrow. 'Well, well. Now what do

174

you suppose the connection *there* is?'

'I don't know.' I tried to think. 'I tell you I'm going to put Ted Cameron behind me and I suddenly realize I hate the television show I'm doing. Why would one lead to the other? Ohwowohwow. I don't know, Marian—I told you I was out of character today.'

'Maybe that's it,' she said. 'I'll bet it's the character you're playing that you don't like. Do you see any connection between your television role and the role you were playing with Ted Cameron?'

I was so shocked I couldn't speak. I wanted to yell, I wanted to hit her, I wanted to deny it at the top of my voice. The character I played in *LeFever* was only a human toy, for God's sake, something for the hero to play with. I wasn't like that, I didn't *think* of myself like that, I knew better . . . at least I thought I knew better. All of a sudden I was filled with doubts, uncertainty. It was an *awful* feeling.

Finally I said, 'Fiona Benedict was wrong about me.' Somehow that came out sounding too much like a question. I made it more positive. 'She was wrong. She had to be.'

Marian looked at me a few moments as if trying to make her mind up about something. Then abruptly she said, 'Kelly. Don't judge the Miss America contest. Call your lawyer friend Howard and see if he can break the contract for you.'

How ironic. How dumb. I started to laugh. It sounded artificial, even to me. 'Relax. I'm not going to judge any Miss America contest. It's all been decided. They cancelled *me*.' Marian didn't say a word; just sat there with her mouth open. 'That's right. Seems my image is no longer wholesome enough for them. What with a killer for my lover and a blackmailer producing my shows, I'm no longer fit to associate with young American virgins. That kind of dirt rubs off, you know.' I sounded even more sarcastic than I'd meant.

Marian let out the breath she'd been holding. 'If I said I was sorry, I'd be lying and you know it. I'm sorry you

175

didn't have the pleasure of telling *them* where to get off, but you're well out of it, Kelly. You don't need that. *You don't have to play those games.* Now for Pete's sake pull yourself together and get back to being your usual peppy self. You make me nervous, the way you're drooping around. You're well rid of all of them, Cameron and Pinking and even Miss God Bless America. You've had just one fortunate escape after another—what are you so gloomy about? Cheer up, damn it! You don't realize how lucky you are.'

She looked and sounded exactly like a sixth-grade teacher I'd once had. 'Yes, ma'am,' I said in a tiny voice. 'Go screw yourself, ma'am.'

'That's better,' she beamed. 'Now I hate like the very devil to leave this sinfully luxurious establishment you've brought me to, but I do have to be getting back. Work awaits.'

Belatedly I realized how much of her time I'd taken and signalled to the waiter. 'Thanks for listening, Marian. What are you working on now—or am I allowed to ask?'

'Sure you are. I'm on the Richard Ormsby case now.'

'Oh?' The waiter brought the bill and I signed; two coffees, fifty dollars. When he'd left, I said, 'That case is still open? It's been a while. Do you really think you'll ever know who killed Richard Ormsby?'

'I already know who killed him,' she said bluntly. 'I even know why he was killed. What I don't know is how the hell I'm going to prove it.'

CHAPTER 17

MARIAN LARCH

Ivan Malecki sat on his spine and scowled at his feet stretched out in front of him. 'I don't believe it. There's no way that can be right.'

I wanted to grab him by the shoulders and give him a good shake. It had taken me the better part of an afternoon to convince Captain Michaels, and now Ivan was being stubborn.

The Captain shifted his considerable weight in the big chair behind his desk. 'I'm not totally convinced myself, Malecki,' he said. 'But if she's wrong, there's no harm done. If she's right, we damn well better follow through.'

'I just don't believe it,' Ivan said mulishly.

One more try. 'Look, Ivan,' I said, 'can you suspend disbelief about one basic matter, for just a moment? Every time we investigate a killing, we go in assuming the victim is dead for a reason that directly involves him. Either he's been killed in the heat of passion, or he's a threat to somebody, or he stands between the killer and something the killer wants, or—'

'Yeah, yeah. This isn't my rookie year, you know.'

'Okay, then, can you just forget about all that? Assume, just for a minute, a man can be killed for reasons that have nothing at all to do with him personally—all right?'

'Sure.' Ivan sat up straight. 'Jesus, Marian, you think I'm dumb or something? The gangs go joyriding and take pot shots at whoever happens to be standing on the sidewalk. Shooting up the neighborhood just for the hell of it. Those people aren't killed for any *personal* reason. Matter of chance.'

'Then assume for just a moment that Richard Ormsby too was killed for reasons that had nothing to do with him.'

'Crap.'

'Maybe it's not, Malecki,' Captain Michaels helped out. 'Scotland Yard turned up a few enemies who wouldn't mind seeing Ormsby out of the way, but every one of them was in England at the time he was shot. Ormsby was in New York only four days before he was killed. Yeah, I know—it's *possible* something happened in those four days that made it necessary for somebody to get rid of him. But it's not very damn *likely*, is it? Well, is it?'

'No,' Ivan muttered reluctantly.

'And we haven't turned up any reason why anyone over here would want him dead except Dr. Fiona Benedict and her damned book, and we know she didn't do it because she was in the lock-up at the time of the killing. So what's left? Do we tell the Commissioner and the British Ambassador and maybe even the Queen herself, gee, we're sorry, we can't find out who killed the visiting celeb so we're going to go work on other cases now, goodbye and thank you? Look, Malecki, he didn't get it for any of the usual reasons, so now we gotta take a look at the *un*usual reasons. And Larch here has come up with a lulu.'

'It's downright weird, Marian,' Ivan grumbled.

I couldn't argue with that. 'The whole case has been weird. Starting with Fiona Benedict's attempt at murder. The police case against her was weak right from the start. Both of you two had trouble believing Fiona was guilty of attempted murder—a lot of people felt that way. But she did try to kill Ormsby. She tried hard. Even though she didn't succeed, her *trying* to kill him is germane to what happened later.'

'You know what happened later?' Ivan cocked an eyebrow at me.

'I think so. If you're willing to assume for a moment that Richard Ormsby was killed for reasons that had nothing to do with him personally—then take a look at the aftermath of the shooting. Three things happened. First, there was a big surge in the sales of *Lord Look-on*. Second, the collapse of Ormsby's planned publicity tour caused a lot of trouble for a lot of people. But it's the third thing that's important.'

Ivan nodded impatiently. 'Fiona Benedict was released from custody. So?'

'So, who benefits from her being out of jail? Who, aside from Fiona Benedict herself, is the one person on this earth *who is better off* because Fiona was released? What did she do when she got out?'

'She went home.'

'She went home, to Washburn, Ohio. To her son Rudy's papers. She is the only person alive who was in any way likely to go through those boxes and boxes of papers and read everything in them. We already had our go at them and didn't find anything—I spent several days there reading just the business papers, and they were only a small fraction of the whole lot. No, Fiona's the only one who could be counted on to look at *all* of Rudy's papers, to check every folder. And she did, coming up with the bit of evidence that gave us both a murderer and a blackmailer. You see? That's what made Fiona Benedict so important. *That's* why Richard Ormsby was killed—so we'd have to let Fiona go. She'd be no help locked up in a cell. Ormsby's killer wanted that evidence found. He wanted it so much he was willing to kill to make it happen.'

Ivan whistled tunelessly a moment and then said, 'You mean one of the Cameron family.'

'No, no, Ivan—it wasn't the murderer he wanted caught. He didn't give a hoot about Ted Cameron.'

'The blackmailer then? Nathan Pinking?'

'Right. And who is it who's benefited from Pinking's arrest?'

The name had been hanging in the air for a long time; it was Captain Michaels who finally spoke it aloud. 'Leonard Zoff.' He mulled it over. 'Far as we can tell, Zoff didn't even know Ormsby. And he sure as hell didn't move in the same circles as Fiona Benedict. He knew Rudy, but he'd never had any reason to meet Rudy's mother. So that means Zoff killed a man he didn't know, in order to get a woman he didn't know released from jail. If Larch is right.'

'It's *weird*,' Ivan pronounced emphatically.

Agreed. 'Leonard Zoff was losing his battle with Nathan Pinking,' I said. 'Pinking was successful and showed every sign of becoming more so. Zoff was keeping his head above water, he was doing all right—but he wasn't hitting it as big as his old enemy was. He had to sit there and watch Pinking pulling away from him. That must have hurt bad. Those two men lived for the pleasure of outdoing each other. Anyway, Zoff had one ace in the hole. Kelly Ingram. Kelly was on her way to stardom, and that's all Leonard needed—one really big star.'

'She'll make it,' Ivan said pontifically. 'She's there now as far as I'm concerned.'

'But then Pinking put her under personal contract when he gave her her role in *LeFever*,' I went on. 'He made it a condition of signing, Kelly told me. Pinking was helping with the star build-up, he cast her in a TV movie, he was going ahead with a new series in which Kelly would star. The bigger a success Kelly became, the more money that meant for Pinking—because he'd see to it that she appeared in nothing but Nathan Pinking productions. And Leonard Zoff had to stand there and watch his one chance at Easy Street gradually being taken over by the man he hated most in the world. No wonder he was moved to action.'

'Wait a minute, wait a minute,' Ivan said. 'How would Zoff know there was any evidence that'd lead to Pinking's arrest? How'd he know about those photos? And where they were? He couldn't have known about them unless Rudy Benedict told him. Are you saying Rudy told Zoff what he was doing?'

Captain Michaels fielded that one. 'No, Rudy didn't tell Zoff anything. But remember what Ted Cameron said—that Pinking had speculated Rudy might have kept back a couple of photographs of the incriminating painting? Then Cameron said Pinking decided the photos would pose no threat once Rudy's mother had all his papers shipped to Ohio. Even if she did find them, she wouldn't know what they meant. What Pinking didn't know was that Marian here had already shown a lotta curiosity about that missing painting, and Fiona Benedict remembered that and mailed her the photos.'

Ivan objected. 'But all that talk about the photos, that was between Cameron and Pinking. Zoff wasn't there. How would he know what—oh. The bug.'

Michaels nodded. 'Zoff would have had Pinking's office

bugged just to keep tabs on what his enemy was up to. The blackmail scheme was a bonus he hadn't counted on.'

I said, 'I had a talk with Leonard Zoff not too long after Rudy Benedict was murdered, and I remember he expressed a kind of mild outrage that we weren't going through everything of Rudy's looking for clues — every file folder, every envelope. At the time I thought it was just the concern of a man who wanted to see a friend's killer caught. But of course that's what I was meant to think. I ended up reassuring him that Rudy's mother was going to check all the papers and she'd let us know if she found something. So Leonard Zoff *knew* Fiona Benedict was going through those files. He knew because I told him.'

'So all he had to do was sit back and wait,' Captain Michaels said. 'Zoff had known Rudy Benedict a long time, and everyone acquainted with the writer knew what a cautious, self-protective man he was. Zoff was sure those photos would be there, and sooner or later Fiona Benedict would find them. She might not know what they meant, but she wouldn't just pass over them the way Pinking thought she would. Zoff knew Dr. Benedict was checking *for the police* as well as for herself — Pinking didn't know that.'

'But it didn't work,' Ivan said, slowly coming to accept the theory. 'Instead of staying in Ohio and reading her son's papers, Dr. Benedict came here and tried to shoot Richard Ormsby. She really did try?'

'She really did try,' I nodded. 'Ormsby hit her where it hurts. She must have thought she was protecting herself.'

'Like mother, like son,' Captain Michaels grunted.

True. Those two had been more alike than either one of them had ever realized. 'I'd like to know when Zoff first began to understand why Rudy had been killed. Would Cameron and Pinking have actually used words like *blackmail* and *murder* while they were working out their private financial arrangements? I can't see that. Zoff must have pieced it together slowly over a number of overheard conversations. Captain, do you remember the missing file folder?'

'What missing file folder?'

'The first time I talked to Nathan Pinking, I asked to
see the file he kept on Rudy Benedict and it was
missing —'

'Yeah, I remember.'

'Well, it's back in the filing cabinet now. I went to
Leonard Zoff's new office after he took over the
production company — Nathan Pinking's old office.
Nothing out of the ordinary in Rudy Benedict's folder.
Same sort of thing I read in Rudy's business files in
Ohio — in fact, I think I remember a few of the letters.
But the file is back.'

'So why was it missing in the first place?' Ivan asked.

'Zoff probably filched it when he first began to puzzle
out what was going on. He may have been looking for
evidence that would tie Pinking to the blackmail of
Rudy's murderer. I think it's more likely he was just trying
to find out whatever he could about the whole Benedict-
Cameron-Pinking situation. Zoff *might* have found
something in Benedict's folder, but I doubt it. He
probably just returned the file intact after he moved into
Pinking's office.'

'Or the secretary had simply misfiled it all along,'
Captain Michaels muttered.

'Mimsy?' Ivan grinned.

'I think it was still Tansy at that point,' I said, grinning
back. 'But even without any help from that particular file
folder, Leonard Zoff was sitting pretty there for a while.
All his problems were going to solve themselves. His
enemy had committed a felony and evidence of a kind
was just waiting to be uncovered in a dead man's papers
in Ohio. Zoff wouldn't have to lift a finger — it'd all take
care of itself. Once Pinking was out of the way, Zoff
would have everything — the production company, the
agency . . . and Kelly Ingram.'

'Then one day it all blows up in his face,' Captain
Michaels said. 'The woman he'd counted on to find the
evidence for him — she's not sitting quietly in Ohio

reading through Rudy's papers at all. She's sitting in a New York detention cell on a charge of attempted murder. Think how he must have felt. To see *everything* he wanted within his grasp—majority ownership of both businesses, a new star in his pocket, the defeat of his enemy. And then to watch it all start to slip away—and why? Because of a book some Englishman wrote. He must have had trouble believing what was happening to him.'

'So he wasn't going to be able to sit back and watch it all work out nicely for him,' Ivan nodded. 'He was going to have to do something to get Fiona Benedict out of jail and back to Ohio. What could he do? Hope her attorney could get her off? Possible, but chancy. And time-consuming. Maybe he felt he was running out of time?'

'Maybe,' the Captain nodded. 'But whatever he was thinking, he ended up convincing himself that his best chance was to make us believe Fiona Benedict wasn't guilty of trying to kill anybody. And the best way to do that was to go ahead and commit the crime she'd been charged with trying to commit. So he was careful to duplicate her method—the TV studio, the gun.' Captain Michaels paused. 'Man lives over half a century without resorting to criminal acts to survive and then suddenly turns to the worst crime of them all—pretty good sign of how much he wants a thing.'

Ivan stood up and stretched. 'Well, it's a good story. What are you going to do with it, sell it to the movies? There's not one bit of evidence that that's the way it happened.'

Captain Michaels grinned broadly. 'That's where you come in.'

'Me?'

'You're going to blackmail Leonard Zoff.'

Ivan sat down again, rather quickly. 'Blackmail. Now there's an original thought.'

'That's the point,' Michaels said. 'The idea's already planted. Zoff has to be superconscious of the fact that blackmail can follow murder. And the shooting did happen in a public place, remember—he can't be *sure* nobody saw him.'

'Jesus, he was hiding in a stairwell behind a door! Only his arm and the hand holding the gun would have been visible. Nobody can identify him from that.'

'Is he going to take a chance on that? Would you? Besides, he wasn't firing blind. At least one eye had to be exposed—part of his face must have been showing. For two seconds, maybe, but it had to be showing. There was a moment there when someone could have seen him. Nobody did, but he doesn't know that. And that's where we get 'im.'

'Okay, he might go for it,' Ivan agreed. 'But why me?'

'Because he doesn't know you, Ivan,' I said. 'He'll be wary of you. If he pays, then that's an admission of guilt. We've got him.'

'Yeah, well, this guy's a killer, you know,' Ivan scowled. 'He might just think of some other little solution, if you know what I mean.'

'Don't worry, you'll go in armed and we'll be only seconds away,' the Captain said. 'We're going to set this up ver-y carefully.'

'Yeah, well, about that,' Ivan said uneasily. 'Isn't that entrapment?'

'Nope,' Captain Michaels said happily. 'Had a long confab with Rothstein in the DA's office. He says only a set-up that leads to the commission of a crime, a new crime, is entrapment. But our set-up will reveal an old crime, one that's already been committed. We aren't going to lead Zoff into doing anything illegal—*paying* blackmail isn't a crime. So we're okay there.'

Ivan had one last objection. 'All right, so we're covered on the entrapment angle. But it's been nearly two months now since Richard Ormsby was killed. Why'd I wait so long to start my squeeze?'

'You had to find out who the man with the gun was first,' I said. 'What you saw at the Ormsby shooting was a face, an unfamiliar face with no name attached to it. But you're good at remembering faces. So you started working backwards from Richard Ormsby. He led you to Fiona

184

Benedict, who led you to Rudy Benedict, who led you to the wonderful world of television and all the magic people in it—especially those gathered under the Nathan Pinking umbrella. So one by one you started checking them out until you came to the face behind the stairwell door. Then you had your man.'

'Yeah.' Ivan frowned. 'An eyewitness who didn't come forward at the time. I suppose it's possible. But will Zoff buy it?'

'He can't afford not to,' Captain Michaels said shortly. 'If he killed Ormsby, he'll at least agree to a meeting.'

Ivan accepted his fate with a big sigh. 'Okay. If he tells me to go to hell, we won't be any worse off than we are now.'

I said, 'And if he doesn't tell you to go to hell, then we can wrap this thing up and go home and *forget* about it. Thank God.'

The men grunted agreement.

CHAPTER 18

KELLY INGRAM

It was that pink dress that finally did it. I went for a costume fitting and they gave me this clingy *pink* thing to wear and I hit the ceiling.

I detest pink. I loathe pink. I hate it so much I embarrass myself, wasting a good strong emotion like hatred on a *color*. The costumers were a brother-sister team called Lesley, they both answered to the same name, no fooling. When we first started *LeFever* I'd made it clear I didn't want to wear pink, ever, and Nathan Pinking (*Pink*ing) had backed me up. But now we had a new producer and Lesley was or were testing the waters, so to speak, indulging in a little muscle-flexing, just what I needed.

'Look,' I told them, 'I'm not going to start off this way.

We both know the game you're playing, and I'm just not going to go along. When you have something I can wear, call me. I'm not even going to try this pink thing on.'

'But Kellylove,' one word, 'it's perfect for you,' Lesley-male cooed. 'It's so y—'

'Call me when you have something I can wear,' I repeated and walked away. I heard him muttering to his sister but the only words I could make out were *prima donna*.

Things had not been going at all well. Nathan Pinking was a blackmailer and a rat and a skunk, but he was also a good organizer. Nathan had delegated a lot of his responsibility, but Leonard Zoff was trying to handle most of the detail work himself and it was too much for him. Once we got rolling he'd probably get the hang of it a little better, but right now things were a bit rough. We were getting ready to start taping the new season of *LeFever*, and the very first script gave me a sour picture of what I had to look forward to. I had only three scenes, and I was to play all three of them in a horizontal position. On a bed, on a towel beside a pool, and on a sofa. I'd convinced Leonard the sofa scene could be just as suggestive if I played it sitting up, but now I had that damned pink dress of Lesley's to worry about.

But what was really bothering me was my new series. The pilot movie was going to show in December; its title was *On Call*—subtle, huh? If NBC bought it, they were going to want the series to keep on with the kind of thing the movie showed. Nathan Pinking had used the *LeFever* writers, and those guys didn't strain themselves any. They'd written the same kind of story they wrote for *LeFever*, except they just switched the male and female roles—as if a woman were just some sort of reverse man. *I* had the adventures, and they'd hired some good-looking actor to gaze adoringly at *me* while I was involved in all those preposterous goings-on. They'd gone at the whole thing wrong, just taking the easy way. It was my series and I wanted it to be right—but I hadn't really been able to make Leonard understand that.

I'd bugged him mercilessly until he showed me the story treatments Nathan Pinking had assembled; Leonard hadn't yet decided which ones to commission writers to turn into shooting scripts. One of them contained a flashback sequence that was supposed to show me just entering college.

'You get to be a student, darling,' Leonard had said loudly. 'Won't that be fun? Pot and protest and free love — just the thing to win the college crowd. Maybe even a classroom scene. Don't you worry none, Kel, you can still pass for eighteen, nineteen, whatever the shit it is. We won't hafta do any close-ups — you just squeeze that fabulous butt of yours into a pair of tight jeans and we got it made.'

Suddenly I'd had enough. I had played the game; I'd let my thirtieth birthday pass without mention. My reason was financial as well as personal: I belonged to a profession where youth was money in the bank. In television, a woman depreciates in value as she grows older, like a car. Men don't; just the women. So maybe there was something wrong with the profession itself, if it made you feel your right and proper age was something to be ashamed of. And there was Leonard Zoff, glibly assuming I'd be delighted at the chance to play a teenager again.

'I'm thirty years old, Leonard,' I said. 'My schoolgirl days are over. I think we can find a better story than this one, don't you?'

He'd argued a little, out of principle; I don't think he really cared one way or the other. But I'd made up my mind right then, I was through pretending to be younger than I was.

That was earlier in the week. But from star of my own (to be) series I'd quickly been bumped back down to mere appurtenance, appendage, accessory, attachment, adjunct to the hero, I did look that one up. My *LeFever* character was more a piece-of-tail role than ever, and the vibes I got from Leonard were telling me my new series would be just more of the same. *Nothing* was right. In

187

short, I was spoiling for a fight. I had to have it out with Leonard.

So on pink-dress day I went charging into his outer office, breathing fire (I hoped). Mimsy looked up from her desk, not at all alarmed. 'Is he in?' I growled in my best tough-broad voice.

'He's out looking over location sites,' she purred at me. 'Anything I can do?'

'Damn it, Mimsy, don't be so friendly—can't you see I'm mad?'

'And you want to stay mad,' she nodded understandingly. 'Would it help to yell at me a little?'

'Naw,' I said, starting to cool down. 'Leonard's got to talk to Lesley, for starters. Did he tell you where he was going?'

Mimsy's face took on tragic overtones that would have done Medea proud. 'Sorry—he didn't. I asked him three times before he left, but he went out without telling me.'

'Did he take his limo?'

She caught on immediately. 'Of course—all I have to do is call the driver.' She punched out a number on the phone.

Leonard never drove himself anywhere. He claimed New York traffic was the one thing in life he was truly afraid of. Mimsy spoke briefly into the phone and then hung up.

'Well?'

'The driver is on his way back to the garage. He said Mr. Zoff got out at the Eastside Airlines Terminal and told him he wouldn't be needing the car any more today.'

'Eastside Terminal? He's not leaving town, is he?'

'No—and I don't think he's meeting anyone. He must just be looking for a shooting site.'

One sure way to find out. I went down to the street and stopped a taxi. Rain was threatening and I didn't have an umbrella, but I didn't want to take the time to go back and get one. Leonard Zoff wasn't going to get away from *me*, he wasn't.

CHAPTER 19

MARIAN LARCH

'Again,' Captain Michaels sniffled. He was catching a cold and his eyes were red and watery.

Ivan cleared his throat. 'At the appointed time I proceed to the designated rendezvous point—'

'Jesus, Malecki, you're not in training class, talk English.' The Captain's cold was making him cranky.

Ivan managed to keep a straight face and started over. 'At five minutes to eleven I go into the Eastside Airlines Terminal. I wait until the last stragglers and latecomers have gotten on the airport buses departing at eleven. Then I approach Zoff.'

Two plainclothes officers would already be inside, one of them behind the counter.

'I tell Zoff I'm the one he's waiting for,' Ivan went on. 'If he wants a name, I tell him Ivan. If he wants to go someplace else to talk, I tell him absolutely not.'

We'd picked the Eastside Terminal because first of all it had to be a public place. No blackmailer who intended to go on living would agree to a private meeting with his victim. The Eastside Terminal had people coming and going, but there were never huge crowds of people there who stayed put for any length of time.

'What if he insists?' I asked Ivan. 'What if he says he won't talk to you in a place where there's a chance you'll be overheard?'

'Then I remind him he's in no position to insist on anything. I tell him my partner is watching from outside, and if Zoff has brought a weapon to force me to go with him, my partner calls the police the minute she sees us walk out the door.'

The 'partner' had been Ivan's idea. He'd thrown himself into the role with gusto, trying to think the way a

189

blackmailer would think—a Method cop. He said the only sure way a blackmailer had of protecting himself was to convince the victim that if anything happened to him, the blackmailer, the victim's guilty secret would immediately be revealed to the world. And the best way of doing that, Ivan said, was not the conventional letter-with-a-lawyer gambit; that's what Nathan Pinking had done and Ted Cameron was already figuring a way around that when things came to a head. No, the best way was to produce a partner, one whose existence was established beyond all shadow of a doubt but whose identity was withheld from the mark.

Since the initial contact was to be made by telephone, we decided the caller should be a woman. Otherwise Zoff might think he was dealing with one man pretending to be two, disguising his voice over the phone. We had a policewoman from Narcotics make the call; Zoff might have recognized my voice. She'd told him she certainly was glad to get hold of him, because she'd spent the *longest* time trying to track him down—ever since the day Richard Ormsby had been killed, in fact.

Zoff had bluffed at first, pretending not to know what she was talking about. Stalling for time. *But he had agreed to a meeting.* An innocent man would have told her to stop bothering him or *he* would call the cops. But Leonard Zoff had instead asked her what she wanted. She'd named the time and place for the meeting, and told him to bring ten thousand dollars with him. Then she had informed him she herself would not be there, that all their dealings would be done through an intermediary, her partner. *All* their dealings, she'd stressed. We wanted Zoff to start thinking this was no one-time payoff, that he was on the hook for good. Push him a little.

Ivan, the ostensible intermediary, would be wired as well as armed. Captain Michaels and I would be in an unmarked car around the corner on Thirty-eighth Street, listening to every word that was said. We were there strictly as back-up. If everything went according to plan, we wouldn't move in until the money had actually changed hands. Ivan would make the arrest; the two police officers planted inside would witness the payoff and provide assistance if needed.

Captain Michaels took out a handkerchief and blew his nose. 'Then what?'

Ivan said, 'Then I ask him for the ten thousand. I tell him my partner and I aren't greedy, we just want enough to live on comfortably.'

'And if he asks when's the next payment?'

'I tell him I'll let him know. But I don't bring it up if he doesn't.'

I said, 'What if he doesn't hand over the money right away and tries to bluff it out instead? What if he says it's only your partner's word against his?'

'I say I'll tell the police I was also present at the Ormsby shooting—that makes *two* eyewitnesses, exactly what the law requires for a positive identification. I'll tell Zoff our story will be that at the time we didn't want to get involved, we didn't know who the killer was anyway. But now that we do know—it's begun to bother us, we feel we should step forward and do our duty, all that stuff. I'll tell him the cops might not believe our reason for keeping quiet so long, but they're sure as hell going to be mighty polite to two people who can ID a killer for them.'

'And if he asks who your partner is?'

'I laugh in his face.'

'If he doesn't bring the money at all?' Captain Michaels coughed.

'I say I'll give him one more chance. Now that he knows we're serious, he either produces the money or he goes to jail.'

'New time and place for the payoff?'

'Noon tomorrow. The fountain at Lincoln Center.'

'What if he claims he can't get his hands on ten thousand in twenty-four hours?'

'I laugh in his face again. Then I quote the balance as of this morning in his Chase Manhattan account.'

'That should rattle him a little,' Captain Michaels grinned. 'Have we thought of everything?' Pause. 'Yeah, I think so. Okay—any questions?'

I couldn't think of any. Ivan shook his head.

'All right then, let's go,' the Captain said. 'If we're lucky we can wrap this up before the weather breaks.'

CHAPTER 20

KELLY INGRAM

It was almost eleven o'clock when the taxi let me out at the Eastside Airlines Terminal. The rain was still holding off, thank goodness. The terminal isn't very large; I pushed the door open and spotted Leonard Zoff right off. He was standing back from the counter, a raincoat over his arm, scanning the faces of the other people there—maybe Mimsy was wrong, maybe he was meeting someone after all. He seemed nervous. I walked up and planted myself in front of him.

He was clearly underjoyed to see me. First he gave a little start, then his features settled into a kind of hound-dog sadness. 'It's you,' he said dully.

I agreed it was. 'Leonard, we've got to talk.'

He nodded. 'But not here. Too public.'

Wasn't he waiting for someone? I looked around. 'Don't you want—'

'No, no, this is no good,' he muttered, suddenly in a great hurry to get out of there. He grabbed my elbow and steered me out the door. 'There's a park about a block from here—if we don't get rained on.'

But we never got there. Two young couples, two *very* young couples (should have been in school) recognized me and proceeded to raise a minor fuss, how nice. I was quite willing to stop for a moment and play the famous television star graciously acknowledging her admiring public, but Leonard had me bundled into a taxi before I quite knew what was happening. He seemed angry for some reason.

He gave the driver the name of a pseudo-Victorian tavern uptown. When we got there, Leonard tossed his raincoat on to the seat of the booth and gestured impatiently to the waiter. It wasn't eleven-thirty yet, but he ordered himself a liquid lunch. I asked for coffee.

When he'd had his first long swallow, he seemed to brace himself. 'All right, spell it out.'

I said, 'First of all, Leonard, we need a basic understanding about where we're going from here. Then we can work out the details as we go along.'

He nodded wearily. 'Yeah, the details. I can hardly wait. Starting with the money, no doubt.'

The budget, he meant. 'Well, there's always room for more money. But I meant other things—the *kind* of show we're going to be turning out, primarily.'

His face grew longer and sadder than ever. 'I was afraid of that. You and your partner won't settle for anything less than total control, will you?'

'My partner?'

'I go through all that shit and come this far only to have a couple of dumb broads take it all away from me, is that it? Who's your partner, Kelly?'

I was stunned. 'Are you actually calling me a *dumb broad*?'

'Yeah, I gotta be careful what I call you now, don't I?' he sneered. Then he seemed to think better of it and shook his head and said, 'Don't mind me, darling, I'm a bit shook, y'understand. This is the last thing in the world I expected. I don't *deserve* this. Kelly—I'm not like Nathan Shithead, I don't enjoy hurting people.'

What on earth? 'I know that, Leonard. I never thought you did.'

'But it didn't stop you, did it? You're just as grabby as all the rest of them. You see an opportunity, you don't give a shit who it is you walk over.'

I was beginning to get mad. 'Now look, Leonard, there's something you better understand right now. You simply cannot talk to me any way you please. From now on you will speak to me with courtesy and respect or you

193

will not speak to me at all.' Since I had absolutely no way whatsoever of backing up that ultimatum, I was pleasantly surprised to see him pale. 'Do you understand me?'

'I understand,' he whispered.

Now *that* got to me. The only time in my life I'd ever before heard Leonard Zoff whisper was when he had laryngitis. Something was greatly out of whack. 'Are you all right?' I asked him. 'Do you feel up to talking now?'

'I'm all right—let's get it settled.' He waved a hand dismissively. 'It's just that *you* are about the last person I'd have thought . . . Kelly, don't you understand? I did it for you as much as for me. Nathan Shithead would have ruined you, he'd have milked you for all he could get for three, four more years and then *phlooey!* Out in the garbage with Kelly baby. He don't care what happens to nobody. Me, I wouldn't do that to you. I'da nursed you along, paced things right so it would go on as long as you wanted it to go on. I had big plans for you, Kelly!'

This was definitely turning into one of the weirdest conversations I'd ever had. 'What do you mean *had*, Leonard? You're still going to do all those wonderful things for me.'

'Not if I can't call the shots. How can I? You breathin' down my neck all the time?'

'Breathing down—Leonard, you don't even know what I want yet!'

'Oh, I have a fair idea! Unless you've changed your mind,' he said, his voice dripping sarcasm. 'Maybe you don't want the money now?'

I slapped at the table in frustration. 'I *always* want money, Leonard—who doesn't? I keep telling you that's not the main thing, but since that's what seems to be bothering you—all right, start with money. I don't want my new series to be the quickie, shoddy thing *LeFever* is. And that takes money. Money for good scripts, money for enough time to do the job right—'

'And money for Kelly?' His lip raised in a sneer.

'Why not?' I said hotly. He'd been sneering at me ever

since we came in. 'Leonard, face it—you're just going to have to shell out. And you might as well start right now.'

He stared at me with open contempt on his face. Then he reached to his inside jacket pocket and pulled out an envelope that he dropped on the table. 'Count it if you want. It's all there.'

Now what? With a sigh I opened the envelope and counted ten one-thousand dollar bills inside. It was an ordinary white envelope, about nine inches wide, no imprinting. I ran the gummed flap across my tongue and sealed the envelope. I sat without speaking for a moment, just holding it in my hand. 'Leonard. I am sitting here quietly, making no fuss, trying to understand why you just handed me *ten thousand dollars*.'

'Keep your voice down,' he muttered. 'Because that's how much your partner said bring, that's why. Don't ask for more because I don't have it.'

'There's that word *partner* again. What partner, Leonard? What are you talking about?'

He was angry. 'What are you trying to pull? Your unidentified sweet-voiced friend on the phone, the one who set up our meeting in the Eastside Terminal. Who'd you think?'

'I still don't know what you're talking about. What meeting? We didn't have a date to meet in the Terminal.'

You know how that comes-the-dawn looks spreads *so-o-o-o* slowly over somebody's face? Well, that's what happened to Leonard just then. At least *he* understood something; I was still floundering. Abruptly he shook his head. 'No, wait a minute—you didn't just happen to run into me there. You came looking for me, don't tell me you didn't.'

'I'm not telling you I didn't.'

'So how'd you know where I was?'

'Mimsy called your driver. He said he let you out at the Eastside Terminal.'

'Oh my God,' he said slowly. 'My God. That simple. It *wasn't* you. I shoulda known it wouldn't be you.' He gave himself a sort of little shake and reached out and took the envelope back from me. 'This was a mistake, Kelly. I thought—well, never mind what I thought. The whole thing was a mistake. Just forget about it, will you?'

But I'd had enough time for a few things to filter through. 'The symptoms were familiar enough, God knows; I'd seen them once before. 'You said the person on the phone who set up the meeting was "unidentified"—right? Does that mean just anybody can call you up and tell you to take ten thousand dollars to the Eastside Terminal and you'll do it? I never knew you were that free and easy with your money.'

'I said forget it, Kelly.'

'You're being blackmailed, aren't you, Leonard?' I asked as gently as I could.

He didn't answer; a tic had developed under his left eye.

'Don't pay,' I urged him. 'I've seen what it can do to a man. Whatever it is your blackmailer has on you, it can't be worse than what's going to happen to you once you give in and start paying. Don't pay.'

He laughed humorlessly and put the envelope back in his pocket. 'Gee, thanks for the swell advice, Kelly.' The tic grew stronger.

'Don't be so quick to dismiss it. You don't know what you're letting yourself in for. Besides, the only blackmail victim I've ever known turned out to be a killer, and you certainly haven't done anything like that.' Which of course started me wondering what he *had* done. *I did it as much for you as for me,* he said. What on earth could that be?

Leonard leaned forward and said in that strange new whispery voice of his, 'I have this terrible feeling about you, darling. I'm afraid you're turning into a problem.'

'Because I made you miss your, er, appointment? You don't know who your blackmailer is, do you? You thought it was me. I. How could you, Leonard? Me, a blackmailer?'

'Yes,' he said heavily. 'It was a bad mistake.'

'Are you worried about what he'll do? Or she. They

were probably there all the time and saw what happened. You'll hear from them again.'

'No doubt.' The tic under his eye seemed to be slowing down.

I did it as much for you as for me. What blackmail-inviting thing could he have done that would have benefited both of us? The only thing that had happened lately that was sheer good news for Leonard was Nathan Pinking's getting himself arrested. From that one event all of Leonard's subsequent blessings flowed. And Leonard was so convinced Nathan Pinking would have ruined my career that his take-over of Nathan's business would have been good for me too, to his way of thinking. (And he may have been right.)

But Leonard didn't have anything to do with Nathan's arrest. What did he *do* that was as much for me as for himself? Nathan was arrested because that horrible Fiona Benedict had found some pictures in Rudy's papers that led Marian Larch to Ted, and Ted blew the whistle on Nathan. None of it would have happened without those photographs Rudy's mother found. And she wouldn't have found them, she would still be sitting here in New York waiting for her trial if somebody hadn't come along and . . . oh. *Oh.*

Oh, goodnessgracioussakesalivemercyme*oh.*

That was it. That was what he'd done. That had to be it. 'You killed Richard Ormsby,' I said stupidly, my own voice little more than a whisper.

Leonard gave a little nod — not in confirmation of what I'd just accused him of, it was more like a little I-was-right nod to himself. As if he'd known all along I'd get there eventually if he just waited long enough.

I put both hands on the table, palms down, helping to steady the room which had suddenly begun to move in a seasick-making kind of way. If he hadn't mistaken me for the blackmailer . . . I would never have . . . and he actually . . . 'And you had the gall to say you did it as much for me as for yourself! Leonard, have you lost your mind?'

'It was *entirely* for you, you stupid bitch!' he hissed. 'You think I was just gonna stand there and let Nathan Shithead take you away from me? You could have been a big star, Kelly. A *great* star.'

I didn't much like that *could have been*. 'Don't you go blaming me, you bastard,' I hissed back. 'You killed one man so you could take another man's business away from him and now you're telling me it was all for *me*? It was all for Leonard Zoff, that's who it was for! Stop kidding yourself.'

'Look under the table.'

'What?'

'Under the table, look under the table.' He jerked his head angrily.

So I looked under the table. What I saw was a gun in Leonard's hand, pointing at me. A gun? Pointing at me?

A *gun*. Pointing at *me*.

I sat back up and said the first thing that came into my head. 'All right, all right, I'll *wear* the pink dress!'

He stared at me. 'Darling, sometimes you just don't make good sense. Now listen. This is what we're going to do. Keep your hands on the table where I can see them—that's right. Now I'm going to signal the waiter. When he gets here, you are going to pay the bill. You got money? Good. Then we're going to get up and walk out of here and get in a cab.'

'And nobody will even notice that you're holding a gun on me?'

'It'll be under my raincoat—nobody'll see it.'

I tried to put a brave face on it. 'What are you going to do if I make a break for it, Leonard? Shoot me in front of all these people?'

'Richard Ormsby was surrounded by a whole buncha people,' he said pointedly.

Oh yeah. I forgot about that.

So we did it the way he said. The waiter brought the bill, and I paid while Leonard *kept me covered* under the table, good heavens. I left a tip on the little tray that was twice the amount of the bill, hoping to catch the waiter's attention. He didn't even deign to look at me.

'Don't try anything,' Leonard warned me as we got up to leave.

My problem was I couldn't convince myself I was in real danger. Sure, I understood the man was a murderer and I was a threat to his safety. But balanced against that was the fact that this was *Leonard*. I was having trouble believing Leonard would hurt me. Not because I was a magic princess that bad things never happened to, but because I represented a long-term investment that was just beginning to pay off. Besides, I'd always looked on Leonard as something of a clown; it was hard recasting him as a killer. He was just Leonard, the man who'd been guiding my career for years. The man whose professional advice I'd followed to pretty good results. The man who . . . had sent me toilet paper as a way of telling me what he really thought of me. Ah yes, *that* man.

The rain had started while we were inside and it was coming down hard now. Which meant, of course, there wasn't a taxi to be had. There was no canopy or overhang to stand under and I didn't have an umbrella, so I was soaked to the skin within seconds. I must have looked ridiculous, standing there on the curb sopping wet. But I couldn't have looked as silly as Leonard, who was equally wet while carrying a perfectly good raincoat over his right arm and hand, his gun hand, oh dear.

Finally a cab stopped. The driver glared at us as we climbed in; he'd have to wipe the seat off. I was surprised to hear Leonard give the address of the *LeFever* soundstage and offices. A weight lifted: that place was just crawling with people.

We were separated from the driver by one of those thick plastic shields; he wouldn't hear us if we talked low. 'Leonard,' I whispered, 'what are you going to do?'

'Don't talk.'

'You aren't really going to shoot me, are you?'

'*Quiet*,' he said.

'I'm whispering,' I whispered. 'Are you really going to *shoot* me?' I decided to change the emphasis. 'Are you really going to shoot *me*? It isn't necessary, you know. If my staying alive depends on keeping my mouth shut, you really think I'm going to talk?'

'Darling, you know I can't risk that.'

'What risk? I will gladly become your *accomplice* before I'll do anything to get myself hurt. Besides, I can't prove a thing—Leonard, you know I can't prove anything. You're safe.'

'You don't understand. I can't even afford the accusation—you could start the police investigating me just by hollering.' He looked at me with something like regret on his face. 'Oh Kelly, Kelly! Where'm I gonna find another face and bod like yours? Why didn't you just mind your own business?'

I'd thought I was minding my own business. 'I'll say it again. I'll never do anything to get myself hurt. Come on, Leonard—do I strike you as the suicidal type?'

He didn't say anything to that, so I pressed my advantage. 'Leonard, I can help you pay off these blackmailers if that's the way you're determined to handle it. I won't say a word to anyone, I certainly won't talk to the police. I'll even stop spleaking to Marian Larch if that'll make you feel better.'

'Spleaking?'

'Spleaking, speaking, you know what I mean.' Was I nervous? 'Leonard—how about it? A kind of partnership?'

'Darling, we both know the minute I let you out of my sight, you'd go screaming to that homely police detective friend of yours.'

'Look in the mirror, buster,' I snapped, angry for the wrong reason. He just laughed. I think he was beginning to enjoy the situation, once he'd made up his mind I had to go.

Speaking of mirrors. I half-turned my back to him and started mugging, I mean I was making these *terrible* faces, hoping the driver would see me in the rear-view mirror. But no, *that* one kept his eyes on the oncoming traffic. He didn't care what was going on in the back seat.

Just as we got out of the cab Leonard pressed the gun into my side and said, low, 'Remember, Kelly, I'll shoot you in front of a witness if I have to. Then I'll shoot the witness.'

So we ran through the rain into the building and I said *hello-isn't-this-awful-yes-we-got-caught-in-it* to the guy who ran the newsstand in the small lobby. I turned automatically toward the elevators but Leonard stopped me.

'Back here,' he said.

The offices and some of the workrooms were upstairs, but the soundstage holding the *LeFever* sets was on the ground level. It suddenly hit me what he was planning and *then* I believed I was in danger. I had to know the place before it became real.

The *LeFever* sets had been repaired and repainted and refurbished and re-whatever else they needed, and Mimsy had distributed a memo (signed by Leonard F. Zoff) threatening everything short of dismemberment to anyone foolhardy enough to venture on to the sets before shooting actually started. That was to be the following Monday. This was Thursday, naturally; disasters always come on Thursdays. He could shoot me and leave me on the set and nobody would find me for four days. Didn't have to worry about an alibi that way, I guess.

My body would be lying there for four days. Four whole days.

'Leonard,' I said, 'I'll *smell*.'

'What?'

'You leave me lying on the set until Monday, I'm going to stink to high heaven by the time they find me.'

He stopped walking and looked at me with a kind of awe. 'Kelly, I don't know of another single person who'd think of that at a time like this.'

'Hell, lots of people would. You'd think of it yourself. Come on, Leonard—you wouldn't want to be found like that, you know you wouldn't. Figure out some other way.'

He just shook his head in amazement and gestured me to go on. He unlocked the outside door to the soundstage and switched on the work lights. These gave barely enough illumination to keep you from tripping over things, and not always then. I shivered; we were both still dripping wet. Leonard put a hand on my shoulder to stop me while he thought about where he wanted to go.

Karate? Kung fu? Aikido? I didn't know any of that stuff. And I couldn't just out-muscle him. *And* I hadn't had any notable success in talking him into or out of anything. About the only thing left I could think of was divine intervention. A lightning bolt to burn him up while missing me altogether. The earth opening up and swallowing him while miraculously leaving me untouched. Any old ordinary Act of God would do. The more scared I am, the weaker the joke.

LeFever had only four permanent sets—LeFever's office, his apartment, a room in a police precinct station, and a plain corridor that changed its fictional location every week. In addition, one or two temporary sets might be needed; one for a gym had been built for the first episode. All the sets were crowded close together; space was at a premium. Leonard took me to the new gym set—because it was the farthest from the outside door?

Speaking of which—it opened! We both heard it; Leonard slapped his free hand over my mouth and pulled me down to the floor. We cowered there in the shadow and listened to a voice say, 'Sumby leffa work lights awn.'

I'd never heard anything so lovely in my life. It was wonderful beautiful terrific Nick Quinlan, and when a feminine murmur answered him, I knew what he was doing there. Showing her the *LeFever* sets, well, that was the excuse. Nick knew the sets would be deserted.

'This here's LeFever's bedroom,' he said.

Feminine murmur.

I felt Leonard tense. If Nick and his lady lingered on the bedroom set, Leonard and I would stay where we were. But if he showed her around the rest of the soundstage, we'd have to move. I was on my knees on the floor with Leonard holding me. I felt around on the floor with my left hand and sure enough it was wet, the floor I

202

mean. Our dripping clothes had made a little puddle there. If Nick turned more lights on and came through and saw the wet floor then maybe—wait, hold it. That meant, first, Nick would have to *notice* the water. Then second, he'd have to *realize* it had no business being there. Then third, he'd have to *investigate*. Forget it.

Nobody was going to come riding to the rescue. If I got out of this, I was going to have to do it myself.

Male and female laughter mingled; they were staying in the bedroom. I'd never have another chance like this one—I was going to have to let them know I was there. I couldn't holler because Leonard's big hand was still covering my mouth, but I could struggle and kick out with my feet and make *some* noise.

So I did. In fact, I almost got away because I caught Leonard by surprise. I kept hitting backwards with my one free elbow and I kicked and squirmed and banged my feet against the floor and made as much racket as I could. Leonard stopped me by turning me over on my front on the floor and laying or lying on top of me, it felt like both. His hand never left my mouth.

'Hey, whazzat?' Nick said from the bedroom set. 'Jeer sumpin?'

Feminine murmur.

'Sumby's here. Lezgo.'

Rustle of clothing, a piece of furniture scraping on the floor, departing footsteps, silence.

Leonard was laughing as he let me up.

CHAPTER 21

MARIAN LARCH

'Judith H. Crist!' Captain Michaels yelled into my ear as Kelly Ingram pushed open the door to the Eastside Airlines Terminal. 'What the hell is *she* doing here?'

The radio speaker attached to the tape recorder on the

car seat between us came to life at about the same time. 'Godalmighty, Kelly Ingram just walked in,' came Ivan's voice. 'What do I do now?' A sign of how rattled he was—Ivan could send but not receive.

'Want me to go take a look?' I said.

'Hell, no,' the Captain barked, his cold making him hoarse. 'Stay put, Ivan'll keep us informed.'

'They're standing there talking to each other,' Ivan's voice said. 'He was surprised to see her but she wasn't surprised to see him—it was like she was looking for him. Captain, I hope you're thinking of something fast because people are starting to look at me funny for talking to my shirt.'

I glanced at Michaels. His face was drawn into a scowl, giving no sign he'd heard. We waited.

'Captain, they're leaving,' Ivan said. 'You know what I think? I think he thinks Kelly's the blackmailer.'

'Damn, damn, *damn*,' Captain Michaels muttered. 'Start the car.'

I started the car. Kelly and Leonard Zoff came out together—but almost immediately were stopped by some kids wanting Kelly's autograph. While that was going on, Ivan slipped out the Terminal door and climbed into the back seat of the car. Up ahead, Zoff had flagged a taxi and he and Kelly were getting in.

'What about the plants?' I asked. The police officers inside the Eastside Terminal building.

'Leave 'em,' Captain Michaels growled. I pulled into the line of traffic behind the taxi.

The whole set-up was shot to hell, all because Kelly Ingram had put in an unscheduled appearance. The situation just might be salvageable—we could try to reschedule for the next day. That wasn't what was worrying me. What was worrying me was the thought of Kelly in the taxi with Leonard Zoff in those circumstances. 'Ivan, you really think Zoff believes she's his blackmailer?'

'Looked that way to me. Remember, we just said "partner" when we called him—we didn't say whether it

204

was a man or a woman.'

Captain Michaels sneezed.

'So what do we do, Captain?' Ivan wanted to know. 'Just tail 'em, make sure she's safe?'

'Let's see where they go first,' Michaels said.

They went to a chi-chi bar on East Seventy-first. I pulled into a no-parking zone and immediately had a fat man in an apron yelling at me until I flashed my badge.

Ivan did a quick check inside the bar. 'There's no other entrance,' he said, climbing back in the car. 'And there's no good place inside for me to stand and watch. They might see me.'

So we sat there without talking for a long time, watching. Finally I said, 'If they separate when they come out, then we're okay—we can go ahead and set up another meet tomorrow. But if they stay together, we just might have a problem.'

'How do you figure?'

'Well, obviously they're in there clearing the air—Zoff can't go on thinking she's a blackmailer much longer. It all depends on whether he gives himself away before she does. If he tips her off that he's being blackmailed and then finds out she isn't involved, well, then Kelly becomes a problem. Let's see what they do when they come out—whether they stay together or not.'

'Mm, maybe. Everything could be okay and they'll just go on back to work together.'

'We ought to be able to tell by the way Kelly carries herself. Whether she's willing or unwilling.'

It started to rain, those heavy gray sheets of water it's impossible to see through. After a few minutes it slacked off into a steady, heavy downpour. The streets had virtually emptied of people. We waited.

Then Kelly Ingram and Leonard Zoff came out and stood in the pouring rain, looking for a taxi.

Captain Michaels sniffled a question.

'Unwilling,' I said.

We all three spotted the raincoat at the same time—the raincoat that was keeping Leonard Zoff's right hand dry while the rest of him got soaking wet. 'Jesus, he's got a gun on her,' Ivan said unnecessarily. I turned on the ignition.

They finally got a taxi—which took them straight to the *LeFever* soundstage on West Fifty-fourth. Ivan did not repeat his suggestion that they might just be going back to work; Zoff's raincoat had taken care of that.

The taxi double-parked and let them out; they both ran for the building entrance, though I didn't see how they could get any wetter than they already were. There wasn't even a no-parking zone for me to pull into this time, so I stopped only long enough to let the two men out. I drove into an alley and left the car there. I made my own dash for the building entrance; the rain was still coming down, hard.

Inside, the lobby was empty except for a man behind a newsstand counter. I hesitated, not knowing which way to turn.

'If you're looking for a fat man and a skinny man who just came running in here,' the newsstand man said, 'they went thataway.' He jerked his thumb past his right ear.

I called out my thanks and took off in the direction he'd indicated. Towards the soundstage where the sets were, not the elevators.

Captain Michaels was leaning on one hand against the soundstage door, catching his breath. ''S locked,' he panted, 'Malecki's gone for a key. Tell me what's inside.'

Briefly I described the layout of the sets. 'It's a lot smaller than it sounds,' I said. 'They don't waste an inch of space. How do you know they're in there?'

'Guy at the newsstand.'

Ivan came back with the building supervisor, who was grumbling. 'Second time I had to do this. What's going on in there?'

'Second time?' Captain Michaels said. 'Who'd you let in before—a man and a woman?'

'Yeah, thass right.'

'Was the woman Kelly Ingram?' I asked him. 'Do you know her?'

'Sure I know her, but it wasn't her. It was some lady friend of his.'

'Of whose?'

'Why, Mr. Quinlan's, acourse. Who we talking about?' He unlocked the door.

Nick Quinlan? Ivan, the Captain, and I all exchanged blank looks—and decided to leave it for later.

'Leonard Zoff—does he have a key to this door?' Captain Michaels asked.

'Sure—he's paying the rent now, ain't he?'

Captain Michaels shooed the building supervisor away. 'We separate once we're inside,' he said. 'And we do it quiet. They could be anywhere.'

One thing I hadn't counted on was the dimness of the light. I crouched to the right of the door until my eyes had time to adjust. I couldn't hear a thing. Then I started to edge my way around the first set, feeling with my foot for the camera cables I remembered as being all over the floor. The way was relatively clear, though. The cables wouldn't be underfoot until next week, probably, not until they started shooting.

I stopped to listen. Captain Michaels and Ivan were both off to my left, neither one of them making a sound. Ivan, you expected to be quiet; but Michaels always surprised me, a big man like that moving like a cat. I'd no sooner thought that than I heard a slight scraping sound. But it came from directly ahead, not from my left. I eased my gun out of my shoulder bag.

I heard another sound from the same place, close, this time like someone bumping into something. If I remembered right, I was right behind the set of the bedroom of LeFever's apartment. I felt my way along to the last flat of the wall. Then I took a big breath, swung around the flat on to the set, went into my crouch, yelled: 'Hold it right there!'—and found myself pointing my gun at a very startled Kelly Ingram.

Who said, peevishly, 'Hold *what* right *where?* For heaven's sake, Marian, put that thing down and stand up! You look ridiculous.'

Slowly I lowered my gun and stood up straight. Kelly, for some reason, was wearing a bedsheet. 'Why,' I asked, 'are you wearing a bedsheet?'

'My clothes are soaked—I'm just trying to get dry. Oh, by the way—it was Leonard Zoff who killed Richard Ormsby. I've got him locked in a closet over there.'

Oh, by the way. Wasn't that overdoing it a bit?

At that moment Captain Michaels and Ivan Malecki erupted around the other end of the set. They too went into a crouch and they both yelled 'Freeze!' at exactly the same moment.

'My goodness, you folks do that a lot, don't you?' Kelly said wonderingly. 'And *freeze?!*' She turned to me. 'You really say that?'

'They do,' I said. 'I don't.'

Captain Michaels decided that was a good time to have a sneezing fit. Ivan was still in his crouch, his arms stretched out holding his gun and his eyes flickering back and forth. Finally he looked at me.

'It's secure,' I said. 'She has him locked in a closet.'

'In a closet.' He stood up. 'Where?'

'Over there,' she flapped a hand vaguely. 'Some sort of janitor's closet—mops and buckets and things.'

The Captain was finished sneezing. 'You locked Leonard Zoff in a closet, you say?'

'Well, he was going to kill me! What else could I do?'

There was this utter silence for the longest moment—and then everyone started talking at once. 'You could have run away!' Ivan kept saying. 'You could have called the police! You could have screamed!'

Captain Michaels finally yelled for quiet. He threw up his hands and said, 'Wonderful. Simply wonderful. Hasn't this been just a *super* day? Not one damned thing has gone the way it was supposed to.' He glared at Kelly. '*We* were supposed to catch Leonard Zoff, not you. Has *anything* gone right today? Anything at all? What next?'

Suddenly an unexpected weight dropped across my shoulders, causing my knees to buckle. 'Hiya,' a familiar voice said in my ear. 'Wha'chall doin'?'

I struggled back up to my normal standing position. 'Nothing—we're not doing a thing, Nick,' I said, and wished Kelly Ingram would stop laughing.

CHAPTER 22

KELLY INGRAM

Leonard was laughing as he let me up, laughing and smug and a little excited—and careless.

It happened so fast I can truthfully say I didn't *think* about it; there wasn't time. It was all kind of dumb, really, more accident than anything else. Leonard stood up and he was so busy laughing and being pleased with himself that he didn't pay any particular attention to where he was putting his feet. Where he put them was right in that big puddle our dripping clothes had made—the set we were on was supposed to be a gym so there wasn't any carpet on the floor.

So when Leonard stood up he slipped on the wet place and I was half up and half down and Leonard threw one arm out for balance and held on to me with the other and there wasn't time to think, remember, that's important, and from my half-and-half position I kicked out one leg and caught him right behind the knees and Leonard went down and cracked his head an *awful* thump against the floor.

I mean, it was a dreadful sound, I thought I'd killed him. I'm ashamed to say it, but that thought gave me a moment of absolutely exquisite pleasure. I got over that, though, and started worrying about what next. I poked him in the chest a couple of times and he didn't even moan. I felt his wrist for a pulse and found one, so he was just knocked out and not dead. Tie him up! Gag him! Handcuff him to the radiator! All these silly things ran through my head. I didn't have handcuffs *or* a radiator, I couldn't even see anything to tie him up with—it was only

209

a make-believe gym, remember.

I knew there was a place nearby where the janitor kept his cleaning supplies and went looking for it, not easy to do in that dim light. I found it, and it had an old lock with a key in it that nobody ever used anymore, I bet. But when I went back to get Leonard I found I couldn't drag him, he was too heavy. So I thought about it a minute and ended up *rolling* him to the closet. He'd wake up with quite a few bumps and bruises from *that* little journey, heh heh heh. The closet was crowded with buckets and things, and when I got Leonard pushed in his head was turned at what looked like a very uncomfortable angle. He'd have a *terribly* stiff neck when he came to. I hoped.

But what if he woke up with some sort of serious injury? Oh wow, guess who'd be in trouble for that! I remember reading about some mugger who was suing because his victim had fought back and permanently damaged some part of his body, the mugger's body, I don't remember what part. What did the law expect me to do when I came up against somebody who wanted to kill me—scream, faint? I decided I'd better tell the police Leonard just slipped and fell. And he did—that was the truth. I just helped him along a little.

I was shivering—from cold, wet, fear, probably all three. The source of the fear was safely locked away, so now I could do something about the cold and the wet. There were no towels in that make-believe gym, I had to find something else. The sheets on LeFever's bed. I'd just gotten my clothes off and wrapped myself up in a sheet when Marian Larch came flying around the corner of the set and scared me out of my wits all over again.

They'd been following all the time, Marian and Ivan Malecki and Captain Michaels. It was the *police* who were Leonard's blackmailers, of all things, and they'd set something up at the Eastside Terminal that I'd spoiled by waltzing in on, at, around, the middle of, whatever, *hate* sentences like that. But when they all came roaring in to save me and I told them I had Leonard locked in a closet, they didn't exactly act as grateful as I thought they should. Ivan Malecki's eyes sort of glazed over and he stood there like a disconnected robot. Marian and Captain Michaels exchanged a quick glance and then looked away. Marian studied the ceiling while the Captain inspected the floor. Then they turned their backs to each other and stared off in opposite directions for a while. Then they looked at each other again—and suddenly everybody started yelling at *me*.

It was easy for Ivan to say I should have done this, that, the other. He wasn't there, he didn't know what it was like. Good thing I didn't tell them I had assisted Leonard in his fall, then they would *really* have let me have it. Nothing I tried on my own had worked—so when Leonard hits the floor with his head I'm just going to walk away and *leave* him there? Hah, yeah, sure I am, don't hold your breath. I was trying to tell them that when Nick Quinlan wandered on to the set and almost drove poor Marian through the floor with that heavy-armed embrace of his.

Seems he'd been there all along. When his lady heard the noise I was making to attract their attention, she got spooked and ran out on him. So Nick just decided to sack out on the set, on the sofa in the living room part of LeFever's apartment. He'd slept through the whole thing.

Anyhow, we eventually got it all straightened out, even though Ivan kept saying *He fell down and bumped his head?* over and over again in this tone of utter disbelief. Marian gave me an *uh-huh* sort of look but just smiled and didn't say anything. Poor Nick—when Marian told him Leonard had tried to kill me, he didn't believe her.

'Naw, he dint,' he said. 'Y'got it wrong summow. 'S bad enough about Nathan.' As if the rules said there could be no more than one rotter among your acquaintances.

'Where's his gun?' Captain Michaels asked me.

'Oh—I guess it's still on the gym set. He had it in his hand when he fell.'

'I'll get it,' Ivan said and left.

'If it's the same gun that killed Ormsby,' the Captain said, 'then we've got our case.'

Nick was shaking his head, still having trouble taking it all in. He went off with Captain Michaels to get Leonard out of the closet, no doubt hoping Leonard would have some explanation that would make everything all right again.

Really peculiar thing, I can't explain it, but I was feeling pretty damned good. Yeah, I can too explain it: it was just knowing all that nastiness was over. And there had been a hell of a lot of nastiness, and it had been going on for a long time, ever since Rudy Benedict decided blackmail would help him magically turn into a World-Famous Playwright. No—it started even earlier than that. It started with a young girl named Mary Rendell who had trusted Ted Cameron.

My grandmother had always told me to be careful of the company I kept, and look at the choice specimens I'd ended up with. My lover was a killer. My producer was a blackmailer. My agent was a killer. A friend had tried to be a blackmailer but got himself murdered instead. His mother had tried to be a killer but managed to mess it up royally. The Benedicts weren't cut out to be criminals—but they sure had tried. Nice crowd I'd been running with. But I was through with them now, I was through with all of them.

There were still loose ends dangling that could trip me up. The network would have to find a new producer for my series—as well as for *LeFever* and the other shows Leonard Zoff had 'inherited' from Nathan Pinking. That meant a delay that would screw up the shooting schedule. It also meant a lot of publicity, publicity of the kind that could so easily turn sour on us this time. There were still hurdles to get over.

But they were all *do*-able things, they weren't the kind of difficulties that made you lie down and pull the covers over your head and not even *try*. The killing and the blackmail and the hatred and the fear and the sheer ugliness of what had happened—*that* was over. It was over, and I felt good that it was over.

And I felt good because now I could think about Ted Cameron without getting a sharp pain in my side and without starting to sweat all over. The Ted Cameron I'd been so hooked on had never really existed; I'd made him up. So I had awakened from my pretty dream to find the real Ted Cameron was only a blank-eyed shadow man who killed people to get what he wanted. His absence would not leave a gaping hole in my life.

Besides, he never danced.

I could hear the men taking Leonard out of the closet where I'd locked him. Marian Larch was seated on the side of LeFever's bed, looking kind of droopy.

'Hey, what's the matter?' I laughed. 'You've got a killer in custody—you should be feeling good.'

'That's not the way it works,' she muttered.

Wow, she was really *down*. 'Marian? What is it?'

She waved a hand. 'Don't mind me—I always get like this when we catch a killer. Depresses me.'

I sat down next to her. 'Some tough cop you are.'

She laughed, a strained little laugh. 'I know. I'm supposed to be hardened by now.'

'It really bothers you, huh?'

'It really bothers me. It bothers me a lot.'

'Well.' I'd never have expected that—from this cool lady who always knew what to do. 'Are you sure you're in the right line of work?'

Big sigh. 'Yes, this is what I want to do. Kelly, don't worry about it—I'll be all right in a day or two.'

'A *day* or two!' Jeez. 'That's far too long to stay depressed. So cheer up, starting right now.'

'Just like that, huh?'

'You once ordered *me* to cheer up, remember? Not long after I'd learned about Ted—we were in my club, having coffee. You said, "Cheer up, damn it!" Remember that? Well, now it's my turn—so cheer up, damn it.'

She managed a smile. 'We don't all have your resilience, Kelly.'

'Hey, you should be cheering me up, not the other way

213

around. After all, *I'm* the one who had four guns pointed at me today, you didn't.'

'*Four* guns?'

'Four, count 'em, four. First, Leonard's. Second, yours—when you were coming on like Supercop. Then two more, in the hands of Captain Michaels and Ivan Malecki. That makes four unless I've forgotten how to count.'

Marian looked stricken, which I guess was better than looking depressed. 'I didn't realize—Kelly, I'm sorry. We should have found a better way of handling it.'

Aha, she was thinking about something else, about me, a good sign. 'Therefore, since you owe me a little cheering up—why don't you come home with me? I can put on some dry clothes and you can put your job aside for a while and we can cheer each other up. How about it?'

But she shook her head and slipped back into the droopy look. 'Not tonight. But thanks for offering.' Damn, I almost had her.

So I just nodded and said, 'Sure, you want familiar surroundings, don't you? Very well, then, I accept.'

'You accept what?'

'I accept your invitation—to go home with you where you will provide me with a bathrobe and a cup of warm liquid of some sort.'

'Uh, well—'

'Come on, Marian, you need company tonight. And I could do with a spot of company myself. What do you do when you get depressed? Sit alone in the dark? Listen to sad music? Eat? A lot of people eat when they get depressed. What do you do?'

She half-moaned, half-laughed. 'I sit alone in the dark listening to sad music while I eat.'

'Thought so.' Although I hadn't, really; I was just talking. 'But tonight we'll turn on every light in the place and tell funny stories and—well, we'll decide about the eating later. I'm getting kind of hungry myself. What do you say? Am I invited?'

She laughed again, and this time it didn't sound

214

strained at all. 'Kelly, I'm kind of glad you're incorrigible. Of course you're invited. You're always welcome—any time at all.'

Aren't those nice words to end a story with?